STRAY MOON

STRAY MOON

A Strays Novel

KELLY MEDING

HARPER
VOYAGER
IMPULSE

An Imprint of HarperCollinsPublishers

STRAY MOON. Copyright © 2019 by Kelly Meding. All rights reserved. Printed in the United States of America. No part of this book may be used or reproduced in any manner whatsoever without written permission except in the case of brief quotations embodied in critical articles and reviews. For information, address HarperCollins Publishers, 195 Broadway, New York, NY 10007.

Digital Edition FEBRUARY 2019 ISBN: 978-0-06-284769-0
Print Edition ISBN: 978-0-06-284770-6

Cover design by Amy Halperin
Cover photographs © Di Studio/Shutterstock (woman) © carloscastilla/ iStock/Getty Images (background)

Harper Voyager, the Harper Voyager logo, and Harper Voyager Impulse are trademarks of HarperCollins Publishers.
HarperCollins is a registered trademark of HarperCollins Publishers in the United States of America and other countries.

FIRST EDITION

19 20 21 22 23   HDC   10 9 8 7 6 5 4 3 2 1

For my parents, who've always stood by me.
You're my Gaius and Elspeth (minus the magic stuff).

STRAY MOON

CHAPTER 1

I was in hell.

Not the literal pit of Hell (never been there, thank Iblis), but a very special kind of hell disguised as an official debriefing on the events of the previous week. A week that happened to star five of the most insane and physically painful days of my life, thank you very much. It's not easy trying to explain my decision to assist a Master vampire in discovering who'd kidnapped a dozen of his kin, especially when the rest of his bloodsucking brood held a trailer park hostage for their own safety.

Surprisingly, my superiors didn't give me as much shit for it as I expected.

No, the biggest issue that I and my dwindling team of US Para-Marshals were facing was credibility, since the brains behind all the bad shit that went down turned out to be one of our own.

I'd been beaten, brought back from the brink of death, and basically destroyed for the better part of a week.

And sitting here was so much worse.

The interrogation room at the US Marshals' field office in Baltimore had all the personality of a prison cell. Three tan walls, a two-way mirror, a plain metal table, a chair on either side. To the naked eye, it was no different than a thousand others across the country. To someone sensitive to magic, though, it was a prison. This room had protective wards beneath the plaster. Tiny holes in the surface of the table could produce a silver nitrate mist capable of sedating a werewolf or vampire (as well as some species of demon). And the suspect's chair could be electrified with the flip of a switch.

Guess where I was sitting?

Only a handful of these Para-equipped interrogation rooms existed around the various field offices, because interrogations of Paras rarely happened in such an official capacity. The two specialized Para-Marshal squads (one of which I unofficially led at the moment, because our former chief was dead) had minimal oversight by the Marshals' Office. As long as we dealt with the threats and kept the violence down, they paid our expenses and let us do our jobs.

The lack of oversight was probably why this whole

mess had gone down in the first place. Not that they'd ever admit that.

And not that it mattered right now. My ass was planted behind the table of that blessed room for three really big reasons.

One: Adam Weller, former leader of the West Coast squad and ex-living person, had used government money and Para-Marshal resources to kidnap vampires from various lines, and to play around with dark magic via his very own necromancer.

Two: our superiors weren't sure who among us to trust, because two of our Para-Marshals turned out to be double agents, working undercover for some other shadow organization interested in paranormal activity.

Three: my version of events kept clashing with those of pretty much everyone else, because I had apparently bargained away all memories of a guy named Jaxon Dearborn.

What in heaven kind of name is that, anyway?

So yeah, the Marshals' Office kind of frowns on traitors, double agents, and uncorroborated stories. Me too. But I didn't know how many more times I could repeat myself to these people before I lost it and unleashed the Quarrel on them.

I wonder if they realized how close I was to exerting the half-djinn legacy my father gave me. Seeing the marshals who were handling this case devolve into their most argumentative and combative nature, quarrelling with each other instead of me—well, that would have been a nice change of pace. Might even have been fun.

But I like my job, so I held my power in check. For now.

The room didn't have a clock, but I'd guess I'd been sitting there staring at my own reflection for almost an hour—ever since Marshal Keene heard my entire version of events for the fourth time, and then stepped out for coffee.

My stomach growled, reminding me it hadn't been fed for ages. I'd been given a soda and turkey sandwich a while ago, long before my last allowed bathroom break. Worse than the boredom and hunger, though, was the lack of communication with anyone I cared about. I hadn't spoken with my teammate Novak, a fallen incubus who'd been tortured with salt water and whose wounds no one would tell me about. Nor my boyfriend, Vincent, who'd been kidnapped by Weller and used as blackmail to make me cooperate. Not with Woodrow Tennyson, either, the Master vampire whose line I'd helped save, and who'd saved my life twice in return. And not even my own mother, who'd been in our team headquarters when the cow shit hit the magical fan on a farm in southern Delaware two days ago.

Two. Blessed. Days. Of me telling the same story over and over again, and no one telling me why I had supposedly forgotten six years' worth of memories of Jaxon. My patience with this entire flipping circus was almost gone.

I stood and stretched, arms over my head, up on my tiptoes. Fatigued muscles burned, and something in my back popped. My abdomen gave a sharp twinge. I pressed a hand over the spot where the necromancer, Lord Robert Adelay, had stabbed me with a silver melon baller (yes that really happened). The thing had punctured a lung and nearly killed me. I would have died, actually, if Tennyson hadn't been there. If I hadn't fed off him—a big, *big* no-no, considering the eternal enmity between djinn and vampires.

Truth is, a week ago, I'd have smacked you in the mouth if you'd suggested I would ever call a vampire a friend, much less call one of the most powerful Master vampires in the world a friend. But Tennyson and I had gone through the wringer together, physically and emotionally, and I'd learned to trust him. He was fiercely loyal to the vampires he'd sired during his five-hundred-plus years, and watching him deal with the violent deaths of twelve of his children had torn at my heart in ways I didn't expect. We'd been together almost constantly for five days, and I actually found myself missing him, the infuriating jerk.

I considered asking for another bathroom break, just to break up the monotony of staring at the walls. I needed to do something, bless it all.

But when I took a step toward the two-way mirror, I found myself standing in mist.

Freaking mist.

The interrogation room was gone. A fine blue mist

swirled all around me, as if stirred by a gentle breeze, but I felt nothing. No sensations of wind, of moisture, even of temperature. This wasn't real.

"Hello?" My voice didn't echo.

A woman appeared in front of me, less than five feet away. She wore a flowing white dress and had white flowers in her black hair. Her ebony skin glowed with an ethereal light, betraying her power. "Shiloh Harrison," she said.

Oh goodie. Powerful people who knew my name. "Who wants to know?"

"Chandra Goodfellow."

It took a moment to place her. After I looked past the white dress and glowy skin, I recognized the West Coast Para-Marshal. We'd only met once before. She was relatively new to Weller's squad, a moon witch recruited about a year ago.

Moon witches are relatively rare and have one of the more interesting origins among the magical folk. More than a thousand years ago, the goddess Brighid was summoned by an Irish queen who was unable to conceive. Brighid agreed to make the woman fertile and grant her six children—children who would grow up strong and powerful and worship Brighid. The woman agreed without insisting on any other terms, such as gender. The queen was desperate to give her husband a son, but bore only daughters. Furious at her inability to provide an heir, the king had his wife killed and the daughters enslaved.

When Brighid found out—the girls were in their thirties by that time, because an immortal goddess's attention tends to wander—she killed the king and gave his land to the daughters. She also gifted them with a drop of her blood, making them strong, extremely intelligent, fertile, and immortal. When one daughter is killed, she is reincarnated into the next child of any woman who carries Brighid's blood, with all of the memories and acquired knowledge of her previous life.

We call them moon witches because their power ebbs and flows with the tides, much like a woman's fertility cycle. Aside from the ability to reverse infertility for a price, moon witches can disappear into shadows, astral-project, and reverse the magical abilities of others. Rumor has it that a drop of their blood is like an insta-steroid, giving the drinker a brief burst of strength, skill, and battle-readiness.

Given the fact that I'd recently met and then pissed off Brighid, meeting one of her little minions in an astral plane made my stomach flip in a bad way.

"I'd say it's a pleasure to meet you, but I'm currently on your boss's shit list, so forgive me for not," I said.

Chandra frowned. "I'm not here for the goddess."

"Then what?"

"I'm here for the Andersons."

"Who?"

"They're one of the mated werewolf couples who have gone missing."

Right. Fourteen mated pairs of werewolves had recently disappeared in California and Florida. All members of registered Packs, their respective Alphas had no information on the missing. Novak and Kathleen, a double-crossing dhampir ex-teammate of ours, (and apparently Jaxon) had visited both Alphas during our investigation, and they'd turned up no real leads. Thirteen of the couples had no children. Only the Andersons had once had children—three, all of whom died one night from carbon monoxide poisoning that somehow didn't kill the parents.

"You knew the Andersons?" I asked.

"Yes, I did. I heard Raymond and Alice's pleas for children, and I went to them. Normally I can only affect the fertility of humans, but they were willing to pay the price to try."

"What was the price?"

She scowled. "The price is between myself and my couples. As I said, they were willing to go against Pack law and use divine intervention. And it worked. They were blessed with three beautiful, healthy pups."

"Until the pups died."

"Yes. Pack laws forbid autopsies, but they were blessed by Brighid's blood. They should have lived long, healthy lives."

I saw where this was going, but asked anyway. "Why are we talking about this?"

"I believe those children were murdered, under orders from the Homme Alpha, and I want answers.

But more than that, I want to bring the Andersons home. The Andersons and the other missing werewolves. I fear for their safety."

"And you want my help?"

"Yes. Our squads are divided, our strength diminished as two separate entities. As one unit, we could solve this."

"We could if we weren't all suspended from active duty."

"The suspension will be lifted once our superiors acknowledge our innocence. We're not responsible for what our leaders have done."

No, we weren't responsible, but that didn't stop a big ugly splotch of guilt from staining my conscience. Guilt that I didn't notice what was going on, or realize that my former boss, Julius Almeida, had also been complicit in these underhanded dealings. A deeper look into his accounts showed a fat little retirement fund in a Swiss bank, fed into a little at a time by blood money. Illegal money.

The double-crossing jerk. The more I learned, the less I mourned for his painful death and brief afterlife as a reanimated head.

He was the past, though. Right now, I really wanted to find those missing werewolves. Considering the fact that Weller had kidnapped forty-six vampires so his necromancer could practice turning them into controllable revenants, the werewolves must have a terrible fate awaiting them. And unlike with vampires, djinn have no issues with werewolves, and I sympathized with their plight. I needed to bring them all home.

"Okay," I said. "Once I get out of this flipping holding cell, I'll help you."

"And your team?"

"I won't force Novak to help, but I'll ask him."

"And Jaxon?"

Crap, I kept forgetting about him. And I wasn't comfortable bringing a stranger into this new mission, but if Chandra knew him, maybe it was okay. "Yeah, sure, him too."

"Thank you."

The mist disappeared, replaced by the drab tan walls of my holding cell. I had no idea if minutes or hours had passed. Judging by the familiar hunger rumbles in my stomach—as opposed to stabbing pain—I'd say minutes. But you never knew how time reacted when you moved to different planes of existence. I'd visited a different plane during my encounter with Brighid, and what had been maybe a thirty-minute conversation had taken the entire day back in the real world.

Magic was a funny bitch.

The door swung inward, and someone not Marshal Keene stepped inside. He was average height, well-built, with sandy hair beneath a US Marshals ball cap, and pale eyes. His face was sharp, too angular to be handsome, but he wasn't hard to look at, either, even though he was clearly exhausted. Sure, he wasn't wearing a smart suit like Keene, but he still screamed Fed under his black t-shirt and jeans.

"Oh, hell, no," I said. "I am not repeating that whole thing for a fifth time. You want to know what happened? Go read the transcripts. I'm done for the day."

Surprise lifted his eyebrows and parted his lips. "I'm not here to debrief you." Nice voice, smooth and comforting, with a faint lilt. Easy to listen to. He must have done a lot of suspect interrogations.

Lucky for his balls, he wasn't here to interrogate me. "Then what do you want?"

He took another step closer, those eyes that weren't quite blue (hazel maybe?) studying me like I was a bug in a jar. I stared right back, a clear challenge, until he . . . kind of deflated. His shoulders drooped right along with his mouth. "It's true, then."

"You want to be more specific?"

"Shiloh, it's me. It's Jaxon."

My supposed teammate who everyone said I'd forgotten about. No, not forgotten. Bargained away my memories of him. "*You're* Jaxon?"

"Yes."

"Okay, good, then maybe you can answer a question for me."

"I'll try."

"Why you?"

"What?"

I circled the table to stand in front of him, out of

reach, but less distant than before. "Why did I lose all memories of you, specifically? No one will tell me."

"Tennyson didn't tell you? He was with you when you woke up in that farmhouse."

"Obviously he didn't if I'm asking you, jackass."

He flinched. "Sorry. This is just . . . surreal. Six years, Shi. Everything's gone?"

"Apparently, and I want to know why. Why you?"

Twin spots of color darkened his cheeks. He looked away. At the floor, the walls, his feet. He was embarrassed. That did not do happy things to my stomach-ulcer-in-the-making.

Finally he said, "In order to find the necromancer's location, you made a bargain with a sidhe. The Fair Folk prefer to bargain in precious things like memory, so you agreed to give up a memory in exchange for her information, which would be erased once the necromancer was killed."

"Okay." Something about all that seemed vaguely familiar. At one point during our questioning, Keene had asked about a memory bargain with a sidhe, but everything around that was hazy, like it was being protected by a film of wet cotton. The sidhe was probably protecting herself by not letting me recall the specifics of our encounter. "I buy all that. Why memories of *you*?"

"You didn't know it would be me at the time," Jaxon said. He was still avoiding eye contact. "The bargain was for all your memories of the . . . the person you loved most."

That socked me right in the gut. My breath caught. I studied the man in front of me more closely, seeking . . . something. Anything to show me why I loved him the most. He had a magical aura, so he wasn't one hundred percent human. Magical creatures of different species rarely worked together well for long periods of time, almost as if their unique differences became like the same ends of a magnet. They pushed the other away.

"We . . . loved each other?" I asked, my voice oddly hoarse.

He looked at me. Hazel eyes swimming with defeat. Hurt. "In our own unique ways, we did. We always cared for each other. Do you remember rescuing your father from a magic abuser about six years ago?"

"Clearly." My father, along with several other magically inclined people, had been kidnapped and held as part of a madman's sick sideshow, making them show off their powers to rich people all around the country.

"I was one of the people you rescued that day. It's how we met."

Something in his words seemed familiar, but I couldn't place him in my own memories of that day. Telling him I didn't remember seemed kind of repetitive, so I stayed silent.

"Four years ago, we gave in to our attraction and

tried for a relationship," he continued. "It only lasted a year, but we stayed the best of friends. We like to give each other grief, but we always have the other's back."

"But . . ." What? I didn't know how to make my swirling thoughts into coherent statements. Or questions. A perfect stranger was telling me we'd had a sexual relationship, and I didn't know this guy from a hole in the wall. The only reason I hadn't called bullshit yet was his demeanor. Sad instead of pushy. Patient instead of demanding I believe him.

"It's a kick in the head, isn't it?" he said, almost to himself. "Finding out how much you mean to someone, only they don't remember a single thing about you."

"I'm sorry." It felt like the right thing to say, even though I hadn't done anything wrong. Had I?

"Your bargain helped us save a lot of lives, Shiloh. I can't fault you for that."

"Maybe not, but I can blame myself for all of the grief you're feeling over this. You lost something, too." Supposedly. But why lie about our shared past? If this guy really did know me, he knew I hated liars, so he had to be telling the truth.

This entire situation was a frustrating mind-fuck, and I really needed to get out of this room before I did unleash the Quarrel.

He didn't say anything, apparently preferring to stare at me like a kicked puppy. I had the oddest urge to hug him and tell him it would all work out. But I

didn't make it a habit of hugging perfect strangers—
even ones who insisted we had six years of forgotten
history. He stared until I got uncomfortable.

"So, what are you doing here?" I asked.

Jaxon shook himself out of whatever deep thought
had caught him. "We're free to go. I thought you'd
like a ride."

"Home?"

"Well, no, you've never told me where you live.
I don't think you told anyone except Julius. I meant
headquarters."

"You know where HQ is?" Okay, stupid question.
"Sorry, of course you must know. Um, you're not
going to pepper me with questions the whole way, are
you?"

His lips twitched. Was that a smile? "No, but I'll
answer any you might have. And we won't be alone.
Novak is coming back. His hands are still healing
from the saltwater bath they got, and he needs a little
help."

"Not that he'd ever admit it."

"Exactly. Elspeth is here, too, and she wants to
stay close. I think she likes being able to mother us
all a little bit."

"My mom's here?" More than anything else, I
wanted to see her. To talk to her and get a nice, big
Mom Hug. I'd dragged her into this investigation,
nearly gotten her killed, and she'd still hung around
to tend our wounds and lend a hand. Maybe she could

help me figure out this whole Jaxon thing. She'd be totally frank with me about anything I asked.

"She's waiting downstairs. She's been raising hell, demanding she see you."

"She's like that. Fiery when she wants something."

"I remember." His eyebrows knit together. "Sorry."

"For what?"

"I don't know. I suppose using words like *remember* feels weird. I'm not trying to insult you or anything."

I raised both shoulders in a shrug. "I know that. I'm not going to suddenly get all sensitive about the word *remember*."

"Okay." He angled his body and indicated the door. "After you."

I didn't like him on my six, because I didn't have a clue who he was, no matter what anyone else said. And it bugged me that I couldn't get any sort of real read on the guy. Even when I spoke with perfect strangers, I could glean something about them by their words, body language, et cetera . . . but not Jaxon. If a sidhe really had taken my memories of him, it could be a side effect of her magic—and that was still a big blessed if.

I squared my shoulders and left the room first. We were in a government building, so it wasn't like he could try anything. Or maybe he could. I had no idea what his Para status was. I strode down a sterile corridor, past other interrogation rooms, to an elevator. In no mood to wait, I took the stairs.

We came out on the first floor in a wide lobby with a scattering of uncomfortable-looking chairs and fake potted plants. Two suited marshals, including Keene, were standing to the side with Novak and my mother, and no one in the group looked happy.

Mom spotted me first. "Shiloh, honey."

She met me halfway, and I didn't care that I was in a building full of colleagues. My mom was here, alive and well, and I was so glad to see her and be out of that awful interrogation room. I let her pull me into a solid hug. Her heart beat wildly against mine, and her hands seemed to be everywhere, testing for injury, reassuring herself that I was real.

"Are you all right?" she asked when she decided to let me breathe better.

"I am now," I replied. "Starving, but otherwise fine. You?"

She took a shuddering breath. "This is exactly what I needed. I heard what happened on that farm, and I needed to see for myself that you're okay. Are you *sure* you're okay?"

Elspeth Ann Juno was in full-on mothering mode.

"Mom, I'm okay, I swear. I would kill for a nice rare steak, though." I winced at my own words, because they made her flinch. I'm an unapologetic carnivore from way back, but I usually went for medium. The whole rare thing was probably a lasting side effect of having drunk Tennyson's blood twice in the last week in order to, you know, not die. The bloodlust wasn't fun, but it also wasn't fatal. I did miss Tennyson's presence, though, which was somewhat alarming.

"I could eat, too," Novak said.

I pulled away from Mom and approached Novak. The fallen incubus among us was a shadow of himself. Six-two, built like a professional linebacker, and gorgeous as sin, Novak had been created to seduce men and women into giving up their souls to Hell. Even when he'd fallen into disgrace and was banished from Hell, he maintained a virility and sex appeal to match even the most popular male movie star. But something had changed after he was imprisoned and tortured on that farm. He seemed distant, almost exhausted. I don't think I've ever even seen him yawn, much less be anything except ready for sex or battle. Now, though—he looked *done*.

"Hey, hot stuff," I said.

His lips flattened out in his best impersonation of a smile. "Hey, kiddo. You really good, or you putting on a front?"

"I'm really okay, but I'll be better once we're out of here." I glanced down at his hands, which were both encased in elbow-length leather gloves. "You?"

"Nothing good food and a lotta sex won't cure."

He was lying. I didn't push, though, not in front of the others. There'd be time to talk later.

But it was then I noticed that not included with the

"others" right now was someone I really needed to talk to as well. "Where's Vincent?"

"He was released from their on-site clinic a few hours ago," Mom said. "They had to give him a transfusion for the blood loss."

Because Kathleen, our dhampir ex-partner, had drained him to unconsciousness so he wouldn't fuss about being locked up in a closet. "But he's all right?"

"Physically, he's fine. We spoke briefly." Mom's smile was forced. I did not like that at all. "He needs a little time to absorb everything."

My heart shriveled into a little ball. "He's dumping me, isn't he?"

"He didn't say that."

"He doesn't have to." I ran both hands through my tangled, grimy hair that really needed a shampoo or six. "I never told him what I did for a living, or what I really am. He's a construction worker, Mom. This isn't his world."

"Give him some time, Shi. He might surprise you."

"Did he at least leave a message for me?"

Mom shook her head no.

Bless it all. Hearing that Vincent had left without a word hurt. Hurt more than I thought it would, considering our relationship had never been serious. We hung out, we had great sex, and then we both went to our jobs. Except the last voice mail Vincent left said he wanted to take things to the next level. He wanted things to be serious between us. Pretty sure he didn't mean "kidnapped and held hostage in a closet by a Para double agent" serious.

So much for that fantasy.

"Your suspension will officially be lifted tomorrow," Agent Keene said, an unwelcome voice in our business. He had a snooty air about him that seemed to suggest the Para-Marshals were more trouble than we were worth. "But you are all on mandatory leave for the next seven days. Your knowledge interface matrix will not be given any new assignments until that time."

Oh great, a forced vacation. Maybe I could use it to wash my hair and pretend my personal and professional lives hadn't just imploded.

"Thank you," Jaxon said. Heavy dose of sarcasm for the win. I could like this guy.

Keene and the other two marshals left the lobby, not bothering to respond. My group angled toward the doors.

"Wait a second," I said. "I'm still playing catch-up here. What happened to Kathleen and Tennyson?"

Jaxon and Novak shared a look. A look I didn't like.

"Kathleen is being placed under arrest until they can figure out who she works for," Jaxon replied. "Same with Lars." Lars Patterson had been a West Coast Para-Marshal, apparently planted in Weller's group by the same shadow agency as Kathleen, and he'd jumped at the chance to get deeper into Weller's back pocket by faking his death and working on the necromancer project. Lars had copped to being the one to help torture a now-dead Master vampire named Piotr into giving up the secrets of necrotic magic. Kathleen . . . well, she'd lied to us all.

She'd also worked by our sides and saved our lives countless times. Yet . . .

"Makes sense," I said. Even though it meant we were another person down in our squad. "Tennyson?"

A muscle under Jaxon's left eye twitched. Not a fan of the Master vampire? "Tennyson is still being detained while the Marshals' Office works with Delaware law enforcement to figure out what to do with him. He's taken full responsibility for what happened at Myrtle's Acres, and the members of his line have been released into Drayden's care."

Drayden was Tennyson's second-in-command. He'd take care of Tennyson's people while he was detained. But something didn't make sense.

"Vampires govern themselves," I said. "The police don't have the authority to punish him."

"No, but the Marshals' Office does. They're weighing his help in unmasking Weller and the necromancer against one hundred and twenty counts of kidnapping."

Ouch. "You don't have to sound so eager for them to lock him up."

"I'm not." Jaxon flashed me an impatient look. "I don't like him, but he did save my life."

"He did?"

Jaxon's impatience melted into sadness. "Yeah," he said, then turned and stalked toward the exit.

I glanced at Mom, who smiled sadly, and the three of us followed Jaxon to the car. This was already going to be a very strange suspension, and I still hadn't told anyone that a moon witch had reached out to me for help via an astral plane.

I kept it to myself for now. Nothing was more important than a hot shower at our headquarters so I could feel half human again. Then we were all going to sit down for a nice, long chat about how to find those missing werewolves.

CHAPTER 2

Even though all four of us wanted to get home and relax—plus a long, hot shower for me to remove three days' worth of grime that couldn't be washed off in a bathroom sink—my stomach started rumbling loudly enough to annoy Novak, who demanded we stop for food. Jaxon swung the car through a drive-thru, and I had to try and sate my hunger for a nice bloody steak on a pair of overcooked double-cheeseburgers.

Novak had trouble holding his sandwich with his mangled hands, which made a mess no one commented on. Mom picked at a salad in the shotgun seat, and Jaxon ate a chicken sandwich with one hand while he drove down the highway as fast as he probably dared. No one spoke, and maybe I didn't remember how Jaxon fit into my life, but I knew that uncomfortable silences were not the norm for our crew.

Then again, nothing was the same as it had been a week ago. Julius was dead. Kathleen was a double agent. Jaxon was a stranger to me. The person I wanted to talk to most right now was a vampire, and he was under arrest. And my boyfriend was likely preparing a polite way to dump me.

After finishing my burgers, I borrowed Mom's phone. Used an app to find Vincent's number, because who memorized phone numbers anymore? Voice mail. "It's me, and this is a safe phone to call. We need to talk. Please."

Simple and to the point. Ball was in his court now.

We had a nice little compound in eastern Maryland built out of what had once been a housing develop-ment. High perimeter fencing now surrounded open land, as well as an invisible magic fence inside that. It unnerved me to see Jaxon punch the security code into the front gate; it also helped me accept that this wasn't some elaborate prank, because Novak would never breach security protocols.

Late afternoon shadows streaked across the yard and driveway, and something on the poured concrete caught my attention: a long line of scattered black splotches that led up to the front porch, like an oil leak, but some of those same specks were on the steps.

"Shi?" Mom asked. "Something wrong?"

"What's that?" I pointed at the droplets.

She glanced at Jaxon, who was watching us from

the front door, still with that same wounded puppy look on his face. "It's blood," Mom replied finally.

"From the other night? When Tennyson and I fought those vamps at the gate?" Three nights ago, Tennyson and I had been returning from an interrogation mission, only to find six necromancer-controlled vampires waiting for us. They wanted the Master vampire we were keeping chained up in our basement, I said no, and things got rough. Tennyson had run reconnaissance to see if the necro was close by, and I'd fought all six alone . . . except that felt wrong.

It's how I remembered the fight, but even I wasn't stupid enough to take on six vamps by myself.

"It is from that night," Mom said with some hesitation in her voice.

Novak hadn't been there for that battle, but he also didn't seem surprised. Someone must have filled him in on events while he was busy being held captive.

"We were both wounded in that fight," Jaxon said quietly. "We both bled. There simply hasn't been time to clean anything."

Something told me there was more to it than that, but I let it go for now—I felt bad enough for downplaying his involvement (even though I still couldn't find it in myself to believe it). We all shuffled inside, and I made a beeline for the stairs and the second-floor bathroom. I got naked, deciding in the moment that I was going to burn the clothes I was wearing. The hot water felt amazing, and I took my time cleaning up. Even braided my hair so it stayed out of my face.

I didn't live at the HQ full-time, but we each had a bedroom we preferred to use in case of overnights or naps. Mine had several extra changes of clothes, some personal items, and a nice, soft bed. A bed that beckoned me to face-plant on it right away. Sleeping in interrogation rooms is next to impossible, and I was running on fumes, despite the food.

Sleeping felt like cheating, though, when we hadn't really talked about anything as a group. I still needed to fill them in about Chandra's plea for help, and I really wanted to speak with Tennyson. Since only one of those two things was actually doable in the near future, I hauled my tired ass downstairs. After that, I could finally get some rest.

The spicy aroma of meat and chili pepper perked me up the instant my feet hit the ground floor. Everyone was in the kitchen, huddled around the island. Mom was stirring a pot of what had to be chili, probably from the freezer, and Novak was practically salivating, despite having eaten a burger and fries not long ago.

He caught me staring and grunted. "What? Food and sex help me heal faster. I'm too blessed exhausted to go looking for tail, so unless someone here wants to help . . ."

"Eat away," I said. "Mom loves to cook."

And there's no way I'm having sex with you, I left unsaid.

"Yes, she does," Mom replied, tossing me a quick smile over her shoulder. "But don't get used to it. Once things settle down here, I have a life to get back to."

"I'm sorry we dragged you into this mess, Elspeth," Jaxon said. He was snacking on a can of peanuts, tossing each one into the air and catching it in his mouth with ease.

I caught myself before asking how he dragged my mom into anything. Someone needed to write down the alternate timeline of events that I no longer remembered, so I could fill in some blanks. Blanks specific to Jaxon's supposed involvement in, oh, the last six years of my life.

For example: if he was the person I loved most, why weren't we together? Or were we actually together, and he was just being super polite about it, because I didn't know him anymore?

This was going to take some time.

"No one dragged me into anything," Mom said. "My daughter asked for help, and I agreed. No one can force me to do something I don't want to do."

"Hashtag truth," I said.

Jaxon chuckled. "I'm not sure if you were agreeing with her, or declaring your own stubborn nature to people who know exactly how stubborn you are." His easygoing grin melted into a sad frown. "Sorry."

"For what? Reminding me I don't know you? Dude, you sitting on that stool reminds me every single second."

The kitchen was quiet. Jaxon looked down, and I knew I'd said the wrong thing. Seemed about right.

"I never properly thanked you, kiddo," Novak said quietly, his dark eyes fixed on the countertop. "You saved my life, and you gave up a big thing to do it."

"Oh . . ." Was that what I'd sacrificed my memories of this other guy for? My throat closed under the onslaught of emotion, probably due to stress and lack of sleep. I kissed his cheek. "You're lucky I like you, demon."

Mom plunked a giant steaming bowl of chili in front of Novak, effectively ending the incubus's rare display of vulnerability. She helped him get a good hold of a long-handled serving spoon with one of his glove-covered hands, so he could eat without making a huge mess. I accepted a smaller bowl for myself, tantalized by the red, meaty goodness.

Jaxon ate some, too, and I caught him glancing at me almost constantly, which was incredibly unsettling. Less like he was trying to figure me out and more like he was making sure I hadn't disappeared on him—not that I could because I hadn't inherited my dad's ability to teleport. He was also still wearing his hat inside, and for some reason, that was really annoying.

"Do you have a premature bald spot or something?" I asked.

He nearly dropped his spoon. "What?"

"The hat. Don't you know it's rude to wear them indoors? Especially at the table."

"We aren't eating at a table."

I seriously dated this guy? "Dude, really?"

"Shiloh, leave it," Mom said.

"It's all right, Elspeth," Jaxon said. "Believe it or not, the hair has already begun to grow back in." He whipped the ball cap off and tossed it onto the counter, then lifted his chin to look me in the eye.

The top left side of his head was nearly bald in a patchy, hand-shaped section, while the rest of his sandy hair was a few inches long. A golden fuzz had overtaken the bald spot, and I kind of wanted to rub my hand over it to see how soft it was. I stared at him, a sense of wrongness about that strange spot I couldn't place.

"I'm guessing that isn't the result of a bad haircut," I said.

"No, it isn't," he replied, the words clipped. "But I should probably trim the rest so it doesn't look quite so strange. I didn't have a chance before we were whisked away to Baltimore for questioning."

I wanted to ask why. What happened? His sharp expression kept me from questioning him further, however. If he wanted to tell me, he could.

"Trim it," Novak said in between mouthfuls of chili. "You look like an idiot."

Jaxon laughed out loud. "Supportive as always, thanks." Then he flipped Novak off.

The easy camaraderie between the pair was both bizarre and familiar, which only fueled my frustration over this supposed memory loss. Novak obviously knew and trusted Jaxon, but that didn't mean I did. Or ever would.

This whole memory loss thing was going to be a long, ongoing mind-fuck of epic proportions. "So I know we're all suspended for seven days, but I have a possible thing to keep us busy in the meantime," I said.

Jaxon blinked at me. "You've been in an interrogation room with no access to phones or the internet for the better part of two days, and you have a thing?"

"She reached out through astral projection."

"A witch reached out to you?" Mom asked.

"A moon witch, yes. Her name is Chandra Good-fellow, and she worked on the other Para-Marshal squad under Weller."

Novak stiffened. "You want to trust one of Weller's people?"

I shrugged. "She seemed sincere and as oblivious to Weller's double-crossing as we were. Besides, she wants help investigating the missing werewolves, and I think we can all agree that's important. She knew one of the mated couples personally."

A familiar gray mist swirled around the room, hiding the walls and appliances, and leaving only the island, me, Jaxon, and Novak. Mom flat-out disappeared. Jaxon leapt from his stool, instantly alert.

Good timing.

"It's okay, it's her," I said.

"Her who?" Jaxon asked.

"My name is Chandra," said the moon witch in

question. She appeared out of the mists, the same as before with the strange, glowy skin and white flowers in her hair. "Chandra Goodfellow. We met a few years ago, very briefly."

"I remember," Jaxon said.

Novak grunted.

"Where's my mom?" I asked.

"Your unknown female companion?" Chandra asked. "Exactly where she last saw you. You haven't physically gone anywhere. This is all happening in your minds."

"Tell us why we should trust you?" Jaxon asked. The brusque, businesslike manner was kind of appealing.

Chandra pinned him with an icy stare. "I was betrayed by my squad leader, the same as you three were. I trusted Adam Weller with my life, and with the lives of all of the Paras we sought to protect and police. I never imagined he would dabble in the black arts, much less be orchestrating such a mass conspiracy against vampires."

"And your other teammates?"

"Lars is, as you know, in custody for being a double agent. I trust my other two team members implicitly. However, they've chosen not to assist me in this private matter that I've described to Shiloh."

"Shiloh didn't get that far before you zipped us here, so why don't you describe it to us?"

She did, repeating what she'd told me about the

Andersons almost word for word. Jaxon's pensive expression never wavered. Novak looked bored and was probably annoyed at having his meal interrupted.

"You're asking us to assist you in investigating the Homme Alpha of the California Pack," Jaxon said. "That's not a small thing. Any crimes committed on Pack land are subject to Pack laws, not man's laws. There's no due process, and we can't drag them in for murder, if the Alpha did, indeed, order those children killed. Further, it would be incredibly dangerous— there's nothing to stop them from simply attacking us if they wanted."

"I'm not asking you to help me in punishing anyone," Chandra said. "I simply wish to locate all the missing werewolf couples and find answers for the Andersons about their dead children. What they choose to do with those answers is their prerogative."

"We've been suspended for seven days," I piped up.

"My team as well, which changes nothing. This has to be an off-the-record investigation, and I'm well aware that limits our backup and resources."

That was pretty much what I figured, anyway, but wanted to her to confirm it.

"You mind ending the mental conference call so we can discuss this as a group?" Jaxon asked. "Maybe give us a phone number we can reach you at?"

Chandra's lips twitched in a half smile. "Cell phones have a habit of bursting into flames near moon witches.

Technology isn't our friend. All Shiloh needs to do is say my name, and I'll hear her."

"Why Shiloh?"

"Because she's a woman."

On that cryptic note, she winked out and the gray swirl disappeared. I blinked hard, suddenly aware of my mother in my face, shaking my shoulder. "Hey, stop, what?" I said.

Mom cupped my chin in her hand. "You went totally blank, Shi. All three of you froze in place, and I sensed magic around you. What happened?"

I jerked my chin out of her grip. "Chandra astral-projected into our heads for a brief conversation."

"Why wasn't I included?"

"You aren't a Marshal. She didn't know you."

Mom huffed. Jaxon took pity, I guess, because he filled her in on what Chandra had to say. "Isn't going after the Homme Alpha very dangerous?" she asked when he finished.

"We aren't going *after* him, exactly," I said. "Apparently the Packs aren't doing much to locate their own. We're hunting down missing werewolves and then finding proof that the Anderson kids were murdered. That's it. No one's putting the Alpha on trial."

"Yet," Jaxon said. Now that he was back in the real world, he didn't seem as defensive or irritated. Maybe he didn't like astral projection?

Actually . . . .

"You're not totally human, right?" I asked.

He stared at me like I'd asked if the sky was polka-dotted. Then the puppy dog thing again. "No, I'm not. I'm a skin-walker."

"Cool." I'd heard of those, but never met one before. "What's your skin?"

"A stag."

I stifled a snort. "Of all the animals you could magic into, you chose a deer?"

Jaxon bristled. "We don't choose our skins, they choose us. And you didn't have a problem with my two-hundred-pound *deer* saving your life the other night." With that, he stalked out of the room, leaving a cloud of anger in his wake.

"Well, that was counterproductive," Novak said.

"I don't remember him!" I curbed the urge to stamp my foot in frustration. "I know this is weird for everyone, but how do you think I feel? You are telling me I bargained away all memories of the person I loved the most, and apparently that's the grumpy blond guy who magics into a big-ass deer. Nothing about the last six years of my life is the same as I believe it to be, and that's a huge thing to get my head around."

"It's going to be an adjustment for everyone," Mom said. "Give yourselves time. But also go a little easier on him? Maybe going to California without him is what's best for now."

My thoughts exactly. I needed to take people I knew and trusted.

"No way." Novak dropped his spoon on the counter with a sauce-flecked *thunk*. "We go as a team, or not at all. The three of us. You, me, and the deer."

"How come you get to call him a deer?" I grumped. "And what did Jaxon mean about saving my life the other night? The vampire fight? He said we both bled." I hadn't seen any wounds in the shower, though— they must have healed when Tennyson gave me his blood. Still didn't remember Jaxon being part of the fight, though. I didn't remember anything, and it was starting to get frustrating as hell.

"Tennyson will be able to give you more details," Mom said. "I only saw some of it from a distance. Mostly I helped with the aftermath." She pulled a face. "I can say that while still in his stag form, Jaxon was wounded very badly. And because he was still using his magic at the time, even when he changed back, the wound was projecting an aura. It wouldn't have healed on its own."

"Head wound?" The hair was kind of a giveaway.

"Yes, a vampire tore off one of his antlers, as well as a patch of skin."

"Ouch." A shiver wiggled up the backs of my legs as a mental image I didn't want flashed through my head. "Really big ouch." I glanced in the direction Jaxon had gone. "But he seems okay now."

"Because Tennyson gave him blood. At your request."

"Shit." No wonder Jaxon was pissy with me. I

vaguely recalled Tennyson and my mom being busy right after the vampire fight, and then my dad poofed into the room to tell me . . . something. But still nothing about Jaxon, though, wounded or not, and no recollection of Tennyson feeding anyone besides me his blood.

"The donation saved Jaxon's life," Mom said. "But the experience left him quite . . . irritable. I don't know that a skin-walker has ever ingested vampire blood before, so I didn't know what to expect. His wounds healed, as we'd hoped, but he was also quick to temper and he lashed out several times, even after we were transferred to Baltimore."

I jumped to my feet. "Did he hurt you?"

"No, it was all verbal. Especially when he wasn't able to see you. After he got the details of what happened on the farm, I think he needed to see for himself that you were alive. He cares for you a great deal, even if you can't feel it. We all do."

"I'm sorry." I hugged her, and she tried to squeeze the life out of me. "I'm sorry I scared you guys." Those few, terrifying seconds between realizing Tennyson was about to make a wish and the cold shock of that melon baller piercing my chest, granting that wish, and fading out, made my entire body tremble. I'd come as close to dying as I ever wanted to get, all to help out a vampire Master I hadn't even known existed a week ago.

Mom made a soft sound that was half sob. "I swear

I have more gray hair because of you and this job. And I suppose I should thank your father for your hearty constitution. Being half-djinn is probably the only reason you survived all of those wounds."

"You're gonna thank Dad?" I pulled back so I could see her eyes. "I want to be there for that. I'll bring popcorn."

My parents coexisted politely, but they both had differing views on my childhood. Mom resented him for being gone all the time—thanks to being an earth djinn who followed the call of Wishers and magic—and he resented her for that. She'd known what he was when they began their affair, and he had to be true to his nature, as he had been true to it for the last eight hundred years. But that didn't make it an easy relationship.

The HQ landline rang before Mom could conjure up a proper retort. Novak didn't look at the phone, and it still felt weird to let Jaxon answer it—if he even tried, from wherever in the house he'd gone—so I grabbed the kitchen handset.

"House of horrors," I said.

A deep, vaguely melodic chuckle filtered over the line. "Are things truly that bad, young djinn?"

"Tennyson?" A flash of genuine happiness hit me hard. Mom's eyebrows rose high on her forehead.

"It does me well to hear your voice, Shiloh. You sound strong."

"I am. I think. I mean, I'm exhausted and could

probably sleep for eighteen hours straight, but I'm not dead, so that's a plus."

"And your bloodlust?"

"I'm still craving a rare steak dinner, but I don't think I'll start drooling if I nick myself shaving my legs." *I hope.* "Hey, how did you get a phone? Did the authorities release you?"

"Not yet. I don't believe they're entirely certain what to do with me. It's not as if a human prison will hold me, if I choose not to be held."

I groaned. "Did you gazelock someone into letting you call me?"

"Perhaps."

"You broke the law so we could chitchat?"

"Yes. You've become important to me, and I needed to know for myself that you were well."

For some reason, that made my heart turn over a little bit. Dad would be horrified that I had any kind of positive feelings for a vampire, but whatever. Tennyson had saved my life twice since I'd met him. He was calling to check up on me. He was officially a friend.

"I'm as well as I can be, I guess, considering the memory loss thing, and the being suspended from work thing. The whole my-boss-was-a-criminal thing."

"You've had a busy week."

Sweet Iblis, I think he cracked a joke for the second time ever. "The week isn't slowing down, either. We still have missing werewolves to find."

"While you're suspended?"

"How did you know?"

"An easy assumption to make, given the circumstances."

Right. "The job is off the books." And I didn't need to share anything else about that. The fewer people involved the better—even if I kind of wanted Tennyson along for the investigation. He was crazy smart, and good in a fight.

"Be careful, Shiloh. From what I've heard, there are greater powers at work here than just your US Marshals' Office. Shadow agencies with hidden agendas. Powerful people with vast resources."

"Aw, you're worried. That's sweet."

He grunted. "We have shared blood. While you are not one of my children, we are now connected, and we always shall be. I cannot sense you the way I could when the sharing was fresh, but if you need me, I will come."

I blinked hard a few times, because no way was I getting misty-eyed over his promise. Nope. "Thank you. I don't suppose the statements I wrote on your behalf have helped?"

"Not so far, but I have faith that my incarceration will end soon. I've reminded my jailers that I need to feed, and none of them seem keen on volunteering."

"Keep eyeballing their necks and lick your lips a lot. Maybe it'll light a fire under their asses."

"Perhaps it will. Be safe on your journey."

"You too." I didn't want to hang up, because Mom

was likely to pepper me with questions. But the instant I dropped the handset into the charger, she wasn't the first voice to speak up.

"The vampire called you?" Jaxon asked. He stood in the archway, arms crossed.

"Yes, he did." I didn't have to ask to know that he and Tennyson didn't get along. It was all over Jaxon's face. "And you can call him by his name. He saved your life, too, you know."

"Elspeth told you about that?"

"Duh." I stifled a yawn, too tired to fight with anyone else today. "I'm sorry I joked about your skin. I shouldn't have done that."

His posture relaxed a fraction. "Thank you. Look, I know it's early, but why don't you go to bed? You look like you're going to collapse any minute. We can talk more about California in the morning."

"I like this plan. Thanks." I turned around. "Mom, are you staying the night?"

She shook her head. "No, honey, I think it's time for me to head home. My plants are overdue for a good watering."

A minor issue sprung to mind. "Uh, how are you getting home? I kind of swung by your house and kidnapped you."

"I'll drive her," Jaxon said. "You get some rest, okay, Shi?"

The nickname sounded incredibly right coming

from his lips, but he was still an unreadable stranger running off with my mom in tow. "Mom?"

"Jaxon is a dear friend," Mom said. She enveloped me into another perfect Mom Hug, and I breathed her in. Soaked in her love and support to tide me over until I saw her again. "I love you so much, my sweet, stubborn girl."

"Love you too, Mom."

I watched them drive away from one of the living room windows, unsettled and exhausted and ready for it all to stop for a while. Except tomorrow would begin a brand-new adventure, and this time, we didn't have any real backup.

"You okay, kiddo?" Novak asked.

"I don't know." I wasn't very okay, but as the default team leader, I had to put on my happy face and be positive for his sake. "But I will be." I had to be.

Right after a nice fourteen-hour nap.

CHAPTER 3

After managing to sleep straight through the night and into the next morning, I finally rolled myself out of bed around ten o'clock and into the shower. More out of habit than anything else. The scent of coffee drew me downstairs like a witch to a ley line. I filled a mug, then dumped in some sugar and an ice cube so I could drink it faster.

The general silence of the house weirded me out. The dining room, where our massive, offline computer system was set up, was empty, and so was the living room. There was one bedroom we mostly used for weapons storage that looked like it had been recently ransacked, and the door to the little-used garage stood half open.

Noises from inside the garage drew me toward it, more curious than alarmed. The rear compartment door of one of our Explorers was open, facing away, but I caught a flash of pale hair and took a chance.

"Jaxon?"

He peeked around the side of the SUV, nothing about him familiar, not even after yesterday. The guy was just . . . there. Taking up space. "Hey, you're awake."

"Sort of." I tapped my coffee mug, not very good at the whole small-talk with strangers thing. "What are you up to?"

"Okay, don't get mad, but Novak and I have already put a plan in motion to get to California."

I blinked at him. "Um, okay. I mean, I was thinking plane tickets?"

He chuckled. "We'd have a difficult time getting our specialty weapons through security, don't you think?"

"So what do you suggest we do? Drive across the country?"

"No, you and I are driving to the crux near your apartment."

I nearly asked how the fuck he knew there was a crux of ley lines near my apartment and thought the comment through. If we had worked together, then he knew Novak occasionally used the intense magic of the crux to teleport me to HQ during emergencies. All anyone knew was that my apartment was about an hour's drive from here, because that's all I'd told my coworkers. Except Julius, but I wasn't going there right now.

I hadn't seen my apartment in over a week, when

it had once contained my naked boyfriend. "Bless me, I still haven't talked to Vincent about all of this."

"Your mom called while you were still asleep. No messages from Vincent on her phone."

Fuck.

I tamped down more frustration over that broken relationship and focused. "Why do we need the crux?" Magical cruxes occurred when three or more ley lines crossed over each other. Witches, warlocks, and magic users loved finding cruxes, because they could use them to increase the power of whatever they were attempting to do. The only reason I used the crux was so I could be teleported by—

"Hey, where's Novak?" I asked.

Jaxon grinned, and he was kind of cute like that. Way better than the wounded puppy eyes I got all day yesterday. "His plane should be touching down in Los Angeles any minute."

"He's already there?"

"Yes. I found Chandra's contact information last night, and I called to see if she could tell us about a local crux for Novak to use in teleporting us."

"But Novak doesn't need to be on a crux to teleport someone to him. The person he's teleporting does." At least, that's how it always worked in the past. If I needed to get to HQ from home fast, I'd go to the crux and let him bring me over.

"Normally, no," Jaxon said. "Except he admitted he's never pulled two people at once, and not across the country while carrying a lot of weapons. He thought the magic boost would help."

I eyeballed him as I sipped the steaming coffee. "You probably don't realize this, but you're going to land in Los Angeles with a woody. Novak is—"

"An incubus whose power is tied to sex and seduction. I know. He's teleported me before."

"Oh." Duh. Teammate. "Sorry."

Jaxon rounded the vehicle and stopped within an arm's reach of me, studying me with a new expression I couldn't readily identify. "It's baffling. You look exactly the same. You talk the same, act the same, but I'm not in there anywhere. Not a single part of me is left."

He sounded so incredibly sad that I nearly reached out and hugged him. "Jaxon, are we a couple?"

"As in lovers? No, not for several years."

"But we were?"

"Yes, we were. We loved each other, but we couldn't make it work out romantically. We stayed great friends, though, and teammates."

"Why didn't we make it, though? Was I too bossy? I'm super bossy."

He laughed. "A lot of things, Shiloh, and it wasn't any one person's fault. We were both excited about working with Julius and the Para-Marshals. We were also both lonely, unique souls who found comfort in each other for a while. And we were smart enough to end it before things got ugly."

"I'm glad." I believed his sincerity, and I was starting to really hate the fact that I'd lost everything of this man I was slowly getting to know.

Maybe the second time was the charm?

Something hung in the air between us, a charge I couldn't describe, but it was over in seconds. Jaxon looked away first.

"So the plan," I said hastily, "is for Novak to teleport us to California ready to rumble with our weapons. Didn't trust Chandra to get us what we'd need when we got there?"

"To be honest? No. Between Julius and Kathleen, I'm done blindly trusting someone because they ask me to, *especially* other Paras. There's too much to lose."

"Have you always been this cynical?"

"No. Believe me, it's a renewed trait."

"Renewed?"

He tilted his head, a little half smile quirking his lips. "I was very much a loner before I met you and Julius. I didn't trust easily, and being held captive in that traveling freak show didn't help at all. But meeting you . . . you have this spark of energy that you take everywhere you go. You live every day to its fullest, and you treasure the world around you. It helped me see the good side of people, rather than all the darkness."

"I'm glad." My heart hurt in a way I didn't understand. "Even if I don't remember any of it."

"It's not your fault. We just need to start building new memories together."

"Like tandem incubus teleportation."

"Exactly. You want to put that coffee in a to-go mug, so we can hit the road?"

"Sounds like a plan."

I got the travel cup—and Pop-Tarts, because toaster pastry—and then we headed out. Except Jaxon idled right outside of the main gate. "What?" I asked.

"You've never told me where you live, so I don't know where I'm going."

"Really? I thought we dated." How had I never invited him back to my place?

"What little off time we had for, uh, activities, usually happened in one of our bedrooms here at HQ." He gave me a funny look. "I told you yesterday I've never been to your place."

"You did?" I groaned. Sometimes magical side effects really sucked. "Sorry. Hopefully, one day something you say will stick."

"Not your fault, Shi."

"Did I ever see your place?"

"I live here at the house. No separate address."

"That whole loner thing?"

He nodded. "And no commute."

"Smart man." I gave him the name of my town, and he started driving again. The crux itself was behind a convenience store, so doing this in the middle of the day was probably going to attract some attention. Couldn't be helped. The cover of darkness was too far away, and we only had a week to figure this out—probably less if anyone at the Marshals' Office realized we weren't exactly "on vacation."

"So why not pick a place closer to HQ?" Jaxon asked after five minutes of silent driving.

"I never told you why?"

"Well, you never told me your address, remember? I had no idea if you lived down the block or in another state, since Novak teleports you over during emergencies."

"Oh. Right. I guess I like knowing I'm far enough away that I can compartmentalize what I do as a Para-Marshal and put it away when I'm off the clock."

"And with Vincent."

"Yeah." I looked at Jaxon, whose easy gaze was fixed on the road ahead. "Did you get a chance to speak with Vincent in Baltimore?"

"I saw him from a distance when your mom talked to him, but no, I haven't spoken to him."

"Oh." Maybe waiting to reach out again was a bad idea, considering how we'd left things before Vincent was kidnapped, but I'd tried, bless it. And I had fourteen mated pairs of werewolves to find before I could fix my personal life—if there was anything left to fix.

"Changing your mind about going to California?"

My hand jerked at the unexpected question. "No. Vincent I were never serious, and he's got a lot to think about. It isn't every day you find out your girlfriend is half djinn, a Para-Marshal, and spends most of her time settling disputes between otherworldly beings."

"True. I knew about magic from a young age, so it's always been part of my life. I can't imagine finding out everything I know now as an adult."

I couldn't image it, either, and it was too blessed depressing to keep discussing. Time to focus on work. "So the werewolves. Any thoughts?"

"Not many. When we went to see the Dame Alpha in Florida last week, she didn't have much to say about her missing wolves. Just that it was an internal matter. She didn't give any indication she was searching for them, either, though. The only reason we know they're missing is because of the National Registry."

All Pack Alphas are required to enter names of any new werewolves—born or forced—into the National Registry, so our government can track their movements and pack sizes. If they're leaving pack lands for an extended period, they have to report that, too, and if anyone goes missing . . . you get the idea. Since Packs govern themselves, a lot of Alphas probably chafed at the scrutiny, but so far, the federal government had never directly interfered.

And we didn't plan on doing that now. Our mission was simply to find the missing werewolves and report their location to their Alphas—and also take down whatever shadow agency had probably taken them for Iblis knew what purpose. After the whole vampire/necromancy thing, nothing would surprise me about this case.

"The only similarity with the missing couples is their history of infertility," Jaxon said. "So it's likely whoever took them is doing fertility experimentation. Maybe trying to find a way to turn humans into werewolves without the horrid bites and near-death experience forced wolves go through."

"Maybe." I wasn't sure how infertility played into making forced wolves transition more easily, but I also wasn't a geneticist, and forced wolves were already infertile.

The majority of Pack members were born wolves, and they were considered the only true werewolves by the Pack and its leadership. But if a shifted wolf bit, mangled, and nearly killed a human—and that human survived—they became what was called a "forced wolf." All the same hypersenses, reflexes, and strength of a born werewolf. The main difference was born wolves responded more readily to their beast nature, while forced wolves were often better able to control the animal within.

I'd only met two forced werewolves in my life—that I know of—and that was six years ago. Will and Kale both lived on a ranch in Colorado, its lands protected by magical wards that had been a gift to Will from my father for helping rescue him from Balthazar's traveling freak show.

Actually, calling Will wasn't a bad idea. He might have some thoughts on the missing pairs we hadn't come up with yet. The problem was I didn't have his number, and I couldn't use our internal computer to find it. That would only put attention on a rogue wolf trying to lay low. And I had a funny feeling he wasn't listed.

"What are you thinking about so hard?" Jaxon asked.

"Someone I used to know. And if what everyone is telling me is true, you knew him briefly, too."

"And who's that?"

"Will Carson."

Jaxon tilted his head slightly, as if pondering the name. If he had no idea who Will was, then maybe Jaxon wasn't actually part of my past like everyone kept telling me, and I wasn't crazy or—

"Oh, yes, the werewolf you and Julius worked with to free us from Balthazar's prison."

Bless it.

"Why do you think he'd know anything?" Jaxon asked.

"A hunch," I replied.

"Because of his and Kale's ranch?"

"Exactly," I said. "He must have a finger on the pulse of the werewolf world. Colorado isn't a Pack state, but he still helps werewolves out."

"Yeah. Did you ever ask about that?"

"I tried, but he wasn't a particularly talkative guy

the whole time I worked with him. And then he and Julius parted ways, and we haven't really had an opportunity to talk since."

"We'll put getting in touch with him on the To-Do List," Jaxon said. He took a breath, as if he had something else to say, and before I could prompt him, said, "Sorry—I hate to keep calling attention to this, but it's so strange listening to you talk about events we've experienced together—hell, the night we first met—and you have no recollection of my involvement."

"It's weird for me, too. It's like, I know there was a sixth cage, a sixth prisoner, but I don't know who it was. All I know is you telling me it was you, and it's so fucking frustrating."

"I'm sorry."

"It's not you that has to be sorry."

Not that it was necessarily me. But, despite only having known him for a day, I liked Jaxon. He was easy to talk to, if a little snippy thanks to his dose of vampire blood, and he seemed incredibly capable, if hatching this plan overnight with Novak was any indication. I could see why I liked working with him. It wasn't exactly fun to be with someone who was so sad just being around you, but in some ways he'd lost a lot more than I had.

We listened to the radio for the rest of the drive, and I gave him directions to the convenience store. The power of the crux danced beneath my breastbone and tickled across my skin, and I was surprised when Jaxon parked exactly on top of it.

He winked at my openmouthed self. "I use magic, too, remember?"

Skin-walker. Big deer. Duh.

Sweet Iblis, I need to start taking notes or something.

We'd all been reissued work phones, which had Wi-Fi and fun stuff like that, but they weren't the same as the special model phones that had once interfaced with the Knowledge Interface Matrix (which we all just called K.I.M.) back at the office. And with her offline, we had to go about things the old-fashioned way. Jaxon whipped out a burner and made the call to Novak . . .

. . . except the blessed crux played havoc with reception, so Jaxon had to back up a few yards to tell Novak we would be in position in exactly ten seconds, and then hung up. Moved the car back in place. And we waited . . .

I always hate this part.

Novak called to me a second later, his voice a distant bass in my head, as seductive as any fully powered incubus. It caressed my mind, my heart, and my body, then sent a flare of arousal between my thighs. His power was in his ability to arouse and claim a person, man or woman, and in order to teleport me to him, I had to want him.

So did poor Jaxon, and I closed my eyes so he

wasn't too embarrassed by the erection he'd be sporting by now. Intense heat surrounded me, followed by the sensation of falling. I fell for a lot longer than usual, probably because of the distance, and the heat fluctuated a few times in intensity. Beside me, Jaxon moaned—a super sexy sound that only fueled my own arousal and powered the incubus pulling us through, using the natural power of multiple ley lines.

Instead of a gentle arrival, I kind of crashed in the sense of a hard landing somewhere, but we didn't actually hit anything. Only appeared in the parking lot of some defunct department store with yellow caution tape around the main entrance. I wanted desperately to give in to the urge to cross my legs and help with the horniness problem, but Jaxon and I weren't alone.

Novak stood a few feet away, his dark skin covered in sweat, and gleaming in the sunshine. Next to him was Chandra herself, and she wasn't quite what I expected. Instead of the flowy robes and shimmering skin, Chandra wore jeans and a leather jacket, and her hair was twisted up into dozens of black braids. She was still pretty, but didn't shine and looked . . . normal.

Chandra laughed. "Your friend Novak had the same reaction when I picked him up from the airport," she said, her voice as normal as her appearance. "It's much easier to blend in like this than how I appear in your minds."

"I bet," I replied. I climbed out of our Explorer

with still slightly quaking knees to shake Chandra's hand. Her skin buzzed warmly with the power of her magic. "Nice to see you again."

"Likewise."

I glanced over at Jaxon, whose forehead was resting against the steering wheel. "I'm sure he'll join us when his problem goes down."

Novak smirked.

Giving Jaxon his privacy, I looked around to get my bearings. The decrepit neighborhood didn't offer any clues, though, and I really should have asked before we teleported. Novak had flown into Siskiyou County Airport, the closest one to the Pack lands, which was about a million acres of forestry and mountains north of Six Rivers National Forest, and not far from the Oregon border.

"Where exactly are we?" I asked.

"Etna, California," Chandra replied. "Population about seven hundred humans. With the crux and all the ley lines, though, I've sensed quite a few Paras who aren't showing themselves."

Something buzzed across the empty street, and I turned to see a pixie cloud disappear behind a brick building. Chandra wasn't wrong.

"So now that we're here, what's next?" I said. "Do we talk to the Homme Alpha?"

"Hopefully, yes."

"Hopefully?"

Chandra shrugged. "When we first became aware

of the missing wolves last week, we tried to get an audience with the Alpha, but he only said it was an internal matter. My hope is that with you three here, he'll change his mind."

"And why would he?" Jaxon asked in his faintly lilting voice. He'd finally joined our group on the pavement.

"Because you assisted in stopping a powerful necromancer, and you freed the missing vampires. If we're lucky, he'll see the value in our assistance and give us any information he or his people have."

"Sounds like a solid plan to me," Novak said. "We couldn't get anywhere with the Dame Alpha of Florida, but that was before we discovered the traitors in our midst. Perhaps the fact that we are not blindly standing by our fellow disgraced Marshals will prove good faith on our part."

I flashed Novak a bright smile. "Be still my heart, you almost sound like a hero."

He flipped me off.

"I'm glad you agree," Chandra said. She was also giving Novak a sweet side-eye, and I couldn't help wondering if they'd find a quiet spot later to give Novak a hand-healing power boost.

"I have one question," Jaxon said. "Yesterday morning, you were able to find Shiloh in Baltimore without her calling for you, and last night you said you could sense her calling because she's a woman."

"That is correct."

"So why can't you get into the head of Alice Anderson, or any of the other missing female wolves?"

Dude, that was a question I hadn't even considered. Made me glad this Jaxon guy was on our team.

"I'll be honest—I don't know why I cannot sense them," Chandra replied. "Moon witches can sense human and werewolf females exclusively, and I've never been unable to locate a mind I've previously touched like this. It is Shiloh's human half which allows me to find her mind in the mist, and I should be able to find Alice, but I can't. I worry it's because she's dead, but it's also possible I'm being blocked."

"Mist?" I repeated.

"The mist of human consciousness."

"Alrighty then. Now that we know that's a thing, let's go see about some werewolves."

CHAPTER 4

Despite them existing in various states for decades, today was the first time in my twenty-eight years on Earth that I set foot on Pack lands. I'd never had a reason before now, and Para-Marshals technically had no jurisdiction, so what was the point? I had no idea what to expect as Chandra drove up a single-lane paved road that snaked through gorgeous countryside. Trees and leaves and mountains, beautiful nature all around us. It would have made a wonderful national park if it hadn't been given to the werewolves.

But humans had plenty of national parks and Pack wolves basically lived in one area their entire lives—which was, believe it or not, not much longer than the average human.

I'd half expected a gate or fancy entrance of some kind, but the only reason I knew when we'd driven into Pack land was the sentries on the sides of the road. Dark-haired shadows dashing from tree to tree, watching without interfering.

The road led us into a small town that could be found in any rural area: wooden homes, a grocery store, a diner, a school, and various other buildings necessary for day-to-day life. Nothing very modern, nothing looking particularly prosperous. Old, faded ads in the stores. The only thing I didn't see was a stoplight or a church. And, of course, we *did* see a lot more wolves than in your typical Main Street. People mingled with them on the sidewalks, and many stopped to look at the unfamiliar car—which is when I noticed there weren't all that many cars anywhere. This little town had been carved out of the forest, and it almost felt like a faded fairy-tale setting.

Chandra knew where to go, because she followed the road through the quaint town, and up another path toward the biggest log cabin I'd ever seen. Three stories, huge, with a wide porch and lots of windows. Had to be the Homme Alpha's residence, and it was as ostentatious as the town was . . . well . . . poor.

I really needed not to form an opinion about this Alpha, but I kind of disliked him already. Every Pack Alpha ruled differently, some with an open hand and others with an iron first. Some adhered to a rigid hierarchy, and others only paid it lip service. I had a funny feeling this was a strict, heavy-handed Alpha who treated his wolves like peons.

This wasn't going to be a fun meeting.

"Are there any forced wolves in this Pack?" I asked.

"None that I'm aware of," Chandra replied. "I checked the registry this morning to make sure no one else had disappeared in the meantime, and all the entries were listed as B."

B for born.

"Why's that important?" Jaxon asked.

"Might not be, but it says something about the Alpha," I replied. "In a state the size of California, you can't tell me there aren't any rogue or forced wolves out there, and if they ever applied for protection with the Pack, they obviously didn't get it."

"Good point."

Chandra parked near two navy SUVs and cut the engine. The front door of the big lodge opened, and two brown-furred beasts walked out, followed by a tall woman in a pantsuit. Her cold gaze did not get my hopes up that this would be productive.

"Who's that?" Jaxon asked.

"Her name is Rosalind," Chandra replied. "She's the Pack Second, and she's a bitch. And not just because she's a dog."

I held back a snort.

We all exited the car, Novak having a bit of trouble with the door handle. Poor guy needed raunchy sex soon so his hands could start to properly heal.

Not that I was volunteering. Ever.

Knowing I had (supposedly) banged another team-mate in the past was awkward enough.

Focusing on the confrontation that was about to unfold—and even though I'd been second on my team, and Chandra third on hers—I deferred to her on this. We were in her territory, after all.

"Para-Marshal Goodfellow," Rosalind said from the porch, flanked by both beasts. "And guests."

"Ma'am," Chandra said. She introduced the three of us. "We wish to speak with Alpha Kennedy."

"On what matter? We have no business with the US Marshals Service at this time."

The she-wolf's superior tone was grating on my blessed nerves.

"It's the continuing matter of your missing wolves," Chandra replied. "Recently, several vampire Lines saw the disappearance of their members, and these Marshals were instrumental in their return. Perhaps we can be of service to you."

"You certainly are persistent," Rosalind said.

"When people are missing, persistence often pays off."

"Hmm. I'll see if the Alpha is prepared for visitors." Rosalind turned and went back into the house. Her lupine escort remained on the steps, alert and waiting.

I'd never fought a shifted werewolf before, and I didn't want to try now. While I had a hearty constitution and was very hard to kill, thanks to my djinn half, I wasn't sure I wanted to wrestle a two-hundred-pound wolf.

Jaxon leaned closer and whispered, "Feel like I need some Scooby Snacks, or something."

I clapped a hand over my mouth so I didn't laugh. One of the wolves tilted his head at us and his ears swiveled forward.

Either the Alpha was busy, or they wanted to make us sweat, but Rosalind took her sweet time returning to the porch. "He will see you," she said.

Thank Iblis.

Chandra led the way, and our quartet ascended the five wood steps to the porch. Both wolves stood on opposite sides of the door and we passed into a wide foyer. Lots of bare wood floors and walls inside. Rosalind walked down a long hallway to a big open doorway. I sensed no wards or other magic charms, only the vague magic werewolves used for their transformations, buzzing just below my skin.

The room reminded me of some bizarre cross between a king's throne and a man cave. A big leather recliner was situated near the center, and on some kind of pedestal that allowed the Alpha to swivel from a big-screen TV to any audience who might collect behind him. A small bar was set up to the right, and a comfortable chair on the left in a soft purple fabric was probably Rosalind's place.

From the recliner, a barrel-chested man with a lot

of silver in his black hair stared down at us with wide copper eyes. Eyes that were both curious and bland, interested and likewise dismissing us right away.

Needless to say, I didn't like the guy.

"Homme Alpha Kennedy," Chandra said. "It is a pleasure to be seen by you once again."

"Madam Goodfellow," Kennedy replied in a deep baritone. "By bringing strangers to my home, you've piqued my interest. How can I assist the Para-Marshals this fine day?"

"Sir, the question is not how you may help us, but how we may help you."

"Oh?" He sniffed in their general direction. "A demon. A skin-walker. And . . . someone unusual."

A majority of Paras had never met a djinn, so my mixed heritage tended to confuse most people I met. I wasn't about to offer Alpha Kennedy any answers as to my odd scent, though.

"How are they of use to me?" Kennedy asked.

"Sir," Chandra replied, "surely you've heard of the many missing vampires who were kidnapped as pawns in a power play by traitors to our Para-Marshal units. These three agents were instrumental in finding the kidnapped vampire children and returning them to their Line Masters." She also introduced us by name, and he turned his attention to me.

"I've heard the name Shiloh Harrison."

Novak grumped and rolled his eyes.

"I helped find answers for Woodrow Tennyson and his fellow Masters," I said. "I'd like to do the same for you, Alpha."

Kennedy sneered. "We do not require the help of outsiders."

"No? Then where are your missing werewolves?"

"Watch your tone, child," Rosalind said. "You are speaking to the Homme Alpha of California."

While the guy could shift quickly and slit my throat with one paw swipe, I was not impressed with the title. Titles meant nothing without something to back it up.

"Lady, I've spoken to the goddess Brighid herself on another plane of existence. One werewolf Alpha does not impress me, and his stubbornness in accepting our help is silly." I looked at Kennedy again, whose face was stony. "You have resources, and so do I. Pack law supersedes US law on your lands, but something tells me your missing wolves aren't on Pack land anymore. You need people on your side who know the outside world, and if you've spent the better part of your life on your high horse, up in these mountains, then it's not you."

Jaxon gave me an *are you crazy?* look, while Novak simply yawned. I ignored Chandra, half expecting someone to lunge at us. Instead, the Alpha threw back his head and laughed.

"You are an interesting one, Shiloh Harrison," Kennedy said. "I don't know what you are, but you show great bravery in the face of deadly odds. If I give the order, none of you will leave these lands alive."

"But you won't do that." I squared my shoulders. "Besides the fact that we're all federal officials who will be missed if we disappear, you need us, even if you can't admit it. Your outside movements are limited, as are your choices. Maybe this will help with your decision, too: we're not here acting as Para-Marshals, Alpha. All of us are here as civilians with special abilities and an interest in finding the missing wolves. I can go home as easily as I came here and not lose a moment's sleep wondering what could have been, but can you say the same? You are charged with the safety of every wolf in your Pack, and now fourteen of your wolves are missing. Seven couples. We're offering our resources to help you get them back, free and clear, with no ulterior motives."

"You would risk your lives for wolves you don't even know, and yet you want no reward?"

I stared blandly at the Alpha, because yes, I'd just said that. Maybe it seemed unbelievably altruistic, but people were missing. Werewolves or humans, they deserved to be found and brought home. And if these disappearances were in any way connected to the people behind the necromancer, I wanted their asses in a jail cell STAT.

"A word in private, Alpha," Rosalind said before I could respond.

Kennedy nodded, and the pair walked to the far

side of the room together. No one in our quartet had super hearing, and I can't read lips, so I shifted my weight and tried to stay patient. So much depended on a chance to explore these lands, and hopefully I hadn't blown it with my big, blunt mouth. We didn't bother whispering amongst ourselves, because what was the point? Kennedy, Rosalind, and the two human-shaped werewolves in the corners of the room could hear anything we said.

I deserve a treat for not tapping my feet with impatience.

The wolf leaders finally returned, Kennedy to his reclining throne, and Rosalind just to his right. "You have permission to remain on Pack lands until dusk tomorrow," Kennedy said. "I will provide a guide for you. You may take nothing from these lands when you leave."

"Alpha," Jaxon said, "does *nothing* also apply to photographs?"

"We shall inspect your photographs before you leave to ensure nothing you've taken will endanger my people or our ways."

"Agreeable, thank you."

So roughly thirty-six hours, give or take, to investigate a million acres. Great. No problem.

"Gideon," Kennedy said.

A black-haired man stepped forward from his corner of the room. Dressed in jeans and a plain black polo, he was good-looking in a grumpy-pup kind of way, and he stopped an arm's reach from me.

"Alpha," Gideon said.

"You will be our guests' guide while they are here," Kennedy replied. "Show them where they'd like to visit, within reason."

"Yes, Alpha."

"May I inquire about accommodations for the night?" Chandra asked. "Or will we be allowed to leave for a human motel?"

Kennedy stared. "You will be allowed to leave for the evening to rest. You are not my prisoners, but while you're on Pack land, Gideon will escort you as a group."

Bless it, splitting up meant covering more ground. But we were lucky Kennedy hadn't simply sent us packing. Hopefully we could at least visit the homes of the missing couples and check for evidence of a struggle.

"If you have further questions about the wolves who are missing," Kennedy added, "Gideon is aware of what he may and may not tell you."

"Understood, Alpha," Chandra said. "We appreciate your patience and generosity in this matter."

Her people skills impressed me all over the place, because I know I'd have struggled being so diplomatic with a guy who clearly didn't like us or want us here— which I'd already proven earlier. Still, you'd think he would be eager to have help in locating his missing Pack members, but what do I know? My interactions with Pack werewolves were extremely limited, and they did things their way.

"If you'll follow me," Gideon said.

Our group did so, but instead of taking us outside, Gideon led us to a different downstairs room of the large house. The small room was lined wall-to-wall with filing cabinets, with a table and three chairs dead center, like some sort of records room, and it barely had enough space for five adults to stand.

"I imagine taking a look at our investigation into the disappearances is a good starting point," Gideon said.

I blinked hard, then exchanged surprised looks with Chandra. Neither of us had expected the Pack to share their internal investigation, so yeah. Good starting point.

"I know Alpha Kennedy comes across as cold in this matter," Gideon added, "but he cannot show his worry to strangers. If the Pack found out, *they'd* worry, and he's doing his best to keep everyone calm until we know who took our brethren and why."

"That makes sense," Jaxon replied. "The Pack looks to him for guidance."

"Exactly."

"Well, we appreciate whatever you can show us," I said. "The Para-Marshals aren't officially investigating, because the Packs haven't asked for our help. The only reason we discovered any Pack members were missing is because a Master vampire told us last week."

"Yes, Alpha Kennedy received a visit from a Line Master two weeks ago," Gideon said. "He was inquiring if the Alpha had heard anything about vampire disappearances, and Alpha Kennedy in turn reported our problem to him. But he rejected the idea of a larger conspiracy at work."

"I don't suppose the vampire's name was Woodrow Tennyson."

"It was."

That absolutely did not surprise me. "Well, good, because that's who told us about the missing wolves."

"Then perhaps Fate was right to send you to us today."

"Guess we'll see."

Gideon produced seven manila folders, none of them very thick. "One for each couple who was taken. All were mated pairs."

"And none of them had offspring, correct?" I already knew the answer to this, but it never hurt to test how truthful our guide was going to be with us.

"Six couples never produced children, correct. However, the Andersons did have three children, but they all perished in a terrible carbon monoxide accident in the home."

Novak grunted.

"May I see the Anderson file, please?" Chandra asked. Gideon handed it over, and we all tried to crowd around it, but the space was limited. "They had permission to live in Sacramento, away from Pack lands, correct?"

"They did," Gideon replied. "Raymond had a brilliant mind for technology, and Alice an aptitude for mathematics. They were able to achieve well-paid careers in the human world, which allowed them to channel funds back into the Pack. While we are somewhat self-sustaining in terms of farming and generating our own electricity, werewolves make poor animal farmers, so we still purchase our meat and other products from outside suppliers. We require income to sustain those purchases."

Dude, that was more information about how the Pack worked than I ever expected to learn today, and it fascinated me. I figured the wolves probably worked in the small towns near their land to get money, but installing smart people in high-paying jobs across the state was pretty brilliant. And it explained how Chandra was able to help the Andersons with their infertility issues without Kennedy's scrutiny—or approval.

"Did any of the other missing couples live outside the Pack land?" Jaxon asked.

"Two others." Gideon produced the files. "The Barrows lived and worked in San Francisco, and the Porters in San Diego."

"Are they the only wolves of yours who live outside this land?"

"They are not." However, Gideon didn't elaborate on that comment, probably because it wasn't relevant to the case.

"Are any of the other couples still working in different cities also barren?" Chandra asked.

Gideon hedged a bit. "One other is, but the rest are not. Because we cannot lose the income, we did send guards to watch their homes and businesses as a precaution."

Smart move. Without knowing why these couples were being targeted specifically, that unnamed barren pair could be in danger.

"So only three of the missing couples lived away from Pack lands," I said so we were all on the same page.

"Which means eight werewolves were somehow taken from here without anyone knowing about it," Jaxon added, his voice taking on a slightly stronger twang as he laid out a subtle implication that their security was lacking.

Wait, how do I know his voice does that?

Gideon gave us both a bland look. "We have over a million acres of land to patrol, and only eighty-one Dominant wolves capable of watching our borders. With only one main road in and out of our settlement, it's difficult to know how they were taken and from which point."

"You didn't scent anyone other than your own?" Chandra asked.

"No, and that's all in those files. We didn't discover that the Andersons, Barrows, or Porters were missing until almost a week after the fact, when our communication with them ceased, so any lingering scents were gone there, too. No signs of a struggle in any of the homes."

"Nothing to suggest they left willingly?" Novak asked. He usually left this kind of stuff to us, but he was watching Gideon with open suspicion now.

"It's difficult to know. A lot of clothing was left behind, food as well. We found suitcases in each residence, so if they left willingly, they didn't take much. And where on earth would they go?"

Exactly what we wanted to know.

I scanned the Porter file, but nothing in it stood out.

"We don't know where," Chandra said, "but based on the fact that six of the seven couples missing were all barren does suggest a why: someone is experimenting on werewolf procreation."

"Which leads to an even bigger *why*," I added. "And also a big blessed *who*. Can we visit the homes of the four couples who lived here?"

"Yes," Gideon replied. "Would you like to go now?"

"Can we take these files with us?"

"No."

Bless it. "Okay, then give us some time to read them before we go."

Gideon nodded.

We pored through the seven slim files, but I didn't see anything terribly useful. They could have been forced out of their homes as easily as they left willingly, but there was no clear sign of which.

"Did you do any fingerprinting?" I asked.

"We do not use that type of technology here, no," Gideon replied.

"Will we be allowed to?"

The expression he leveled at me reminded me of when a dog's ears go flat. "I will inquire with Rosalind about your request. Excuse me, please."

He left us alone in the room, which was kind of ballsy, considering the dozens of filing cabinets containing decades of Pack information. All at our fingertips. But he was trusting us, so I kept my curiosity in check.

"There isn't much in these files," Jaxon said after a few minutes of silent reading. "Then again, these guys aren't trained investigators. At least, not in the sense of a thorough investigation. I mean, fingerprinting? Who doesn't do that?"

"Pack animals who rely more on scent than human technology," Chandra replied. "Remember, born wolves rely more on their inner beasts than their human minds."

"Except wolves like the Andersons who are allowed to be educated on human technology for the benefit of the Pack?"

"Exactly."

"Oh, hey, that reminds me," I said. "When we get to our motel tonight and find some workable Wi-Fi, I need to get online and track down a forced wolf I used to know. He keeps his ear to the Para underground, specifically with werewolves, so he could be a useful resource."

"You haven't contacted him yet?"

"I've been a little busy, and he's off the grid, so finding him isn't as easy as Google."

"Understood. I don't suppose he has any female companions I could find?"

"None I'm aware of."

Jaxon's face went slack, a sure sign he knew something but wasn't sure he should say it, and godsdammit, instinctively knowing these things about the guy without understanding why was going to give me a migraine.

"What is it?" I asked him.

"Look, we talked a little that day after the freak house bust," Jaxon said. "He let it slip that he has a daughter."

"Really?"

"Yeah, she was a kid then, so she'd be early teens by now, I guess."

"If she's achieved her first cycle of the moon, I can find her," Chandra said.

Jaxon blinked dumbly at her.

"Her first period," I said.

"Oh." His cheeks pinked in an adorable way. "Uh, okay."

"The middle of the Homme Alpha's house might not be the best time for a mental phone call, though, so maybe we can reach out later?"

Chandra nodded.

Gideon returned with a shocking yes from Rosalind for taking fingerprints, and with nothing left to see or do here, he led us outside. "I'll lead you to the Chandler home first," he said. "They're closest. You can follow my truck."

We got back in the Jeep, Chandra behind the wheel. Novak and I were in the back, and I reached into the rear compartment to dig out a fingerprint kit. Gideon led us back down the main road toward the little town, and then onto a narrow road that split rows of various kinds of homes. Some were single-wide trailers that had seen better days, others were simple log cabins, and a few looked like pre-fab homes, probably added over the years as the Pack grew.

He stopped in the yard of a log cabin, so Chandra pulled up behind him. The yard was a little messy, but hey, no one had been home to tend it for a while. Gideon walked right in like he owned the place.

"Don't you guys use keys?" I asked as I followed him.

"No need," Gideon replied. "Theft is one of gravest crimes and receives swift punishment. The Pack must work together to survive, so we share freely and know better than to disrespect another."

Too bad humans can't be as well behaved as Pack wolves.

"How are they punished?" Jaxon asked.

"For a first offense, they lose their tail, which places them at the bottom as a disgraced wolf." Gideon glanced around the small interior as if bored. "As a disgraced wolf, they no longer run with the Pack during the full moon. If they offend again, they are put down."

"Sorry I asked."

Iblis—I was sorry he asked, too.

"As I said, we must work as a Pack to ensure our survival. Mankind won't do it for us, and honestly, you could learn from our laws."

I snorted. "Dude, in some places on Earth, countries cut the hand off a thief for a first offense, and it still doesn't deter crime. Desperate people will do desperate things, no matter the consequences."

"Perhaps if your people did more to help each other, they would be less desperate."

"Mister, I am right there with you, and unfortunately, we aren't here to confab about ways to save the world from hunger. Can we look around?"

"Of course."

I handed the fingerprint kit off to Jaxon—trusting he knew how to use it—so I could poke around. Chandra and I were both sensitive to certain kinds of magic, so we moved through the cabin. Novak, too, because he could sense if demons had been in an area within a certain time frame—not that we had any indication that something demonic was at work here.

The downstairs was a big open space with a kitchen, living room, and eating area. The bedrooms were near the back, one with the standard furniture, and other an office of some kind.

No kids.

No overt sense that anything magical had happened here from me or Chandra. The bedroom had clothes, the bed was neatly made. Food was rotting in the fridge like whoever had left had intended to come back one day—or had been forced out with nothing. No real signs of a struggle anywhere in the place. The Chandlers had simply . . . vanished.

Which, knowing what I know about magic, teleportation, and other stuff, was entirely possible. Oh, hey!

"What about teleportation?" I said to the group at large, who'd reassembled in the living room, where Jaxon was painstakingly trying to lift prints. "I mean, Novak popped me and Jaxon across the country, so couldn't someone have potentially teleported the werewolves to another location?"

"It's definitely possible," Novak replied. "How it's done depends on who's doing the teleporting. For an incubus, I rely on my target being aroused, whereas a djinn can pop wherever he or she chooses."

"But djinn can't teleport someone else unless it's part of a wish." The air around me shifted in an odd way, as if invisible waves of magic had rippled outward from a disturbance. I caught Novak's deep frown; he'd sensed it, too.

"So who else can teleport?" Gideon asked, seemingly quite interested in our magical conversation. Werewolves knew of the existence of fae, demons, and other creatures, but he probably didn't get off Pack land often enough to experience it. Who else indeed—

Good evening, Shiloh, Tennyson's voice boomed in my head. *Miss me?*

"What the ever-loving heaven?" I turned around and my mouth fell open, stunned stupid to see Woodrow Tennyson, vampire Master, standing in the cabin's open doorway.

CHAPTER 5

The first time Tennyson spoke directly into my head, I thought my brain was going to explode. Or simply liquefy and leak out my ears. Once we got our telepathic mojo going, though, it was less brain-explodey, but it was always uncomfortable.

Until today. He'd spoken in my head at a pretty normal voice level, and the instant our eyes met, something deep inside me quivered, as if sensing the connection we'd made by him sharing his blood. It also made my mouth water for a nice, bloody steak, and that was bad.

Yet probably not as bad as him suddenly showing up on Pack land.

"What are you doing here?" I asked.

Before Tennyson could respond, Gideon inserted

himself between him and us—not that Tennyson could enter a private residence without permission from someone non-vampiric. "Does Alpha Kennedy know you're here, vampire?"

"He does not," Tennyson replied. Outside my head, his voice had a deeper pedigree and the inflections of someone from high-society Europe—and it occurred to me I'd never asked Tennyson where he originally came from. He was five hundred plus-years old and obviously not Native American, so unless he came over on the *Nina*, *Pinta*, or *Santa Maria* . . . .

And where on earth could he have come from to have hair like that? It flowed down to his mid-back in thick layers of ethereal colors—every imaginable shade of brown, black, red, copper, gold, blond, silver, and white separating the individual strands. Maybe that's what happened to the hair of really, really old vampires? But paired with his pale skin and sharp jawline, he was both incredibly handsome and an obvious predator, even when he wasn't baring his fangs or changing his eye color with his emotions.

"My business is with the Para-Marshals, not your Alpha," Tennyson continued.

"Announcing yourself to the Alpha is a sign of respect," Gideon replied, the first edge of a growl in his voice.

"Respect goes both ways, wolf. I seem to recall your Alpha ordering me off his lands and to keep my ridiculous conspiracy theories to myself, and yet now

I find you are employing Para-Marshals in your efforts to locate your missing Pack members."

"We haven't employed anyone. They came to my Alpha and asked permission to carry out an independent investigation. Our missing are still considered an internal matter."

"Hmm." Tennyson looked right over Gideon's head. "Shiloh, you look well. I am pleased to see this for myself."

"Thanks," I replied. "Uh, you too." Suddenly the pulse point on the side of Jaxon's neck looked way too interesting. "You came all the way to California to find us? You couldn't have called first?" Wait a minute. "How *did* you find us?"

"You and I are connected, remember? I can sense you if I reach out far enough."

"Oh."

"That is really creepy," Jaxon said under his breath. Novak grunted his agreement.

Tennyson's lips twitched. "Skin-walker. How are your wounds?"

Holy crap, he's asking how Jaxon is?

I didn't remember any of Jaxon and Tennyson's previous interactions, but I was smart enough to know they'd been strained. Maybe because of me? Tennyson and I had spent a lot of time alone together this past week, and if Jaxon and I had been together once, maybe he was jealous? No, that didn't fit my impression of Jaxon as a person.

Overprotective?

Jaxon took off his baseball cap to reveal closely shorn hair. "Healing, thanks."

"I am glad," Tennyson replied. "You fought bravely that night, and you are important to Shiloh."

"Uh-huh."

Yeah, definitely overprotective.

"Vampire," Gideon said, clearly not enjoying this casual banter, "If my Alpha ordered you off our lands, then you have no business here. Leave."

"No," Tennyson said without looking at Gideon.

"Okay, let me handle this," I said. I inserted myself between the posturing vampire and werewolf. "Tennyson? Outside."

His mouth twitched as he bowed slightly and left the cabin's small porch. I followed him onto the porch and shut the door, and this close to Tennyson, his power crackle-popped across my skin. I licked my lips, remembering the addictive taste of his blood, and positive this was a bad idea. But despite the fact that vampires and djinn are mortal enemies—even though myth tells us we're cousins—I considered Tennyson a friend. And he'd sought me out for a reason.

"I told you on the phone that I'm fine," I said. "Why are you really here?"

Tennyson tilted his head at me. He wore a thick cloak to protect himself from direct sunlight, the hood now down in the shade of the porch's roof. "Three days ago, you were near death, and now you're here, searching for missing werewolves, instead of spending time repairing your broken relationship with a man you say you care about."

For a split second, I thought he mean Jaxon, who was right here with me, until I remembered Vincent. "I tried calling Vincent but so far he's ignoring me. And it's hard to ignore a moon witch when she gets into your head and asks for help," I replied. Off his curious frown, I gave him a condensed version of why we were here.

"You have found no sign that these mated pairs were taken by force?" Tennyson asked.

"Not yet, but we haven't been investigating for long. So far, there's no evidence, no leads, nothing in this house that helps us. It's like they vanished into thin air."

"Such a fate is possible, but unlikely, considering thirteen of the fourteen pairs taken from both California and Florida were barren."

"Spoiler alert. The fourteenth pair only had children because Chandra intervened with magic."

"Interesting. The witch admitted this?"

"Yup. Also spoiler alert. All three of those kids are dead."

Tennyson narrowed his eyes. "Alpha Kennedy or his Second likely had those children killed."

My entire body jerked at how bluntly he'd stated something we had only suspected. "That's a bold accusation."

"Pack werewolves are extremely suspicious of modern medicine, preferring the old ways when one falls ill. They'd see infertility as a punishment from their goddess Danu, not as something to be overcome. If the Alpha became aware of this witch helping a mated pair conceive, he'd see it as a bad omen and fear retaliation from Danu. The only way to regain balance would be to eliminate the unnatural children."

"Yeah, but assuming Danu is real, is any goddess genuinely appeased by the murder of children?"

He gave me a droll look. "You'd be shocked."

No doubt.

"I don't suppose you have a personal relationship with Danu like you did with Brighid?" I asked.

"Even if I did, young djinn, what would motivate me to assist you in this endeavor? With Brighid, my own children's lives were at stake."

"No pun intended."

He quirked a slim eyebrow. "My point is, what do I have to gain by arranging an audience with Danu?"

"Wait a minute." I studied his blank face, unable to tell if he was leading me on or not. But Tennyson had been completely genuine in all our previous interactions, so I had no reason to doubt he wasn't sincere with his question. "Are you telling me Danu is real and you know her?"

"I'm merely asking a question."

"So am I. Tennyson, please." I reached for his arm, then pulled back, uncertain if physical contact was okay. Just because I'd drunk his blood more than once didn't give me the right to get handsy with a Master. "You may not like werewolves as a general rule, but twenty-eight lives are at stake, and it's possible three innocent children were murdered. And you didn't just come out here to check up on me. Can you help?"

Tennyson watched me with eyes that sparkled with flecks of green. The air around us charged with a warm, sweet scent I'd begun to associate with him being curious about something. And the weirdness of the fact that I could scent his emotions was still bizarre, but nothing about my life could be considered normal.

Other than maybe the desire to fix things with my boyfriend, but how do you reconcile getting kidnapped by a necromancer intent on controlling an entire line of vampires? Especially when you won't freaking call your girlfriend back?

Yeah.

"Vampires are not altruistic by nature," Tennyson finally said. "We are, in fact, quite selfish. As a Master of some age, I have acquired a wealth of knowledge over the past five centuries, and I cannot merely parcel it out to anyone who asks."

I nearly asked why not before I remembered the selfish part. "So, what do you want in return for said information?"

"I find the work you do fascinating, Marshal Harrison, and I quite enjoyed our previous partnership. I also find you fascinating with your dual nature, and I am rarely so enticed these days. My general assistance comes with a simple request: I wish to, as they say in the vernacular, tag along."

"You want a ride-along on a missing werewolf case?"

"I do."

"Sweet Iblis, but you vampires are weird."

Tennyson smiled. "I can easily say the same about yourself and the creatures you associate with. You went above and beyond helping me save the kidnapped vampires, and while my children were sacrificed, you also sacrificed a great deal of yourself to your work, and I admire that. As I've previously said, I have never found myself in the position of admiring a djinn before, and I find the experience unique. I would like to continue our professional relationship."

Jaxon is going to shit himself if I say yes.

But as Tennyson himself admitted, he was five centuries old and he knew things. He wasn't going to give his vast knowledge away for nothing, not even permission to tag along while we investigated. And then his words came back to me.

"You said your general assistance in exchange for the ride-along." I crossed my arms and dared hold his gaze. "What about contributing your own personal resources and contacts, such as an audience with Danu? What will that cost?"

His lips twitched. "You are learning, young djinn."

"Figuring out people is part of my job."

"For additional information such as my contacts and resources, I may request small favors in exchange."

"Favors from whom?"

"As you are the only person on your team who does not appear to despise me, they will likely come from you, or those you can influence on my behalf."

I huffed. "You know, part of being on a team is pooling your resources for the good of the job."

"And as the skin-walker is fond of pointing out, I am not part of your team. I am, as you might say, a civilian."

"A civilian with information we could use."

He tilted his head, his expression bordering on smug without tipping over. And the bastard had every right to be smug, because he could potentially help us, and he knew it. As I internally debated his involvement, a rather sickening thought popped in my head:

What would Julius do?

In the past, that was my go-to question when I had to make a difficult decision regarding the team. And in the past, the answer rarely steered me wrong. But Julius had betrayed the team and died a reanimated head. I needed to trust my own intuition. Listen to my gut.

My gut said Tennyson's future favors might give me an ulcer, but they would probably be worth it. His intel and assistance had been beneficial thus far, and he had yet to abuse my trust or my faith in him.

"Jaxon is going to murder me," I said.

Tennyson's lips twitched. "Is that a yes to my proposal?"

"Not yet. First, how did you get out of jail?"

"I may have made a very sizable monetary donation to both local and state law enforcement in exchange for the charges being dropped. No humans were actively injured, and I also offered monetary compensation to every person held captive in their home in Myrtle's Acres."

"You bought your way out of it?"

"I believe the technical term is *bribed*," he said with a smirk. "Wealth has its perks. Besides, your judiciary system is ill-equipped to not only try a vampire in court, but to enforce their judgments upon me."

He wasn't wrong about that, which is why the Para-Marshals deal with paranormal crimes, not human police.

Dealt with. Whatever. I loved my job and needed to believe we'd come back from this and function as a unit again.

"Okay—maybe don't mention that to the others."

"I will restrain myself."

"Appreciate that," I said dryly. "Can you wait out here while I break the news to my team?" I asked. "I don't want to piss Gideon off by inviting you inside."

Tennyson quirked one eyebrow, probably because he didn't get to witness the fallout of my decision. I wasn't entirely sure it was the smartest move, but I had to trust my instincts here. We needed every extra brain and set of eyes on this case if we were going to find the missing werewolves. And we *did* work well together.

I went back inside the cabin and found all four people staring back at me with expectant expressions. Well, three were expectant, and Jaxon looked irritated. "Why is he here?" Jaxon asked.

"He wants to help," I replied, straightening my spine. "And I said he could join our investigation."

"Are you *kidding* me?" He threw his hands up. "Shiloh, why?"

"Because he's got five hundred years of experience behind him, and he has ties to stronger paranormal beings than us that could be incredibly useful. He got me an audience with Brighid last week, remember?"

"He did?" Chandra closed the few feet of space between us, her dark eyes lighting up. "You've actually met the goddess?"

"Yes, and she's a haughty, sex-crazed bitch, but she gave us useful information while we were tracking the necromancer."

"She's the goddess of fertility, of course she loves sex. I'd do almost anything for a face-to-face with my mother goddess."

"I hope you mean that, because Tennyson's favors will require something in repayment."

"Of course they will," Jaxon said with a snort. "That creature doesn't do anything without an ulterior motive."

"It's part of his nature, okay?" I snapped. "Vampires don't do favors for nothing—they don't have the same altruistic nature as the rest of us. He has nothing at stake in finding the werewolves, so he won't interfere or be a burden. All he wants to do is be part of this, and like I said, potential useful info in his head."

"And stay close to you." Jaxon's narrowed eyes and tight fists clearly spoke to his feelings on *that*. "If he hurts you or anyone else in this room, I will drive a stake through his heart without hesitation." He doubled over, hands flying to his temples. "Get out of my head!"

"Tennyson!"

Apologies, Shiloh. I merely told the skin-walker he has nothing to fear from me.

Maybe wait and tell him in person. Your voice is hard to handle.

I didn't get an answer.

"So vampires are telepathic," Chandra said. "Fascinating."

"Some are, some aren't," I replied. "I guess different Masters develop different abilities as they get older, and that's one of his tricks. But if you aren't used to it, it's like someone talking through a bullhorn right into your ear."

"That sounds awful."

"It fucking is awful," Jaxon said. "He better not do that again unless it's life or death."

"Can we focus, or what?" Novak asked. "The vampire can wait until we're done here."

"You're right," I said.

"I must protest this," Gideon said. The young wolf had been shockingly quiet for a while, but his glare for Tennyson hadn't eased. "Alpha Kennedy must be informed of the vampire's arrival and inclusion in this investigation."

"Can't you wait for a couple of hours? What if your Alpha changes his mind and makes us all leave? We'll never find your missing brethren without a thorough search, and Tennyson can sense different kinds of magic than the rest of us. Please."

Gideon held my gaze, his eyes steely, before nodding once. "Continue."

"Thank you. Jaxon, how are you doing with fingerprints?" Even though I'd handed the task to him without thought, I still didn't *know* he was any good at lifting prints.

"I've got plenty, and so far all appear to be were-wolf," he replied, "but I won't know whose they are until I can get into a human town, find some Wi-Fi and send them to the Registry. And I found 'em all over the place, so it doesn't look like anything got wiped down."

Werewolf fingerprints were remarkably different than other humanoid species, such as vampires, djinn or, well, humans. The friction ridges were spaced wider apart and the whorls went sideways instead of vertical. All this told us was that no one else except wolves had been in this cabin recently—or at least, no one except wolves had touched anything.

It was once more pointing to the theory the two Chandlers had simply vanished into thin air.

"Would you like to see the next home?" Gideon asked, his tone a bit less friendly now that he was helping us hide Tennyson from the Alpha for a few hours.

"Yes, please," Chandra replied. "It's unlikely we'll find anything new at the other homes, but it's worth investigating."

Outside, Tennyson was waiting in the shade of the porch, his expression benign. Novak and Jaxon barely glanced at him on the way to the Jeep, but Chandra approached and introduced herself. Tennyson did the same and gave a polite, old-school bow.

"I have met a few vampires in my time," Chandra said, "but never a Master of a Line, and certainly not one who knows my mother goddess."

Tennyson glanced at me, and I mouthed, "Brighid," at him.

"Ah yes, the goddess of warfare," he replied. "I didn't realize she created the moon witch line."

"She did, and while I've heard her voice in my head at the full moon several times, I've never been graced with her presence."

"Consider yourself lucky, witch. Brighid is clever and not without her sharp edges."

"I have edges of my own, vampire."

With Tennyson and Chandra standing beside each other, another option became crystal clear and super-obvious. "If Brighid is your mother goddess," I said, "wouldn't she be interested in knowing the children one of her daughters created have possibly been murdered?"

Chandra's lips parted. "It's possible. Perhaps she'd know or be able to learn something for us."

"Remember: Brighid's help always comes at a price," Tennyson said. "Speaking with Shiloh was my favor, as we were seeking my children. If you ask this of her, she'll require something of you."

And that price would be steep. I shoved away the memory of Tennyson kneeling between Brighid's spread legs with his teeth in her thigh. Apparently vampire bites near the groin give goddesses a super-max orgasm, but goddess blood tastes like pig shit to vampires. Tennyson had done me a big favor last week.

But that wasn't the only problem.

"Is she still located in Newark, Delaware, or did she move?" I asked Tennyson.

"She moves frequently, as she has a distaste for screwing the same human twice," he replied. "I would have to reach out to my contacts in order to find her new home."

"Can you do that sometime soon?"

"Certainly. I can do it in the car on the way to our next location." He tapped the side of his head, and yeah, telepathy was going to be a big asset for us going forward. Jaxon and Novak could hate it all they wanted, but Tennyson was useful.

Tennyson put his hood up, and after a brief argument, Jaxon drove with Novak shotgun. I sat in the middle in the back seat, which put me in a great position to get annoyed glares from Jaxon in the rearview mirror. Gideon led us down another quiet street to a yellow trailer that had seen better days. A few kids played in one yard, and they stopped to watch our crew go inside. Tennyson stayed in the car to make his brain-calls.

The Drake house was in the same condition as the Chandler house: everything left in such a way that the two people who lived here could have simply vanished during the Revelation. Someone had even left a half-eaten sandwich on the counter. And Jaxon once again found only werewolf fingerprints.

"Brighid is not currently on the mortal plane," Tennyson reported when we returned to the Jeep. "I have a contact who will advise me when she returns."

"Thanks for trying," I said.

On the drive to the Riggs house, I studied the yards and roads. For such a tight-knit community, no one seemed to be around. Had Alpha Kennedy issued some sort of directive that everyone stay inside while we toured the lands, so we couldn't interact with them? Possible, but what about the kids near the Drakes' house?

Maybe this Pack was simply wary of strangers. I'd seen very few vehicles around, and our Jeep wasn't exactly subtle. At the Riggs home, I asked Gideon, "Will we be permitted to speak to the neighbors? Ask if anyone saw anything suspicious?"

"We have already done so," Gideon replied. "No one had anything remarkable to tell us, which is why nothing was noted in our reports."

That felt like a dodge. "Well, I am a trained investigator, so maybe I can help them recall something new? Sometimes the tiniest nugget of information can unravel a whole case and reveal answers."

He hedged a moment longer, before nodding his assent. "I'll take you next door."

"Thank you."

Tennyson was waiting in the Jeep, and I felt his eyes following me to the house next door. Gideon rang the bell, and it took several long moments before an elderly woman opened the door.

"Hello, young master Gideon," she said in a paper-thin voice. "And who is this pretty young lady?"

"My name is Shiloh Harrison," I said. "I'm part of a team that's doing an independent investigation into the disappearances of your Pack members, and I was hoping to ask you a few questions about your neighbors."

She looked at Gideon, who nodded. "I suppose,

but only a few minutes. I exhaust myself quite easily these days."

"Mrs. Aaron is one of our Pack elders," Gideon said as we stepped into a very tidy home. "We will be celebrating her one hundred twelfth birthday next month."

"Congratulations," I said.

"Yes, yes." Mrs. Aaron eased her frail body into a recliner, then put a knit blanket over her lap. "Not sure I'll be any use to you. Didn't see a thing."

"I'm more interested in the Riggses as people, ma'am." I sat on the couch across from her, while Gideon lingered near the door. "Were you friendly with them?"

"Of course, we're all friendly with each other. We're Pack."

Okay, not direct enough. "Did you speak to them often? Share meals?"

"Laura brought me freshly baked cookies every week. She was such a nice young lady. Such a shame she and Peter couldn't whelp a pup."

That phrasing conjured up uncomfortable images of a woman birthing a litter of puppies. I cleared my head.

"Yes, I heard that all the couples who disappeared from Pack land had trouble conceiving. Is that unusual for werewolves?"

"Oh, my, yes. When I was a girl and first mated, you couldn't go a lunar cycle without someone you knew giving birth. Every mated couple had multiple children. But the young ones these days." Her dark eyes went distant. "Fewer pups hurts the Pack in the long run. There'll be too many elderly to care for and not enough young ones to do it."

"Yes, I can see how that could be concerning. Alpha Kennedy doesn't seem to think it's a problem worth exploring through human medicine, though."

"No, no, we don't mess with those things. If Danu blesses a couple with a pup, it's because they deserve to raise him or her. Those children are blessings."

Except this Danu didn't seem up on current events with her werewolves—or she was, and she simply didn't care. And in the meantime, this "religious objection" to medicine was going to wipe the werewolves out, if they didn't look into it . . .

Something struck me.

What if the infertility is medical? Maybe a sabotage of some kind? Keep the wolves segregated and clinging to their old-school beliefs, until those beliefs killed them off?

"I understand," I said. "Just one more question, Mrs. Aaron, and then I'll leave you to rest. Are there any other young mated couples who have been trying for children and who aren't conceiving?"

"You could try the Mastersons. Been mated three years now, and those poor folks have yet to conceive. Gideon knows where they live."

Gideon looked like he'd rather chew glass than take me to see the Mastersons, but it was a lead worth exploring, and I told him as much outside. "Have you done any sort of blood tests on these infertile couples?" I asked.

"No, we don't rely on those human methods," he replied. "You know this."

"Yeah, I do, and I also had a bit of an epiphany just now."

"About what?"

I crooked my finger at him, and we returned to the Riggs house, where my people were finishing up finding absolutely nothing useful.

"How old was the oldest couple taken from Pack lands here?" I asked Gideon.

"Twenty-five. They were all in their early twenties."

"What about the Andersons, Barrows, and Porters?"

"They were all in their early thirties. Established professionals."

"What are you thinking, Shiloh?" Jaxon asked.

"It's just a hunch based on what the neighbor said," I replied. "She told me in her day, every mated pair had multiple children, and she's over a hundred. That's several generations ago, and now you have these seven barren pairs, plus she said there are more in the Pack. Young without kids, even after trying."

"Children are our lifeblood," Gideon said. "We cannot reproduce with humans or forced wolves, so without offspring, our species dies off."

"Exactly. So what if someone is doing this on purpose, either with a pathogen or magic?"

"You believe someone could be causing this infertility?" Chandra asked.

"It's possible. I mean, sure, werewolves helped us win World War II in only a few weeks, but in the last thirty years or so, a lot of politicians have based their platforms on being anti-Para, anti-vampire, anti-werewolf. Taunting the public with how easy it would be for them to take over and murder us all in our sleep."

"So they kill us off slowly," Gideon said with a deep, dangerous edge to his voice. "Invisibly."

"It's a theory, yes."

"It's a clever theory, Marshal Harrison. One I believe I must bring before Alpha Kennedy immediately."

"Really?"

"Yes. If he agrees with your reasoning, then an investigation must begin. We cannot afford to let our people die." Gideon glanced around our small group. "While I know other childless werewolves have been taken from Florida, I also overheard Alpha discussing the issue with Rosalind. They said other Packs have also been experiencing high rates of infertility in the current generation of childbearing age."

"So this isn't just the two Packs," Jaxon said.

"No, and we must go. Now."

We still hadn't looked at the Davis house, but the other three hadn't been any real help. I told Tennyson what was going on during the trip back to the Alpha's home. He didn't have much of a reaction, and

I couldn't help wondering if he'd already suspected as much about the other Packs—and whether or not he was holding on to information.

Both Rosalind and Kennedy bristled when they recognized Tennyson, but Gideon didn't give either of them a chance to complain. He laid out what we'd discussed in the Riggs home. Kennedy didn't look happy that Gideon had eavesdropped, but he paid attention to the whole idea of a pathogen or magical whammy causing the widespread infertility. He and Rosalind excused themselves to the corner of the room to discuss, and I couldn't hear them, but Gideon stood with his ear tilted in their direction.

Gideon gave us a subtle thumbs-up moments before Kennedy resumed his throne, with Rosalind at his side.

"I must extend my thanks to you and your friends, Marshal Harrison," Kennedy said, and my respect for the guy increased because he actually sounded sincere. "You were able to see our problem from a new perspective. All eighteen Pack Alphas have been in contact about the unusually high number of young people unable to conceive. We realize it's a widespread problem."

"But your *religion*, for lack of a better word," I said, "prevents you from using medical science or forensics to investigate why your young people are infertile."

"We do not consider ourselves to be religious in the way humans do. Spiritual, yes, because we live with two spirits inside of us. The spirit and soul of our human shape, and also the spirit of our mother goddess Danu. We live as our ancestors have lived for millennia to honor Danu. It's why forced wolves are not treated as Pack. They lack her spirit."

"I understand honoring your mother goddess, but you allow some Pack to live in man's world, to use and create technology, and to act like any other human being."

"It's necessary to sustain our Packs. We can grow our own food, but we can't produce the amount of meat we need to eat, even by hunting these lands, not with so many mouths to feed daily."

Something about that struck a chord with me. "Who do you get your meat from?"

He deferred that to Rosalind, who replied, "We have three independent contracts with both cattle and hog farmers. Organic only."

"So given our theory of a pathogen, is it possible your meat supply has been contaminated?"

"We have highly developed senses, Marshal." I swear she sneered right down her nose at me. "We'd be able to taste any foreign chemical in the meat."

"Not if it was developed by someone with access to werewolf physiology. You and your people are extremely isolated here, and I imagine you don't watch a lot of CNN. There are shadow agencies, and maybe even legit ones, who are experimenting on Paras. If someone really wanted to sabotage the Packs, they'd have the know-how to hide it from your super taste buds."

A touch less sarcasm, djinn—the werewolves are proud people.

I clenched my jaw. *I'm proud, too. So get the hell out of my head.*

Rosalind's expression remained mild, but fire glinted in her eyes.

"Please, Alpha," Chandra said. "If you won't allow us to do blood tests on your Pack members, then allow us to test samples of your meat. We have access to labs that can search for anything artificial."

Alpha Kennedy nodded. "That is a compromise I will allow. However, if our meat supply is somehow tainted, why isn't it affecting all of our people? We currently have fifteen active pregnancies with females under the age of thirty. And those missing who lived in the outside world purchase their food from big box chains."

"I don't know, and that's what we're trying to find out. It's possible whoever is poisoning your meat supply is tied to your missing wolves, and it's also possible it's a coincidence, but I do not believe so."

"It's also possible there is no contamination," I said, "and that the cause is magical in origin."

"Why would any magical being have an issue with the Packs?" Alpha Kennedy asked.

"I don't know. And it's entirely possible that if the

infertility is magical, the magic user is being forced or coerced right now." And I really wished my mother was here, because she has a keen sense of magic. We could stick her at a crux and Novak could—no. Oh no, not going there.

Ew.

Chandra had to know someone local who could give the place a read for magical signatures. And if she didn't, maybe Will Carson did. Either way, I was committed to finding the missing werewolves, discovering the source of their (likely) unnatural infertility, and I wouldn't stop until I brought them all safely home.

CHAPTER 6

Chandra took the Jeep halfway back to town so she could get enough internet signal to send our finger-prints to the Werewolf Registry, as well as deliver our meat samples to whatever lab she had in mind.

The rest of us continued exploring the Davis house, as well as speaking to other neighbors of the missing werewolves. The younger Pack members were upset and worried about their missing friends. The elder members were concerned, but confident the missing would be found, because Alpha Kennedy wouldn't relent until that happened.

I bit my tongue more than once over their faith in Kennedy, because I saw no sign he was doing any-thing to find the kidnapped wolves. But he wasn't my leader, and I didn't need to have unshakable faith in him like his people did. All I needed to do was watch my tongue and find those wolves.

Despite the Pack having nearly a million acres—and being the largest Pack in the States—the members lived fairly close together in what amounted to one single town, with only a few outliers in the vast forestry. It gave them huge swaths of safe, private lands on which to run during the full moon, or any time they wanted to shift and go on a hunt. While I understood having a dual nature, I didn't understand what it felt like or meant to shift into a completely different physical form.

The only one of us who did was Jaxon.

I found myself watching him more intently as he interacted with the wolves. Many sniffed him, but few inquired what he was. They all knew we had abilities, and skin-walkers were rare enough that most people have never met one. And he'd told me he transformed into a stag, but I had no visual for it. No clue what he actually looked like in that form.

As we chatted with several families in a large park, he caught me staring and winked. The simple gesture should not have sent a little wobble through my belly. It shouldn't have but it did. He didn't seem like the type of guy I normally went for. Then again, the only person I'd "seriously" dated in the last six years was Vincent.

Except I'd apparently dated Jaxon, too. And I still

loved him, or I wouldn't have lost those memories. But I had no actual feelings toward the man one way or the other right now. Less a stranger the more time we spent together today, but still not a friend. Barely an acquaintance. We worked well together professionally, but there was also a blank aura around him I couldn't explain. As if magical residue from the sidhe's spell was still blocking me from truly getting to know the man.

I caught Jaxon staring again and glared. He looked away.

This is impossible. He's a distraction I should have left in Maryland.

He was also a heck of a good investigator.

Chandra returned to the land around six, and we met her back at the Alpha's house. Her face said it before she announced, "The meat isn't contaminated with any foreign substances that we could detect."

"So if your theory that we're being targeted is correct," Rosalind said, "then the infertility is being caused by a magical source."

"That's our working theory now, yes. I'm sensitive to certain kinds of magic, but not all, and I'm not powerful enough to sense older magic or spells cast by men."

"So we need a different magic user to figure out if the Pack is being whammied," I said.

"Exactly."

"Do you know any?"

Chandra shook her head. "I know my fellow moon witches, but no other magic users. I reached out to my other squad-mates while I was off Pack lands and made a few inquiries, but nothing has panned out yet."

Novak eyeballed me, but I cut him a hard stare and hoped he interpreted it as, *Don't you fucking dare bring up my mom.*

He didn't speak.

"We shall not solve this problem tonight," Kennedy said. "I invite you all to stay for dinner. We'll be eating quite soon."

We all exchanged looks, probably individually hoping dinner wasn't raw meat, because I honestly have no idea what a werewolf diet looks like.

"We accept your generous offer, Alpha," Chandra said.

Considering how the morning started, being asked to stay shocked the shit out of me. Rosalind led us through another door and into a huge dining room. The long wood table looked like something out of a medieval castle, with heavy wooden chairs lining both sides. Two big chandeliers hung over it, with actual lit candles on them, and at the far end, a stone fireplace roared with a stunning blaze.

A woman and six kids of various ages were arranging themselves around the table. Rosalind introduced us to the woman—the Alpha's mate, Claire—and the six children, who were their collective spawn. When Kennedy entered the room, the youngest—a round-cheeked boy who couldn't be older than three—toddled over and reached up. Kennedy swooped the boy into his arms and kissed his cheeks.

In fact, he went around and kissed all his children, before kissing Claire. And it wasn't a show for us. It looked so natural and practiced that I believed it was simply how he behaved. The big, bad Pack Alpha was completely owned by his family.

The kids were curious about us, too, and Kennedy explained we were helping him find the missing Pack members. As platters of roasted pork and vegetables went around the table, I found myself quizzed by a pixie-faced girl who was probably eight or nine. They'd interspersed their guests amongst the children, and I wasn't prepared to deal with kids and their blunt questions.

"You look too young to be a Marshal," the girl said.

"Well, I am twenty-eight," I replied as I cut into a piece of pork that smelled amazing.

"Oh wow, that's old."

Across the table, Jaxon snickered.

"But you don't *look* that old."

Iblis save me from annoying children. "I have really good genes."

"So do you have any really cool superpowers?"

I shoved a roasted carrot into my mouth to stall.

"Shiloh is very strong," Jaxon replied for me. "It takes a lot to hurt her. She's also very smart, a good leader, and she cares about other people. Those are incredible superpowers, don't you think?"

The girl shrugged. "I guess." To Jaxon, she asked, "What do you do?"

He leaned across the wide table, which was ripe with chatter from all ends, and said, "I'm a skin-walker. I can shift into a stag."

"What's a stag?"

"A really big deer," I replied.

"Oooh, can I see?"

"Maybe after dinner," Jaxon said with a wink meant for the child, but Sweet Iblis, why was that so adorable?

He's good with kids. Do I already know this about him? Did we talk about kids when we dated?

The conversation around us shifted, and I paid attention to my food. The only person not at the table with us was Tennyson. He'd volunteered to remain outside now that the sun had gone down, so he could concentrate on his vampire voodoo and telepathically conference call his information sources.

I have to admit, the telepathy made me all kinds of jealous. It was the only reason I was able to "tell" him the words to bind me to the Rules of Wishing last week. Thankfully, a wisher can only bind a djinn once, unless they know magic, too, so Tennyson shouldn't be able to do that again.

I hoped. Vampires and djinn were cousin races, so

theoretically he shouldn't have been able to bind me at all.

The werewolves consumed a lot of food, even the kids. Gideon and Rosalind were also there, as well as two others whose names I didn't catch, both older females. Everything about the meal was homey, comfortable, and warm—exactly as I imagined a family meal would be. I didn't remember many meals like this growing up, because my dad was frequently away on djinn business, or because he'd been summoned.

But no matter where he was in the world, no matter what business had his attention, he was always there for my birthday. Mom, too.

"Shi?" Jaxon said.

I snapped my head up. "Yeah?"

"You okay? You went a million miles away just now."

"Thinking about the past when I should be focusing on the present."

The two older women cleaned up the empty plates and platters, and then presented us with a massive peach cobbler. I was stuffed and turned it down, but the little girl next to me who'd already cleaned her plate of a huge portions of meat, potatoes, and carrots took a hand-sized slab of cobbler.

My hand-sized, not hers.

I mean, my djinn side comes with a very healthy metabolism, but wow.

Shiloh, I have information, Tennyson said in my head. *I do not wish to disturb the meal by entering.*

I pinched the bridge of my nose to stave off the slight throb in my head from that little telegraph. Unsure of the protocol for leaving a werewolf dinner table, I angled toward the head of the table. "Alpha Kennedy, excuse the interruption, but my associate has news to share," I said.

Kennedy waved a hand at me. "You may leave, don't worry. We aren't terribly formal about that."

"Thank you. The food was amazing."

Chandra, Jaxon, Novak, and Gideon all excused themselves, and we approached Tennyson in the foyer. He seemed smugly impressed with himself which, let's face it, is really his factory default setting.

"What's the news?" I asked.

"I have located Danu on the mortal plane."

Gideon's eyes bugged out. "Seriously? Danu is here?"

"She is."

"Where?"

Tennyson's gaze never left mine, and his eyes flashed bit bits of blue. I groaned out loud, because this was the part of our deal I hated.

"What do you want?" I asked.

"What do you mean, what does he want?" Jaxon replied. "Shiloh, what kind of deal do you have with this guy?"

"Favors in exchange for his help, okay? And if he located Danu, then he's being helpful."

Jaxon scowled. "What kind of favors?"

"The favors are between myself and Shiloh," Tennyson said. "This was our agreement."

"Don't worry," I said to both Jaxon and Novak. "Tennyson isn't out to hurt me, and anything sexual is one hundred percent off the table." That didn't really mollify my fuming teammates, but whatever.

"Oh, did we agree to that?" Tennyson asked, knowing it would make Jaxon fume—which, of course, the skin-walker did.

"Yes," I said through gritted teeth. "What's the favor?"

"A single drop of your blood."

Surprise jolted down my spine, but before I could react, Jaxon was in Tennyson's face with a gun pointed at his temple. "What the fuck do you want her blood for, vampire?" he snarled.

Whoa.

Tennyson merely smiled at him, his eyes swirling depths of crimson. He was fast enough to snap Jaxon's neck, though, so I grabbed the butt of my own gun, which was full of silver nitrate bullets. I trusted Tennyson, but only so far.

He didn't move, though. "The young djinn has tasted my blood more than once," Tennyson simply said. "I think it's only fair I be allowed a taste of my own."

"Yeah?" Jaxon replied. "And what if you can't stop after just one drop? What if you decide you want to turn her?"

"I have never in my five hundred-plus years turned an unwilling human, and shan't begin now. Shiloh is too rare of a find to alter her thusly."

Rare a find? Am I an antique now?

"Jaxon, back off," I said. I squeezed his shoulder hard enough for him to flinch, then lower the gun from Tennyson's head. "Thank you for caring, but I can handle this."

Jaxon holstered his gun and turned to face me. His eyes gleamed with anger and fear, and deep inside them, I spotted a hint of the mighty stag waiting inside to free itself and protect me. "I agree you're a rare find, Shi," he said with a hitch in his voice. "I can't lose you."

My heart absolutely did not pitter-pat over that statement. Nope.

"I'm a tough girl," I said. "It took multiple direct blows to the head, a concussion, a fractured skull, and melon-baller to the lung to take me down last time."

"And my blood is the only reason she is alive now," Tennyson said. "Shiloh, do you agree to the price of my assistance in locating Danu?"

I held Jaxon's gaze another beat, telegraphing as much confidence as I could. Hoping he really did know me well enough to trust me and back off. "The risk is worth speaking to Danu. Maybe a goddess can get us a direct line to the missing wolves and we can end this."

His scowl only deepened before he nodded his assent.

"Thank you." To Tennyson, I said, "Yes, I agree. A pinprick on my finger somewhere in private."

"Agreed," Tennyson replied so smugly I kind of wanted to punch him.

Blessed vampires.

"She's a few hours north of here," Tennyson continued. "I will drive as the sun has set and take Marshal Harrison."

"Oh no," Novak said. "You two aren't road-tripping to see another goddess and leave us behind to worry the vampire hasn't taken Shiloh and run when we can't speak to you for eight hours. Fuck that."

"I will accompany them," Rosalind said. She stood on the periphery of our group and the stony look on her face meant no argument would sway against it.

"I'm going too," Jaxon said.

"No, you cannot," Chandra replied. "From what little I know of Danu, she despises other shifters not her creation. She will not react well to you. I will go. Shiloh and I still need to reach out to her contact in Colorado, and we can do that on the drive."

"Fine." He sounded anything but.

"Save your warnings, skin-walker," Tennyson said. "I will not betray Shiloh's trust. You have my word."

Jaxon still looked pissed. The overprotectiveness was both charming and annoying. I get he had feelings for me and wanted to protect me, but I could handle myself and had since I was a teenager. And if we had dated, I had to wonder if that was one of the reasons why we broke up. Hard to work side by side with a lover when you're both getting shot at or attacked by an angry pixie cloud, and you are too focused on saving them rather than getting the job done.

"It's going to be okay," I said to him.

"I said fine," he growled, but the anger was softened by an equal part of concern. "Just be careful."

"I got this."

He nodded.

"This is adorable, but we should really leave now," Tennyson said. "Unless the incubus can be of some use?"

Novak snorted. "Doesn't work that way. I can only teleport to me, but trust me, I'd gladly send you to the other side of the planet if I could."

Jaxon fought a grin.

"Then let's go," I said. "Anyone need to pee before we hit the road?"

Chandra and I sat in back so we could do her mistsearch thing on Will's daughter and not be distracted. Rosalind didn't seem happy to be up front with a vampire, but she's the one who'd volunteered. Werewolves are generally suspicious, and she likely wanted to hear firsthand what Danu had to say, rather than getting it secondhand from us.

Once Tennyson had us speeding along the highway going north into Oregon, Chandra asked, "Do you know anything more specific about Will's daughter? Name? Age?"

"I'm sorry, I don't," I replied. "All I know is what Jaxon said about her being in her early teens. And she lives in Colorado on a ranch out in the middle of nowhere."

"All right, I'll do my best." She closed her eyes, and a slight hum of magic filled the car as she did her mistwalking thing. It was both spooky and kind of cool that she could locate other women anywhere in the world and telepathically communicate with them.

Nothing happened right away, so I watched the forest speed by and listened to the radio. After about an hour, without opening her eyes, Chandra said, "I think I've found her. I'm bringing you into my mind, Shiloh."

The car immediately disappeared. Chandra and I stood in a gray mist, as before, and a teenage girl gawked at us from a few feet away. She had a hairbrush in one hand and wore a nightgown.

"What the hell?" she squawked. "Who are you?"

"I'm someone who knew your dad a long time ago," I replied. The girl wielded her hairbrush like a weapon, and I instantly liked her. "His name is Will Carson. I'm Shiloh Harrison."

She squinted at me. "I know that name, I think."

"I'm a Para-Marshal, and I was involved in the

vampire kidnapping case that recently broke on the news."

"Oh, right. Dad was really sad when he heard your unit leader died."

"Julius and I knew your dad six years ago. We worked together to free other magical creatures from a warlock who'd imprisoned him."

"Okay. Then who's she and where are we?"

"My name is Marshal Chandra Goodfellow," Chandra replied. "I'm a moon witch, and we haven't gone anywhere. We're communicating telepathically. You have not physically left the place you previously stood."

"Oh. Um, hi. I'm Lacey."

"A pleasure to meet you."

"Yeah, so why are we meeting, exactly?"

Kid got right to the point. I liked her. Reminded me of her dad.

"We're unofficially investigating the disappearances of a number of Pack werewolves," I said. "I was hoping to ask your father if he'd heard anything about the missing wolves, or if he had any ideas of where to look."

"He hasn't mentioned anything to me," Lacey replied, and good goddess, she even looked like her father. Same dark hair and eyes. "But then again, I don't ask about that stuff, because he doesn't talk to me about it. Him and Kale don't want me involved, because I'm human."

"He's trying to protect you and that's smart."

"I mean, do you want me to go ask him for you?"

"Actually," Chandra said, "if you are in close physical proximity to him, within ten feet or so, I can include him in this group chat."

"I think he's downstairs in the kitchen, but I'm not sure. I guess if you let me sign out or whatever, I can go get him, and then you can log us back in?"

I grinned at the text-speak.

"I can do that. I'll know when you're near him."

"Can I warn him what's about to happen?"

"Please do."

Lacey winked out.

"She has a gentle soul, but a troubled mind," Chandra said. "The poor thing has experienced tragedy and pain."

I grunted, unhappy knowing that, but also not surprised. I hated seeing children suffer, and Lacey seemed like a sweet girl. She'd taken us at our word and wanted to help.

Maybe a minute or two passed before Lacey and a much-aged Will Carson appeared in the mist.

"Whoa," he said as he blinked hard several times. "Shiloh. It's been a while."

"Yes, it has," I replied. Will had more flecks of gray in his hair and new wrinkles around his eyes, but he looked fit and alert.

And suspicious.

Chandra introduced herself and summed up what we'd already told Lacey.

Will chewed on his thumb cuticle while he thought. "I don't deal at all with Kennedy's Pack, because they're so far away. I've also heard rumblings of infertility but nothing too specific. And I haven't dealt directly with any Pack wolves in over a year. Mostly I help strays and other magic users who want to disappear."

"Speaking of magic users," I said, "our biggest suspicion right now is that magic is what's been causing the infertility. Chandra helped one of the missing couples become pregnant, but she can no longer sense the mother in her mind."

"Sure she's not just dead?"

"It's possible, but we're hoping not. That said, Chandra's magic is limited, and she can't sense if there is outside magical interference going on within Pack lands. We need someone who can tell us if the couples were whammied on purpose."

"What about Irena?" Lacey asked.

Will cut a sharp look at her.

"Who is Irena?" Chandra asked.

"She's a Caster who came to my land to live her life in peace," Will replied, clearly unhappy Lacey had mentioned the woman. "She comes from a line of powerful Ukrainian witches, but is estranged from her coven."

"Do you think she'd be willing to assist us?"

"As in fly to California and go onto Pack lands?" Will looked like he'd rather eat horse shit than ask her to do such a thing.

"Please, Will," I said. "I know it's a big ask, but I'll owe you a favor. A big favor. Twenty-eight souls are missing, and we all fear they've been taken for experimentation."

He growled softly. "I know what it's like to be held against your will. I'll ask Irena."

"Thank you."

"If she agrees, I'll get her there."

"We're based in Etna." I gave him my cell number, which Lacey promptly began repeating under her breath.

Hard to write things down in an astral plane.

"Good luck," Will said.

I blinked the interior of the Jeep back into focus, surprised by the abrupt shutdown of the chat.

"So," Tennyson said, "was your search useful?"

"I hope so," I replied. "Will didn't know anything about the missing Pack wolves, but he may know a witch powerful enough to sense if there are any spells on the Pack."

"Did your friend mention from whence the witch is descended?"

"Um, Ukrainian line?"

"Hmm. Powerful, indeed."

His depth of knowledge about random things never ceased to amaze me. "You know, you really should try out for *Jeopardy!*"

Chandra snickered.

"So how long of a drive is this exactly?" I asked.

He was coasting along at ludicrous speed, which could easily get us pulled over and heavily fined, but Tennyson could in turn gazelock any trooper and send them on their way, so I appreciated the haste.

"We should arrive at our destination in about four more hours," he replied.

"And our destination is where, exactly?"

"Portland."

"Danu is in hipster land?"

"Yes."

A goddess hanging out amongst knitting shops, fair trade coffee, and techno-geeks. What could possibly go wrong?

CHAPTER 7

My worst nightmare came true when Tennyson parked in a public garage around midnight, and then led us to a street teeming with teenagers and young adults going in and out of bars, restaurants, and coffee shops. Our destination appeared to be a place called Java Bytes, which had a full-service coffee bar, as well as several rooms where gamers played on consoles connected to huge seventy-two-inch screens on the wall.

The noise was incredible, the coffee smelled amazing, and way too many guys had mustaches. When had those become popular again?

Tennyson paused a moment, and we got some stares. Not only was he six-four, with his multicolored long hair, the black robe, and dead-white skin, he could have just walked in and screamed, "I'm a vampire!" He didn't seem to notice, though, simply closed his eyes and . . . felt? Reached? Did that thing he did to sense where goddesses hung out.

At least Danu wasn't hanging out at a frat house having sex with three college students. I still couldn't scrub that memory of first meeting Brighid out of my head.

Rosalind growled at someone who got too close, and the poor guy looked like he was going to pee himself.

"This way," Tennyson said. He led us to one of the rooms where two young women were playing some kind of car racing game, with at least a dozen others watching and cheering. He pointed at the player with short black hair cut page-boy style, heavy eyeliner, a red plaid skirt, and black suspenders over a white t-shirt. "That's Danu."

Our werewolf goddess was a Goth hipster?

As if sensing our arrival, Danu paused the game. Groans and protests erupted in the room, but she cut it off with a sharp look as she stood. Turned. She eyed Tennyson a beat before saying, "Clear the room. Now." Her voice lacked volume, but the command was clear.

Everyone left except us. Chandra closed the door.

"It's been at least two centuries, Woodrow Tennyson, Line Master," Danu said. "What brings you here at this late hour?"

"A favor for a friend, love," he replied.

Rosalind gaped at Danu, and I couldn't figure out if she was starstruck or dumbstruck. Danu was five-three if she was lucky and didn't look like she could wrestle a small dog, much less shift into a werewolf.

"A favor," Danu said. She tapped a red-painted nail against equally red lips. "After what happened in Germany, I didn't expect we'd ever meet again, much less you'd seek me out."

I glanced at Chandra; we both wanted *that* story.

Danu finally looked at the rest of us, her gaze dismissing Chandra out of hand. She lingered on me a bit longer, before acknowledging Rosalind. "A daughter of mine. I sense strength in you, Child of Ossory."

I'd never heard that particular phrase before.

Ossory, Ireland, is the birthplace of Danu and her werewolves.

Oh, thank you. For once, I was kind of grateful for our telepathic connection.

"It is an honor to meet you, Goddess," Rosalind replied. "I come on behalf of my Alpha and our Pack to beg for your assistance."

Danu rolled her eyes. "Geez, don't be so formal. I haven't been off this world in so long I don't really remember what it's like to be all goddessy and stuff. Just spit it out."

Rosalind blinked hard several times, probably thrown by her goddess's laissez-faire attitude, before finding her voice again. "Twenty-eight werewolves have disappeared from Pack lands, and we have no clear leads in discovering what happened to them."

"What does that have to do with me? You interrupted my forty-eight-hour tournament for missing werewolves? Don't you have cops for that?"

"That's what we are," I said, pointing between myself and Chandra. "We're assisting the Packs in locating their missing wolves, and we came here for information."

Danu took a step toward me, her nose twitching. "You're not human. I smell earth djinn blood in you."

"My father is an earth djinn."

"Intriguing. A very, very unusual find." She turned suddenly silver eyes onto Tennyson. "If I help can I keep her?"

Before I could squawk a protest, Tennyson said, "No. Shiloh and her friends are under my protection, and they are not for trade."

"Shame. Then I might have helped you."

"Goddess, please," Rosalind said. She went to her knees in front of the smaller woman. "Your daughter begs you for your help. Your people have followed your rules for centuries, forgoing man's technology and medical intervention, living as a Pack, praying to you every night."

"Oh, wow." Danu stared at Rosalind like she'd lost her mind. "I don't give a crap if you guys have cell phones or pop Vicodin. Do you know how boring it is to sit in an astral plane and listen to other people praying, begging, and promising things? Setting a world record on *Hell Racer 4* is way more interesting. Humans are weak, but they sure are fun."

Rosalind's entire body wilted and her head went down. I kind of felt sorry for her. It's not every day you find out the deity your people have faithfully served doesn't give a shit about you, and that the rules you thought were so important were being flouted by the very person who made them. Rosalind made a soft noise, and I couldn't swear to it, but it sounded like a sob.

It also got Danu's attention. She squatted in front of Rosalind and tipped her head up. The sight of a tear track on Rosalind's cheek shocked the hell out of me. Danu wiped it away with one finger, then touched her cheek. The silver in Danu's eyes gleamed brighter.

"Oh," Danu said softly. "I'd forgotten."

"Forgotten what?" Tennyson asked.

"What it's like to be worshipped by my children. There are so few werewolves in Portland, and I haven't been home in decades. I apologize for my harsh words, daughter, but I want you to know you are free to live your lives as you see fit. Do not shy from technology that could aid you, nor from medicine that could save you. Be well and enjoy the life you have."

"Thank you, Goddess," Rosalind said in a choked voice. "Thank you."

"You're welcome." Danu kissed her forehead before rising. "My power is slightly diminished and rusty from having lived here for so long, but I am willing to try."

"Thank you," I said.

"Not here, though." She snapped her fingers.

Everything went briefly white, and then I was standing in a dark, outdoor space somewhere, surrounded by trees. The others were there, too. Only Danu and Tennyson were not disoriented from the teleportation.

"Trippy," I said. "Where are we?"

"MacLeay Park," Danu replied. "It's closed at this hour, so we won't be disturbed."

"Disturbed?"

"I need to shift in order to reinvigorate my power and reach out to my people. There are so many."

Danu stripped right out of her little Goth-girl outfit and immediately shifted. Most werewolves take anywhere from thirty seconds to a full minute to shift, depending on their age and experience, and it's an actual change anyone watching can see. The fur sprouting, the limbs repositioning.

Not Danu. From woman to beast in the blink of an eye and hot sizzle of magic that ripped down my spine. She was enormous, about the size of a horse, with golden fur that also glittered with hundreds of other colors. Similar to Tennyson's hair, but more complex.

I attempted pushing a thought at Tennyson. *Does your matching hair have anything to do with Germany?*

Leave it for now, young djinn.

I want that story.

Perhaps one day.

Danu stretched once before resting on her haunches, closing her eyes and tilting her head up to the half moon in the sky above. The power of her shift had Rosalind shaking all over, until she gave in and shifted as well. Her wolf lay in front of Danu and stretched out on her belly in a prone position.

Long minutes ticked by. I checked my phone. No new texts or messages since the previous one from Jaxon about the motel they'd checked into in Etna. I texted Jaxon what we were up to, as well as Danu's unexpected location and appearance. I didn't expect him to be up, but he replied, Goddesses are never what you expect, huh?

Nope.

My phone chirped from an unknown number, location blocked. Where should we meet you in Etna? —Will

I grinned and texted back the address to the motel. Speaking while a goddess was telepathically looking for her werewolves seemed rude, so I showed the text to both Chandra and Tennyson. It meant help was either on the way, or just now leaving.

I learned that one about thirty minutes of silence later, when Jaxon texted that Will and Irena had arrived at the motel. I sent back a thumbs-up.

Bored and tired, I sat with my back against a tree.

I'd be blessed if I knew how long this would take, and I was ready to say screw rudeness and play a game on my phone. But the battery was low, and our middle-of-nowhere location didn't exactly have a charging station.

I didn't realize I'd dozed off until a shock of magic jostled me awake. Danu and Rosalind had shifted back, and while Rosalind dressed right away, Danu just stood there in her birthday suit—although I guess goddesses don't really have birthdays—and frowned at the ground.

"I sense so many across the world," Danu said. "It's been so long since I've connected to my children. I didn't realize how much I missed it. Even the forced wolves are clear to me in their joy or distress."

Rosalind blinked hard at that one—probably because born wolves assumed their goddess had no time or inclination to protect the unnatural werewolves.

Lots of shocks tonight for her.

"But the twenty-eight I feel in my bones exist," Danu continued, "I cannot find. Not clearly. I feel cornfields and open spaces. The center of this country. The heartland."

"Would looking at a map help?" Chandra asked.

"Perhaps. I'm only familiar with coastal states in America."

Chandra brought up a map on her phone and showed it to Danu. Danu studied it, closing her eyes several times, probably reaching out. Testing borders and boundaries. Finally, Danu opened her eyes and said, "Kansas." Although her pronunciation was more like "can-sass," but whatever. Goddesses didn't know everything.

"Thank you, Goddess," Rosalind said. "This is the best, tightest lead we've ever had."

"You're welcome, child," Danu replied. "You do your Alpha proud. Return to him with my words of peace and joy. And the best of luck in finding your people."

"I don't suppose you could flash your way to Kansas," I said, "and help us find them?"

"I cannot interfere in mankind in such a way. All I can offer is information."

"Worth a try. And it's been a really long day."

Danu put her clothes back on. "Come. Let us return to Java Bytes. I have a tournament to complete."

She winked us back into the game room and the goddess facade faded away, leaving behind a surly young woman intent on playing her video game. She opened the door and her adoring fans swarmed in, so our little quartet left. I considered a coffee for the road, but Tennyson was driving, so I slept instead.

I woke as the first hint of the sun appeared on the horizon. We were back in Etna, close to the motel, and Tennyson had his hood up. After he parked next to an unfamiliar SUV, I stretched as I climbed out. Novak had given me two different room numbers, side by side, so I knocked on one.

Novak opened the door. I'd never assigned the

phrase "bright-eyed and bushy-tailed" to the incubus before, but I'll be blessed if he didn't kind of glow. He'd also taken off his gloves, and his hands looked nearly back to normal.

"Someone got laid last night," I said.

He winked, then stepped aside so Tennyson could bolt inside. With public places, he didn't need an invite. Chandra and Rosalind followed us inside. The small room had two double beds and décor that hadn't been updated in at least thirty years. Jaxon stood from his bed and came over, me clearly his target. He looked me over as if expecting to find a mark or blemish, or some other proof Tennyson couldn't be trusted.

"How did it go with the wolf goddess?" Novak asked.

"We got Kansas out of her," I replied. "But that's as close as she can get. Whatever is protecting them is strong enough to keep a goddess's nose out of their business, and that's kind of scary."

Someone must have texted them, because a knock echoed on the door, and then it opened. Will entered first with a slender, pale woman behind him. She had long, dark brown hair and wore a belted tunic over a colorful peasant skirt.

"Shiloh, it's good to see you in person again," Will said. "You look well."

"Thank you, same." I shook his hand.

"This is Irena Petrova. She's a good friend, so be gentle with her."

"Hi, Irena. Shiloh Harrison."

"Pleasure," Irena said in a small voice. For being a powerful witch—and she did snap and buzz with magic—she seemed extremely timid. Maybe it was all the supernatural people in the room. "Will told me everything. I owe the world a few good deeds, so I have agreed to assist you in any way I can."

"I appreciate it, thank you." I introduced them to Chandra, Tennyson—they both seemed crazy wary of him—and finally Rosalind.

Rosalind stared at Will with the start of a sneer on her lips, and too late I forgot that born wolves generally despised forced wolves—until her expression softened. Hopefully, she remembered Danu felt and loved all her wolves, not just born ones. "I'm second of the Homme Alpha's California Pack, and I thank you for your assistance on his behalf."

"You're welcome," Will said. His expression suggested he hadn't expected such a polite response. "I may live in a Pack-less state, but I understand wanting to protect your family."

"Your daughter?"

"Yes, and others."

"Are you good to fill everyone else in on our visit with the goddess of video games?" I asked Chandra. "I desperately need a shower, a change of clothes, and coffee, in that order."

"Certainly," she replied.

"Your bag is in the room next door," Jaxon said.

"Thanks."

The shower helped wake me up, after only about five hours of sleep in the last twenty-four. I wasn't unused to strange working hours and long periods of no sleep, but I also had jet lag from jumping coasts and time zones.

I exited the bathroom wrapped in a towel and yelped when I saw Jaxon sitting on the bed nearest the door. "Do want me to hurt you?"

Jaxon tilted his head, lips twitching. "You've said that to me before."

"Yeah, well, maybe learn boundaries."

"I've seen you naked, Shi."

"I don't remember being naked in front of you, though, so close your eyes."

He did. I retrieved clothes from my closet and dashed back into the bathroom to dress.

"Do you remember last week when Piotr was first captured at our gate, and you were bit by that magic spider?" he asked, apropos of nothing.

"Yeah, hard to forget nearly dying of a spider bite, drinking Tennyson's blood to fight off the deadly infection, and then going vampirey on my mom and trying to bite her neck."

"Touché. Do you remember when you were healing? Your first shower after?"

"Yeah, Mom braided my hair and helped me get in."

"Who dried you afterward and helped you get dressed?"

I paused to think. Those memories were fuzzier. I'd somehow dried off and put on clothes, and then struggled downstairs to join my crew. But they were less distinct than the memory of my mother's help. Clothes on, I returned to the bedroom and crossed my arms. "Let me guess. You?"

He nodded. "Do you remember any of it? The things we said to each other?"

"No. You know I wish I did."

Wish. Ha ha.

Jaxon's face fell. "Yeah. I guess this situation was similar and I hoped it might jog your memory."

"Except for the nearly dying part." I sat beside him, close without touching. He was still a stranger, known to me less than thirty-six hours, and yet . . . not. And those two things together continued to drive me nuts. "My memories were magically taken from me, Jaxon. And unless whoever took them decides to give them back, I'm pretty sure they're gone, and that sucks for both of us. I hate that everyone in my life remembers us together, but I don't. It's disorienting and frustrating, and I don't—"

Warm lips cut off my small rant, and I froze in place. Jaxon's kiss was tentative, curious, and undemanding. I didn't kiss him back, but I also didn't rear away and slap him for being so bold. To me, we'd met a few days ago. To him, we had six years of history, both professional and sexual. I wouldn't shame him for this boldness.

When he pulled back, he clearly expected to be smacked or berated. All I could do was touch his cheek and say, "Sorry, Prince Charming, you didn't break the spell."

He laughed, and it broke the tension in the room. "Figured it was worth a shot. Come on, we've got breakfast and coffee in the other room."

"Fantastic."

We returned to the slightly crowded room, where breakfast sandwiches and fast food coffee were being passed around. I accepted a sausage and egg biscuit, which pleased my rumbling belly. Tennyson hung off in the corner, his nose wrinkled against the greasy food smells. And maybe the strong mix of paranormal odors. It wasn't every day a Line Master was squished into a motel room with two werewolves, a skin-walker, two witches, an incubus, and me.

Fun times.

"So—plan for the day?" I asked after starting on my second sandwich.

"We return to one of the missing's homes," Chandra replied, "and we allow Irena to explore."

"I must check in with Alpha Kennedy posthaste," Rosalind said. "He must be informed of last night's encounter with Danu."

I glanced at Will, who sat with Irena on the opposite side of the room from Rosalind. "Probably a good idea," I said. "Considering some of the things Danu said."

"Agreed."

"I would like to remain here," Will said to me. "Irena trusts you because I trust you, but I don't think I'll be welcome on Pack land. Keep her safe for me."

"I will, I promise," I replied. Some sort of genuine affection existed between the pair, but I didn't get the sense they were romantically involved.

Chandra's phone beeped. "Results on the werewolf fingerprints we sent last night." She scanned the file. "Every print is registered except one. There is no information in our database about the unregistered print, or who it might belong to."

"Which house was it found in?" Rosalind asked.

"Davis."

"An unregistered wolf was on Pack lands without the Alpha's permission and absconded with our people." Her expression promised bodily harm to whoever that print belonged to.

I truly do not ever want to be on a werewolf's bad side.

"If everyone's done eating," Jaxon said, "let's get this show on the road."

Since we couldn't all fit comfortably in the Jeep—Jaxon had borrowed the SUV from the Pack—I, Irena, Jaxon, Tennyson, and Chandra headed straight for the Davis house. Novak drew the short straw in driving Rosalind to the Alpha's house, and then joining us. Irena watched through the window as we entered the protected lands and took in the beauty of these mountains and forests.

Northern California in all its natural glory.

Plus the occasional blur of a passing werewolf sentry.

At the Davis home, Irena stood in front of the front door with her eyes closed. For the first time, I noticed a small burlap pouch attached to her wide leather belt. "There is an unnatural force here," she said. "I don't have to enter to sense it, but I cannot pinpoint it yet."

I opened the door and let Irena go inside first. She settled on the floor of the living room, cross-legged, and opened the pouch. Our group watched from a slight distance, giving the witch room to work. She removed two bundles of dried herbs, a leather cloth, and a matchbook. Lit a match, then held one bundle over the leather cloth until it caught fire. An acrid odor stung my nose.

"Angelica root enhances natural abilities for a brief period of time," she said without looking away from the smoldering leaves. Once it had burned to the tips and made Jaxon cough twice, she did the same to the second bundle. "Bay leaves will protect me from the source of this unnatural power."

Pro-tip: don't ever burn bay leaves in an enclosed area. Just don't.

None of us opened a window, though.

Irena put the matches and burnt end of the bay

leaves on the leather, rested her hands on her knees, and closed her eyes. Deep, even breaths marked by the gentle rise and fall of her chest. Power snapped around her and caressed my skin. Everyone seemed affected in some way by the strength of Irena's magic. Tennyson's eyes gleamed like cobalt blue headlights. Jaxon's entire body trembled in a way that suggested all he wanted to do was let his stag skin take over.

She *was* from a powerful line. An old, powerful line.

How had she and Will met?

We waited.

Novak showed up with Gideon in tow, and Chandra shushed their questions. No one wanted to break Irena's concentration, and within moments of being exposed to her power, Novak had a boner he couldn't hide. I simply let the magic dance across my skin, its strength second only to the power of the djinn.

Or a goddess herself.

I lost track of time and was almost disappointed when Irena's eyes snapped open.

"There is an object in this house that does not belong here," Irena said. "Check beneath the floorboards under the marriage bed."

I beat everyone and shoved the bed against the far wall, out of my way. Jaxon and Chandra joined me, and we poked at the boards until one came loose under Chandra's hand. She lifted it out of place, and a waft of something sour hit me—but it wasn't a smell everyone could detect.

It was the odor of black magic. Necrotic magic.

I looked up. Tennyson hovered in the doorway, cloak up around his head to protect himself from the home's many windows. He met my gaze and nodded.

"Looks like we found our whammy," I said. "Anyone have a tissue handy? I don't want to touch that thing."

Novak handed me something, and it took me a second to realize it was a sock from a laundry basket. I turned it inside out, picked up the pulsing copper square inside the recessed space, and pulled it out. Looked innocent enough, but the power filling it worried me.

"Has anyone seen anything like this before?" I asked.

"I have," Tennyson replied. "About three hundred years ago now. A scorned witch used it to punish her philandering husband. She put a similar rock beneath their bed, and over the course of weeks, he was subjected to boils on his nethers, as well as infection. In time, they were removed by a surgeon to save his life."

Jaxon and Novak both made faces. Gideon looked flat-out appalled.

"And how do you know this?" I asked Tennyson.

His lips twitched. "I was one of the men helping him cheat on his wife. In my own defense, I did not know he was married until our liaison ended due to . . . faulty equipment."

"You've got an interesting way with words." I rolled the sock up and around the cube, but it did little for the power still dripping from it. "On to house number two?"

Irena didn't have to mojo any other homes. We split up to search not only the houses of the three missing couples, but also the other young mated wolves having trouble conceiving. In each one, we found another copper cube beneath the couple's bed, hidden in the flooring somehow. Socks worked well to wrap them up, so we had eleven cotton bundles by the time we finished and met up at the Chandler house.

"You need to contain their power so it doesn't affect anyone else," Irena said. "It needs a natural container."

"We don't really have time to carve a box for them," Jaxon said.

"I have an idea," I replied. An idea that would hurt, but I've had worse. I walked to the nearest thickly branched tree and yanked on it. A heavy branch of black oak wood fell to the ground. One of the handy things I do as a half djinn is vibrate my body fast enough that I can pass through solid, natural materials, like wood or dirt. Not metal, though.

Two at a time, I inserted those wrapped cubes into the center of the tree branch. My hand was on fire, scorching from the inside out by the time I finished, and I collapsed onto the lawn, clutching my right hand to my chest. Jaxon knelt beside me and rubbed my back, and Sweet Iblis, that felt amazing. A warm, grounding touch.

"Wow," Gideon said. "That was amazing."

"I get wild applause at parties," I deadpanned.

"You okay?" Jaxon asked.

"I'll live. So we found the source of the infertility."

"The question now," Chandra continued, "is finding out who put them here."

"Bingo."

"You may be able to use their magic signature to trace them back to the missing wolves," Irena said. "But that is beyond my power, and I must rest."

"Of course," Chandra said. "You've been incredibly helpful, thank you."

"You're welcome."

Irena went into the Chandler home to rest, while we hashed out the problem in a circle on the lawn.

"So we found cubes in every home that was having fertility issues," Jaxon said. "Seven other couples had one, so why were the others taken and not them?"

"Good question," I said. And something else occurred to me that I'd never asked before. "Gideon, did your mated couples disappear all at once, or was it over a period of time?"

"We figure based on when neighbors last saw them that the disappearances happened over the course of about a week. The last couple, the Riggses, went missing about a day before the vampires taking a trailer park hostage broke on the news."

"Coinciding with the same time the Para-Marshals

learned any werewolves had gone missing, thanks to Tennyson."

"So, theoretically," Jaxon said, tracking my thoughts, "whoever did this had plans to come back for all the infertile couples. I will bet the bank on that."

"Agreed."

"Hopefully the cubes did not cause lasting damage," Chandra added. "I do hope the young couples who were affected have luck conceiving in the future, and that their infertility was only a temporary side effect of this black magic."

So did I. I wasn't maternal and had no real desire to have kids—heck, I didn't know if my dual nature would allow me to conceive in the first place—but I understood the Pack's need for continued offspring in order to remain strong and viable. Djinn could live for up to a thousand years, and my dad had other full-djinn kids I've never met.

But would Mom want grandkids?

Not a freaking clue.

"We should report our findings to Alpha Kennedy," Gideon said.

"Yes," Chandra replied.

Irena requested to stay behind and Novak volunteered to chill with her, so the rest of us headed up to the big house. Alpha Kennedy and Rosalind were in deep discussion with several other werewolves, and his mate, Claire, was the only one I recognized.

But he saw us immediately. I had the cube-embedded branch in my hands, and I tag-teamed the story with Gideon, from Irena's arrival to me vibrating the offending magical items into a tree.

"It's unbelievable that anyone would sabotage the Packs like this," Kennedy said with a snarl. "Targeting innocent people, and to what end? Why plant these and then steal my Pack members?"

"We don't know," I replied. "And that isn't all, sir." I told him about the sole unknown fingerprint, which only enraged the guy further.

"A strange wolf made it onto our lands?" Kennedy turned the force of his rage onto Rosalind, who had that flattened-ears look going on. "How did that happen?"

"Alpha," Jaxon said in a firm tone, "when magic is involved, anything is possible. I'm certain that, under your guidance, your people patrol your lands with the utmost diligence. Sometimes events are impossible to control."

His words seemed to calm Kennedy, who said, "You're right, Marshal. It's frustrating to think our borders were violated, when we have autonomy over our lands and people. Those damned rogues and forced wolves. No Pack wolf would cross into another Pack's land without permission."

I bristled on Will's behalf, even though he wasn't in the room.

"Alpha," Rosalind said. "Remember the words from Danu's lips herself. Even the forced wolves and rogues are her children and part of her consciousness."

Kennedy growled once more, before relaxing again. "You're right, Rosalind. Change will not occur overnight, but we must do better."

Well, knock me over with a fucking feather.

"I need to call the other Pack Alphas and tell them exactly what to look for in their homes," Kennedy continued. "Please extend my sincere thanks to the human witch who found those cubes. I am in her debt."

Something told me Irena wasn't the type to collect, but I said I would share his thanks. "It was a forced wolf who brought Irena to your land, Alpha."

He squinted. "Then he has my thanks, as well."

"I'll be sure to pass along your message."

Jaxon nudged me in the ribs; guess he heard the slight edge of sarcasm.

"What is the next step in your investigation?" Rosalind asked.

"Well, we know the missing wolves are somewhere in Kansas," I replied, "but we can't exactly go door to door. It's a big flat state. Hopefully we can use these magic cubes as some kind of anti-homing beacon thingie and trace back to the wolves."

"Now that we are involved, I have a request."

You're involved? *That is news to me.* "Um, okay."

"I would like Gideon to join your group as a liaison between your team and us here at home."

I glanced at Gideon, who looked like a happy puppy, so he was obviously on board. No one in my group threw up any objections. Gideon had been immensely helpful so far, and having a werewolf nose in the mix couldn't hurt. "We agree to your request, Alpha's Second."

She smiled at my use of her formal title.

"I'll need a few hours to prepare," Gideon said.

"Take your time," I replied. "I doubt we're leaving town today. You can meet us at the motel when you're ready."

"Thank you, Marshal."

"Would you all like to stay for lunch?" Kennedy asked.

"Thank you, Alpha, but no," I replied. "Irena is exhausted, and I imagine she's eager to return to her home. But we thank you for your generosity."

"You're welcome. You've found more answers than I ever expected, and I'm grateful to you all." His gaze flickered up and past my head, where Tennyson was probably standing. "Even you, vampire. I should have taken you more seriously during your first visit."

Well, dang, that was practically an apology. I looked over my shoulder in time to see Tennyson execute a half bow that was somehow both serious and snarky. He was good at that. Still, Kennedy accepted it as genuine, and I couldn't help but wonder if he wasn't quite as obnoxious as I'd first believed when we met.

I'd have to think about that some more.

Not now, though. Armed with a magic-cube-filled log, we needed time to regroup and come up with a plan for finding twenty-eight missing werewolves in the great corn state of Kansas.

CHAPTER 8

Irena was, indeed, ready to go home, which was fine. She'd come of her own volition and done the job we'd asked of her. I was sad to say good-bye to Will, though. Six years later, he still had the same drive and determination to help others that he'd had when we first met. "Save my number," I said as we stood by his rental car. "I owe you guys for this, so if there's anything I can do for you in the future, please call."

"I will, thank you." Will smiled, but it never reached his haunted eyes. "Good luck with your hunt, Shiloh. I hope you find the missing wolves."

"Me too. Take care."

We shook hands again. Then I stood in the midday sun and watched them drive away to the nearest airport. They were replaced almost instantly by a sheriff's car that trundled into the motel's parking lot. It stopped next to me, and a man with a handlebar mustache rolled his window down.

"Afternoon, Officer," I said, in no mood to play nice with the locals.

"You folks in town on business or pleasure?" he asked.

Pretty loaded question, considering this was a small town situated very close to the Pack border. I pulled out my badge. "Guess."

"Don't usually get any trouble from the folk in the Pack lands, unless something else in town is awry."

"I'm not at liberty to say, but I assure you, there is no immediate threat to the residents of this town." Out of the corner of my eye, I saw the same pixie cloud from arrival day burst in and out of view, and I nearly laughed. It amused me how humans couldn't see most fey unless the fey allowed it, but I saw them interacting with humans all the time. Following them around, reading books over their shoulders.

The deputy nodded. "I expect if that changes, I'll be notified." He handed me his card, so I swapped it for one of mine.

"Count on it," I replied.

"Surprised it took the locals so long to realize they'd been invaded by out-of-towners," Jaxon said. He appeared on my right side, hazel eyes fixed on the departing car.

"I guess it's a good thing we'll be heading for Kansas soon."

"First we need to figure out how to use the cubes as homing beacons to find the exact location we're looking for." He angled toward me and lowered his voice. "What about your mom?"

I grimaced. "I don't want to get her involved."

"I know, but she might be our best option. She used Julius's severed head to lead you guys to where he was turned into a revenant."

The fact that I knew that but didn't remember *he* knew that threatened to give me a blessed headache. "Just . . . let me be the one who brings my mom up as an option. Please?"

"Of course."

Novak and Chandra returned with takeout for lunch, so we settled into one motel room to eat and discuss our options. Tennyson lurked in the corner of the room, a silent statue, and I refused to ask him if he knew someone who could track the werewolves. I still owed him for his first favor. Chandra put a call in to a fellow moon witch to ask for leads within the human magic users community.

But tracing magic to its source was a tricky and rare gift that few people would ever admit to possessing, because it made that person a valuable commodity to other magic users. Especially magic abusers who might use the tracer against his enemies. I didn't want my mom to get on anyone's radar by helping us again.

I also wasn't sure we had another choice.

While you waffle over the inevitable decision to in-

volve your mother, Tennyson said, *we have unfinished business.*

I glared at him. "Does anyone have a pin or other sharp object?"

"What for?" Novak asked. He had a smear of mustard on his cheek from the deluxe burger he was chowing down on.

"I owe Tennyson a favor."

"You're gonna poke him full of holes?"

Jaxon choked on his soda.

"A drop of blood, remember?" I said.

"My fang will do just fine," Tennyson replied.

"No way, you are not biting me. That was not part of the deal."

"As you wish."

"I should have a safety pin in my makeup kit," Chandra said.

I followed her to the room next door and wasn't surprised Tennyson trailed us. I had asked for this to be a private moment. After Chandra dug the pin out of her kit, she left and shut the door. The fact that I was now alone in a motel room with a Master vampire was not lost on me. Nor was the way his power crackled the air around us and made my pulse race. My mouth watered with the memory of how his blood tasted.

"You still feel it, don't you, young djinn?" he asked. "Our connection."

"Yes. I kind of hate you for it, but you saved my life, so that makes it impossible to try and stake you."

His lips quirked. "You lack the speed to success-fully kill me, but I do admire your forthrightness and tenacity." He lifted his right index finger to his mouth and punctured the tip with his fang.

The sight of that crimson liquid had me taking two steps toward him, before I stopped myself. Resisting the lure of his blood was not fucking easy. I'd ingested too much not to be drawn to it, to the power that would surge in my veins directly after—but the blood-lust. The bloodlust made me attack my mom once. I wouldn't risk my friends' safety for a hit of my new favorite drug.

"You're an asshole," I said.

He threw his head back and laughed. "You are indeed strong. Few who have tasted vampire blood once can resist its call."

"Put the finger away, Tennyson." My annoyance at his manipulation attempt tweaked at the Quarrel, and the last thing I needed to do was let it loose this close to a roomful of people I care about, especially knowing it wouldn't affect the vampire at all. He wasn't done, though.

"Is that what you truly want?"

Bless it. "Yes," I said between gritted teeth.

"As you wish." He licked the drop of blood off and no more welled up. The tangy scent lingered in the air, though. "Your turn."

I grunted, then stabbed the pin into the pad of my left thumb. The sharp prick became a throb. I hadn't poked it in very deep, just enough to squeeze a drop of blood to the surface. Tennyson's sweet scent surrounded me, as did he and his power. He'd moved so fast his cloak still swirled around him to catch up. Solid blue eyes flashed, and I nearly recoiled. Nearly. This was our agreement. My dad would flip his ever-loving shit if he found out about this, but I held still while Tennyson raised my hand to his mouth. A cool tongue flicked across my thumb, and then he was on the other side of the room in a whoosh of air movement.

He stared at me with those headlight eyes, both pale hands pressed to his mouth.

"Was it that bad?" I asked.

"Oh, Shiloh, I'm sorry," he said from behind his hands. "I should not have done that."

This was not the reaction I'd expected. "Why? What happened?"

Despite his height, he seemed to shrink, using his cloak to cover himself. Shield himself. "Your blood . . . it's the sweetest thing I've ever tasted." The words were muffled behind his hands and tinged with . . . fear? No. Tennyson didn't get scared. "No honey, no plant, no other thing I've tasted on earth compares. Heaven and earth, what have I done?" His entire body quaked once.

Sweet Iblis, what on earth is happening?

"Okay, you're scaring me," I said. "If I tasted good, what's the problem?"

He lowered his hands to reveal low-hanging fangs

the length of my thumb. Vampires always had short fangs that extended during feeding or distress, like a fight. His fangs now were horrifyingly impressive, and I understood.

Tennyson wanted more of my blood.

"You must leave the room, Shiloh, or else."

Didn't have to tell me twice. I put the room door between me and him, then yelped at the sight of Jaxon waiting for me outside. "What happened?" he asked.

"He liked it a little too much."

"Meaning?"

"Meaning Tennyson asked me to leave the room, so I left the room."

"Shiloh—"

"It's fine. If he can't control himself going forward, he stays behind."

Jaxon scowled. "Good luck making him stay behind."

"If I have to put a silver bullet in his foot to keep him down, I will." I looked at the other room's open door, where Novak was doing a terrible job pretending not to eavesdrop. "Did you guys come up with anything?"

"No. We've all put out feelers to our contacts and informants, but so far, no one is powerful enough to do what we need, especially over such a big area."

"So we're back to asking my mom?"

"Pretty much. And on the plus side, we know we can trust your mom."

"True." I palmed my phone. *But can she trust us to keep her safe?* "All I can do is call her and ask, right?"

Jaxon's answering smile was both supportive and sympathetic, and I stared at his lips a bit too long that time. Instead of doing it in front of everyone, I wandered to the other side of the parking lot near the main road, and leaned against an electric pole.

"Hey, Shiloh," Mom said in a bright tone. "How's the hunt for the werewolves?"

"Progressing, actually." I filled her in on what we'd learned about the infertility, meeting Danu, and finding the cubes. "So this is where we're stuck."

She was silent a beat. "You want to use the magic cubes as a way to find the person who created them. Track the magic to its source."

My mom always was sharp. "Yes. We're asking around, but none of us know anyone else strong enough to do it. And Kansas is kind of huge."

"You're right, it is. When I used Julius to find the source, we at least had a sense it had been done semi-locally. Trying to do the same in Kansas is like literally looking for a needle in a haystack."

"Or a cornfield."

A car buzzed by and blew its horn at me. I flipped them off.

"Where are you?" Mom asked.

"Small town near California Pack lands. I wanted to call you in private. You don't have to help us."

"I didn't have to marry your father, either, but that happened."

"Mom."

"I'm sorry, I'm not dissing your father. I only meant no one makes me do anything I don't want to do. If you ask for my help, daughter, I'll help you. And since this isn't an official investigation, you don't have to worry about misspeaking in front of me."

"True. Okay. Will you help us?"

"Of course. When and where?"

"Probably not until tomorrow, and most likely in Kansas somewhere, so I'll text you once I've talked to the team."

"All right. Be safe."

"Always am, Mom."

Despite her assurances, my stomach was a little uneasy over involving my mother in one of my cases. Last time, she'd been attacked by a magical snare and nearly choked to death on a spider. What if this magic user put up snares, too? She could be hurt again. Or killed. Any of us could, but it was our job to take the risk.

I returned to the room and informed my companions of the news.

Jaxon brought up a map of Kansas on his phone. "Wichita is a fairly central location with a big airport. Might be a good place to meet up with your mom."

"Our other decision," Novak said, "is of our own

transportation. I require a lot more sex before I could possibly teleport the Jeep and multiple passengers such a distance."

"Guess there aren't any brothels nearby, huh?" I asked.

"No, there aren't. The best I managed last night was a blow job behind the convenience store."

Chandra was eyeballing Novak with interest, so I made a slashing motion with my hand. "No, don't even think about it," I said. "If you two want to fuck when we aren't on a case, that's one thing."

"It's an unofficial case," she replied.

"It's also a twenty-five-hour drive from here to there," Jaxon added. "Some of us can fly into Wichita, while two stay behind and take turns driving the Jeep."

I will drive. I flinched at Tennyson's voice, but it lacked the booming volume I'd gotten used to. *I do not require that kind of sleep, and I can drive straight through. And I need a bit of distance from you, Shiloh.*

"Shi?" Jaxon said, staring at me. "The vampire?"

"Yeah, he volunteered to drive. Says he can do it without sleeping."

"Are the windshields tinted enough?"

I'm touched. I didn't know the skin-walker cared.

I rolled my eyes. "Apparently so. With our badges, we'll be able to carry our service weapons onto a regular plane, but we'll be sans our special guns and toys until Tennyson arrives with the Jeep."

"Then maybe he should get a head start," Chandra said. "We can use Gideon's vehicle to get to the airport from here."

As you wish.

"He's gonna get on that," I reported.

"I'll go outside and make sure we don't need anything else from the Jeep," Jaxon said. "Lord knows if we'll ever see it again." His tone was more teasing than serious, and in my head, Tennyson laughed.

Gideon arrived with a black SUV similar to the first one about an hour after Tennyson hit the road with our Jeep. We filled him in on the plan—he was highly impressed by my mom's powers—then checked out of the motel. The tree branch barely fit inside my carry-on, but it was better than trying to check it as luggage. Hopefully, there weren't any other magic users on the plane with us who'd be tempted by its power. The wood diminished it, but didn't completely mask it.

Last-minute tickets from Podunk, California, to Wichita, Kansas, weren't terribly cheap—or easy to come by—but we put them on the company card, so to speak. Then I called ahead for two hotel rooms near the airport. Mom was joining us first thing in the morning.

Did I mention I hate flying? Hate it. And not because of heights, or because we were in a giant, four-hundred-ton canister carrying two thousand pounds of jet fuel, speeding along at Mach 0.85. It was the complete loss of control over my environment. Once I was on it, I was stuck on it until we landed. I also hate being crammed into a small space with a lot of people, which is why I also avoid rock concerts and Black Friday shopping. I was terrified of losing control of the Quarrel again.

Doing it on an airplane? Disaster.

So I bought a vodka on ice as soon as the refreshment cart came around, closed my eyes, and tried to catch up on some of the sleep I'd missed last night. Even with only one layover, we didn't land until ten hours later, and in another time zone. I was starving, exhausted, and completely wired after spending so much time cooped up and in my seat.

Exhausted won out. As soon as I got into one of the hotel rooms, I unzipped my boots, crawled under the covers, and fell asleep.

I woke sometime later to sunlight streaming in from the room's wide window. I was in the bed closest to it, and I rolled over, expecting to see Chandra in the other double. Instead, I saw Jaxon's sleeping face and another lump beside him.

"What the . . . ?" I sat up, and both noise and action startled the other men awake. Yeah, that was definitely Jaxon and Gideon, but why— Oh no. Really? "Novak and Chandra slept together?"

Jaxon shrugged while rubbing sleep out of his eyes.

"I apologize if you're offended, Marshal," Gideon said. "You were asleep when rooming negotiations began in the hall."

"I'm a big girl, and please, call me Shiloh."

"Thank you. And if you don't mind my asking, I'm curious. What does an incubus add to a US Marshals team like yours?"

"Sarcasm?"

Jaxon snorted. "I think we all bring that."

"Well, besides the teleportation, he's strong and a fierce fighter," I added. The day we stopped the necromancer on that cow farm, Novak had fought like the demon he was, and for one horrifying moment, he'd genuinely scared me. I'd expected an attack. But he'd recognized me as his ally and backed down. "Plus, he knows things. We all have knowledge of different Paras relevant to our own backgrounds."

"That makes sense," Gideon said. "I've had little experience with other Paras in the past, as I've spent most of my life on Pack lands. This is my first trip away from home." For an instant, that brave werewolf facade cracked, and I saw a fearful young man far from his family and life. Then he blinked and the bravado returned.

"Well, something tells me your first trip will be a memorable one." I stumbled into the bathroom to pee and brush my teeth.

The room was typical of newer chain hotels, with the bathroom situated near the door, so I was closest to it when someone knocked. I yanked the chain back and opened the door, toothbrush in my mouth, fully expecting Chandra or Novak.

Instead, Kathleen Allard stood in the hallway with a calm smile on her face—a smile I hauled off and punched without a second blessed thought.

The traitorous dhampir went flying onto her skinny ass and I lunged.

CHAPTER 9

Strong arms looped around my waist and held me back. The toothbrush flew out of my mouth and hit the carpet with a *splat*. Gideon put himself between me and Kathleen.

"What the fuck are you doing here?" I asked, spitting out the toothpaste.

"Hello to you, too," Kathleen drawled.

"Answer me."

"May I stand?" She sat up. Gideon growled and she froze. "I'd rather talk in private, Shiloh."

"So you can stab us in the back again?" I said. "Fat fucking chance."

The door across from ours opened and Novak stepped out, dressed in only a pair of boxers. His broad chest and bare arms glistened with perspiration, and he was breathing heavily. "What is— Kathleen?"

She was pinned between us, but she also wasn't making any move to attack.

"Novak?" Chandra appeared behind him with the bedspread wrapped around her torso. "What's she doing here?"

"She would be pleased to explain," Kathleen said, "if my former teammates will allow me to stand."

"Why are you two hugging like that?" Novak asked.

Jaxon released his hold on me, and I stepped to the side, startled to realize I hadn't noticed his arms around me. It had felt good. Too good. He stepped back into our room, and when he returned, had his service weapon trained on Kathleen. Silver nitrate bullets to the heart killed dhampirs, too.

"Come on in," Jaxon said.

Kathleen stood with familiar grace and strode into our room. Novak, Gideon, and I followed him and left the door propped open so Chandra could join us when she was decent. Kathleen wrinkled her nose in Novak's general direction, and Gideon gave him a wide berth too. The guy reeked of sex. Kathleen stood near the room's desk, hands clasped in front of her like we'd invited her in for tea.

"First off, how did you find us?" Jaxon asked.

"You used your real name at registration," she replied to me. "It was not all that difficult."

"Okay, next question. Why shouldn't I put a bullet in you for betraying us for so long?"

"Because I did not betray you. Never once did I

pass along your sensitive information to our joint enemy. I worked alongside you as an equal and never shirked my duties as a Para-Marshal."

"You sure as shit shirked the whole 'my teammates can trust me' thing," I said. "You were working with the necromancer."

"Yes, on behalf of my actual employer, who planted me in the Para-Marshals first, in order to entice Marshal Weller to bring me into his inner circle. My goal was always the same as yours: stop the necromancer's plan to control a vampire Line."

I kind of wanted to believe her, but I no longer trusted her. Period. "Why are you here?"

"The same reason as you. To find the missing werewolves and the people responsible for their disappearances."

"Because your mystery employer wants them found?"

"Precisely."

"So you just happened to show up on our doorstep after we did all the legwork to even get this far?" I grunted. "Convenient."

"Hardly. With all of you officially on leave, and no plane tickets departing from BWI or Philadelphia in your names, it took me this long to track you down. None of your old phone numbers are working, and even if they were, I suspected you wouldn't speak to me. So I arrived in person to offer my assistance."

"No."

Kathleen's lips twitched. "So hasty to deny me?"

"I don't fucking trust you, lady."

"I don't trust her, either," Novak said. "But I think I believe her. Kathleen's a lot of things, but she's never been a bald-faced liar."

"How is being a fucking double agent not bald-faced lying?"

"Because no one asked if I was a double agent?"

"I swear to—"

Kathleen's lips twitched. "Sorry—I couldn't resist. But you're not wrong. I do seem to have a talent for secrecy. I am also old enough to eat crow when necessary. It was never my intention to deceive or hurt any of you." She looked from Novak to Jaxon to me. "I was doing my job, and for whatever distress I caused, I offer my apologies."

I scowled, but Novak simply nodded. He had been closer than anyone else had been with the secretive dhampir, and I trusted Novak's instincts. I didn't trust Kathleen, but that didn't mean I couldn't work with her. "I believe you," I said.

She nodded. Her green eyes fixed on mine while her nostrils twitched. "I admit, the human witch's scent on Novak does not surprise me, but why does the scent of Master Tennyson still linger on you?"

"Because he's working with us again."

"Oh?"

"The vampire found us in California and he wants

to help," Jaxon said. "He's driving our Jeep and equipment cross-country for us."

"Oh? How generous." She flashed me knowing smirk, as if I'd somehow earned the favor of Tennyson driving our stuff in a salacious way. Ugh.

I flipped her off. "What sort of help could you even offer us?" I asked. "We have a plan, we are executing it, we do not need you."

"My employer has narrowed down our search field to within one hundred square miles. The magic protecting it prevents him from focusing any closer."

I looked first at Jaxon, then Novak. Even Gideon had the same wary surprise on his face. Chandra chose that pause to join us, and we brought her up to speed, including Kathleen's final bombshell.

"We have someone sensitive to magic who's on their way to locate the missing wolves," I said, hedging a bit. She didn't seem to know about the magically infused tree branch in my luggage, and I wasn't about to offer that up freely to her lying ass.

"There are few more powerful than my employer," Kathleen said, a bit of suspicion leaking into her voice. "And they could only get as close as one hundred miles. How will your magic user do better?"

"Kathleen's information would give our person a more focused area to search," Chandra said.

I glared, but Chandra only met me with a hard stare of her own. She understood betrayal, and she knew how hard this was on us. But we all understood the stakes. Twenty-eight innocent lives and who knows what they were going through.

Gideon looked like he wanted to knock all our heads together, but he was deferring to those of us with more experience at this.

Someone knocked on the door for the second time that morning, and it could only be one person. Chandra was closest, so she answered. Spoke quiet words at the door, and then shut it again. "Our person is here," she said.

Kathleen laughed. "Don't bother, I can scent her. You might as well allow Elspeth inside. We've met."

Chandra cut her eyes at me; I nodded. No sense in keeping up the charade. Mom entered the room with her spine straight, and a disdainful look she threw right at Kathleen. I walked over to hug her hello. She barely glanced at Novak's nearly naked state and hugged Jaxon, too. Huh. Jaxon introduced her to Gideon.

"So that happened," I said, jacking my thumb at Kathleen.

"I see." Mom kept a reasonable distance from the dhampir. "Shiloh, your clothes look slept in."

"Because they are. Someone's unexpected arrival interrupted my morning routine."

"I saw no reason to delay my request," Kathleen said.

"What request?" Mom asked.

I huffed. "Kathleen claims her employer has located

the missing wolves to within a hundred square miles. She wants to work with us in exchange for the information."

"And you believe her?"

"I don't know."

"I have no reason to lie," Kathleen said. "By coming here, I risked being shot as a traitor. I promise you, my information is accurate."

Haughty as ever, but I also believed her. She had nothing to gain by lying to or tricking us. But . . . "Who's your employer?" I asked.

She slowly blinked, then yawned.

M'kay. "As soon as Tennyson gets here with the Jeep, tie her up with silver chains."

"Wait," Kathleen said. "I know you feel slighted by me—"

"Slighted doesn't begin to cover it, lady."

"But did we not work together in the end to stop the necromancer from taking control of Master Tennyson? I proved we are on the same side."

"You hit me in the back!"

"After you elbowed me in the stomach. I was playing a part, Shiloh, and I continued to play it until myself and Lars could make our moves."

"Where is Lars anyway? And how exactly did you get out of holding?"

"Lars is still in holding, while I am not. My employer believed you more likely to accept my help than his, since you know me."

"I don't know you," Chandra said. "And I don't trust you *or* Lars."

"I don't know who *any* of you are," Gideon snapped. "I just want to find my people. What if the woman's telling the truth?"

"She's a dhampir," I replied.

"And I'm a werewolf. And you're half djinn—I don't care. What if she can get us closer? It'll be that much easier for your mother to trace the cubes back to their creator, right?"

Kathleen tilted her head. "Cubes?"

"What?" I said. "Your employer doesn't know about those?"

"If she does, she did not inform me."

So the employer was definitely a she. Interesting, but also not useful at the moment. I crossed my arms and angled back toward Kathleen. "How do we know you aren't actually working for the people who stole the missing wolves?"

"Because we believe the same person who bank-rolled Weller and the necromancer is bankrolling this operation, as well. We are committed to bringing this individual down."

"Why? Who are they?"

She squinted at me.

"Tit for tat, Kathleen. You want me to believe your information is real? Give me something more than mysterious *she*'s and *they*'s."

"The man my employer and I seek to bring down is

referred to only as Damian. He has great wealth, great resources, and much reach within the US government. He is a very real threat to the continued existence of Paras on this plane. As you know, vampires and werewolves have always been tangled up in this mortal world of ours, but those who chose to come here? They can leave. If a cleansing happens, all manner of vampire, dhampir, suphir, and werewolf may be eradicated."

A chill raced down my spine. "This Damian person wants to cleanse the world of Paras?"

She nodded once.

That was pretty heavy shit, because it meant my extinction, too. Like vampires, djinn were bound to the earth, because we were created here. We didn't cross another plane to visit this planet, like the fey or pixies, or even creations from Hell, like demons and hobgoblins. If Kathleen was right, Damian wanted to bring down a fucking apocalypse against Paras.

Not. Gonna. Happen.

"Okay, we work together," I said. "But you are not to be out of our sight at any time."

"We may not have a choice down the road," Kathleen replied.

"That's down the road. Agreed?"

She arched a slim eyebrow. "Agreed. The sector we should search is to the west of Highway 283 and south of I-70."

Jaxon brought that up on his phone. Southwest corner of the state, and less than two hours' drive to get to the outer edges. But I could not blindly trust her, so I fetched the tree branch from my carry-on. Mom put both hands on it and closed her eyes. Magic pulsed around her, and the power in those eleven cubes buzzed, making my skin crawl with unease.

She shook her head and opened her eyes. "This is different than the revenant magic, and we were much closer to the source. I can't say for sure if she's correct in our destination, but it has better odds of bearing fruit than us blindly wandering the state."

"Listen to your mother, Shiloh," Kathleen said. "We have work to do."

I glared at her. "Yeah, well, work can wait until after I've changed my clothes. Novak, go take a shower. We bug out in ten minutes."

It ended up being closer to fifteen, because Chandra ended up in the shower, too, and I couldn't really begrudge them some good sex. I loved seeing Novak back at full power, and his hands had completely healed now. And it wasn't as if anyone else was getting any. My last attempt at blowing off some sexual steam had been interrupted by the phone call about Tennyson and the trailer park.

I was also a little jealous, because the pair seemed to have hit it off personally, too.

A moon witch and an incubus. Who'd have thought?

While we probably could have squished the seven of us into one vehicle, it made more sense to take Mom's rental as well as our own. Jaxon and I rode with her, while the others got the pleasure of riding with Kathleen in our rented SUV to keep an eye on her. Jaxon drove our car, with Mom shotgun, the tree branch on her lap. We swung by fast food for breakfast before hitting the open road.

There wasn't much to see in southern Kansas, mostly open plains, wheat fields, and farmland, so we mostly listened to music while Mom concentrated on the branch. After about half an hour, I remembered Tennyson was on his way to Wichita, but we wouldn't be there when he arrived. And the man annoyingly did not use cell phones.

The telepathy had only been used while in proximity to each other, but if he was close enough to Kansas, maybe I could reach him. Worth a try.

Tennyson? Can you hear me?

Silence.

I drew on not only the rush of power I remembered from drinking his blood, but also the magical tether that had previously bound us when Tennyson spoke the binding words for the Rules of Wishing. We'd connected through each of our personal strengths and powers, and we had to still be connected somehow.

Tennyson? Hello?

Shiloh? This is unusual. Are you no longer in Kansas?

Still in Kansas but moving west, toward you. I ex-

plained Kathleen and our morning so far. *Once I know more, I'll tell you.*

All right. I am still about an hour from the Kansas border and the sun is quite bright. I am eager for respite from the glare.

I bet. Uh, signing off.

I swear, I heard him chuckle in my head.

"Tennyson is up to date," I said.

Jaxon's hand jerked on the wheel. "He found you this far away?"

"Uh, no. I reached out."

I could only see his profile, but it showed enough. He was pissed and doing a bad job hiding it. Apparently blood-share meant brain-share, and Jaxon could get over it.

"It's concerning that your connection to the vampire is strengthening," Mom said, echoing Jaxon's thoughts, albeit with a bit more diplomacy. She turned around to look at me, her face twisted with worry. "I fear you'll lose yourself to his power."

"I won't, Mom. I know who I am. The daughter of Elspeth Juno and Gaius Oakenjin. Suspected Para-Marshal Du Jour. Also terrible cook."

Mom laughed and some of that worry faded. "Stubborn girl. You are your father's daughter."

"Hey, you're just as stubborn as he is."

"All of y'all are a special kind of stubborn," Jaxon said.

"True. We are."

"Hey, wait a sec." He glanced at Mom, then at me before reverting his eyes to the road. "Your mom's last name is Juno, and your dad's is Oakenjin, so how come your last name is Harrison?"

"Protection," Mom replied. "My father was a powerful warlock, descended from the equally powerful Juno line. He and my mother were murdered by a coven of witches in Chicago when I was a child, because he refused to side with them during a turf war. I kept the Juno name, because it was the name I knew and a way to honor my heritage. But I also knew if that coven discovered I was alive, or that I had a daughter, they could come looking for us. So when I gave birth, I listed Gaius Harrison as the birth father and Shiloh took his name."

I cut my eyes at Jaxon. "In the six years we've supposedly known each other, you never asked before today?"

"No, it honestly never dawned on me. But your mom also never used to be active in our cases, so the name difference caught me off guard."

"Oh."

Jaxon met my eyes in the rearview mirror, and I didn't miss the open hurt over me saying "supposedly." I was trying, bless it. "So I guess Shiloh didn't inherit any of her grandfather's powers?"

"None that she's displayed so far," Mom replied.

"But I also never taught her how to find and harness them, for fear of discovery. It's why I lead a quiet life and rarely use my own magic."

"So wait a sec." All this was freaking news to me! "I could have hidden abilities I don't know about?"

"It's possible, Shi, but not a guarantee. The power of a magical line is secured by marrying those of equal or higher abilities, but instead, my father married my mother. While she was attuned to nature and sensitive to magic, she possessed no real power. So his line was diluted through me, and what you received was further altered by your father's genes. And I was too scared to explore your abilities, because I didn't want us to be found."

I scrunched down in the back seat and pondered the new turn in my life. I totally understood my mom's desire to protect me from these bad Chicago witches, but I was twenty-eight years old. She could have told me all this sooner, maybe even in private so we could really talk. Not while we were on a road trip with five other Paras on the hunt for missing werewolves.

Sweet Iblis, sometimes my life well and truly sucked.

On the other hand, those bad witches *hadn't* found us, and Mom was taking a big risk helping us again. Choosing to live in a tiny town in Delaware made a lot more sense now.

"Hey, what if telepathy is something I can do on my own?" I asked, sitting up straighter, excited by the idea. "I never tried doing it before I met Tennyson. What if his power is helping draw mine out? I reached out to him just now, after all."

"Try saying something in my head," Jaxon replied.

"Okay. Um." I wasn't sure how to do that. I had a previous link to Tennyson's mind, but I didn't have one with Jaxon. Except we apparently had six years of friendship and a few months of great sex between us.

I closed my eyes and pictured his smiling face. Tried to put it into a new context. The beach, maybe, with sun glinting in his blond hair. Laughter. His lightly accented voice calling my name as he splashed in the surf. Warm hands rubbing suntan lotion onto my back. Such a beautiful . . . memory?

Not my memory.

His memory.

"Are you thinking about us at the beach?" I asked.

Jaxon's head snapped in my direction, his eyebrows furrowed, then just as quickly returned to the road. "How did you know that?"

"I saw it." An odd kind of joy bubbled up inside me. "I saw you thinking about us at the beach. Why are you thinking about us at the beach?"

"Figured if you really could read my mind, you'd like to hear something positive. We had a great time that weekend. Only one we ever got to spend as a mini-vacation when we dated."

"Where were we?"

"Bethany Beach."

"Oh. It's so odd, because I couldn't hear any specific thing in your head, but I saw the memories playing out. I did hear you call my name, but it matched the memory of you doing it on the beach."

"That's an impressive gift," Mom said. She didn't sound happy about it, though. "Perhaps we should leave your exercising it to later, though? We're getting close enough that I need to concentrate on the cubes. I can sense their magic more intensely now, and it's definitely pulling me in this direction."

"Yeah, of course, Mom. Job first, self-discovery later."

I refocused my energy into the task at hand, but we would definitely be revisiting the topic of my visual telepathy at another time. "What are you sensing?"

"It's still so vague. I think the wood is blocking it too much."

Oh fun. Mom passed the branch to me, and I held back a pained scream as I vibrated my hand and pulled one cube out. "Ugh. Here."

She took the sock-wrapped cube with a grimace, then held it in both palms. The dark magic crawled over my skin, so I put the branch in the empty seat and tried to scrunch away from my mom.

My mom, who started shaking in the front seat, before flinging the cube onto the dash in front of Jaxon.

I jackknifed up and reached for her shoulder. "Mom?"

"Elspeth, what's wrong?" Jaxon asked.

"I can feel it now that it's free of the wood." Mom's voice was an odd tangle of terrified and furious. "All magic has a signature unique to the source, especially among witches and trained users."

"You know this signature?" I said.

She twisted to face me, her skin pale, but her eyes blazed with fury. "It's the same magical signature as the witches who killed your grandfather."

CHAPTER 10

I gaped at my mom. "It's the *same* signature? Are you shitting me?"

"I'm perfectly serious," Mom replied. "I was a child when my parents died, but I've never forgotten the sound of their screams, or the scorched earth smell of the witch who cursed them. They didn't know I existed or that I was hiding under their bed, because my mother had kept my birth a secret. From my first memory, they instilled in me how I must hide myself from the magical world for all our sakes, just as I kept you hidden until adulthood."

Shock and horror rolled through my system, and I reached for one of her hands to squeeze. "The witch who killed my grandparents created those cubes?"

"Yes. Copper is a strong absorber of magic. Those

cubes would have been effective for months, if not years, even without a boost from the witch." Mom let out a sound not unlike a growl. "To curse young people barren is an insult to Mother Earth herself. It is dark magic no respectable witch would dabble in, but these Chicago witches have no morals. They answer only to themselves. We must be cautious going forward, Shiloh."

"I understand. I need you safe, Mom."

A few minutes passed before Jaxon said, "I know this is painful for you guys, but Elspeth, can you sense the direction we need to go?"

"Northwest. We're too far south."

"Okay, thank you." On the next route advertising north, he turned. The SUV behind us followed. I called Chandra and filled her in on what Mom learned about the witch and that this was the area. In the background, I heard Kathleen say, "I told you so."

"It sounds like this case just got personal to you," Chandra said.

"It did. I don't know why this witch is working with Damian, or what they want with all those werewolves, but I am going to find out. That woman killed my grandparents."

"Keep a clear head, Shiloh. This isn't the time for personal revenge."

I didn't entirely agree, but I understood needing to keep my head in the game. In the present and not the past. I also desperately wanted to tell the others what I'd learned about my own powers, but it could keep. Maybe it would be surprisingly useful down the road.

We kept going on a long, twisty road through farmland that, I hoped, would lead us to our missing werewolves—and if we were lucky, this Damian person, too. He was not going to cause a Para Apocalypse on my watch. No fucking way.

After ten miles, Mom pointed to another road, marked by a sign that said "Gabriel, KS, Pop. 890."

"Gabriel," Jaxon said. "If that's our destination, there's some irony to it. The name means *God's messenger.*"

"Which Damian seems to think he is if he wants to destroy Paras?" I asked.

"Bingo."

"I believe it's our destination," Mom said. "The power is concentrating, and I don't sense it extending beyond the next town."

"Terrific."

I passed the information to the other car, and then pushed the information at Tennyson. He responded with a simple, *"I will see you soon."*

I also kept a close eye on my mom, but so far, we hadn't encountered any magical snares. The people behind this place weren't doing much to protect it from people sensitive to magic.

Then again, how many magically sensitive people randomly traveled through Bumfuck, Kansas? The

Midwest was a great place to hide illicit paranormal activity.

The small town of Gabriel rose on the horizon suddenly, from flat earth to distant buildings. A scattering of homes lined the main street, along with a handful of businesses and a mom-and-pop grocery store. A municipal building and an antique store. A gas station/repair shop. Nothing unusual until we'd gotten to the other side of town, where a professional-looking building appeared. Brick, two stories, with a sign that advertised a dentist, a family doctor, and the oddly named DM Clinic.

"Here," Mom said. "It's centered here."

"This building here?" I asked.

"Yes."

The parking lot had about a dozen cars in it, so we didn't stand out too much pulling into two rear spaces, side by side. We rolled windows down on the sides of our vehicles that faced each other. Chandra was in the back seat facing me, so I asked, "Do you sense any of the werewolves?"

"Not yet," she replied. "The cube may be interfering somehow, or the place has protective shields. I'm uncertain which."

"I don't scent them, either," Gideon said from the driver's seat. "Something may be interfering, or they simply haven't been outside the clinic in a long enough period of time that their scents faded." From somewhere inside the SUV, Kathleen concurred.

Well, I could take care of the cube problem. Jaxon fetched it from the dash and I vibrated it back into the branch. My hand tingled with annoyance long after. I moved through objects so rarely that doing it this many times in two days was taking its toll.

"Better?" I asked.

"I feel better," Mom replied.

Chandra closed her eyes. "Yes, I can sense Alice now. Her mind is fuzzy but no longer hidden from me. There is still something interfering, though."

"Can you get into her head?" I asked. "Do that misty thing you do?"

"I'll try. Would you like to join me?"

"Definitely."

The car disappeared, leaving Chandra and me again standing in the swirling gray mists of human consciousness. For as bizarre and trippy it had been the first time, this was old hat now, and I kind of liked it. For all I wasn't entirely sure of the extent of Chandra's powers, this had been crazy useful so far.

Her eyes remained closed as she sought out Alice Anderson's mind. A faint bluish charge ripped across the mists a few times, and I bet that was the interference. Probably a protective ward of some kind, not only to hide their activities from other Paras, but likely from the residents of Gabriel itself.

The shape of a woman appeared. Curvy and tall, standing half-bent as if looking down at something.

Her silhouette angled toward us, as if sensing our presence, but she remained grayed out.

"Alice? It's Chandra Goodfellow. Can you hear me?"

Alice nodded, and more details appeared. She wore a simple linen dress. Had dark brown hair, like many of the other werewolves we'd encountered. But she never fully materialized like Lacey and Will had. That blue electricity jolted all around us, probably unhappy that Chandra had broken through.

"Chandra?" Alice's voice was tinny, as if coming from a great distance when her shape was only a few feet away. "What are you doing here? Who's she?"

"This is a Para-Marshal associate of mine, Shiloh Harrison. We've been working with your Alpha to find you and the other missing werewolves."

Alice blinked at us several times. "Well, you've wasted your efforts. We all left the Pack of our own free will. We want to be here."

My hand jerked, and I met Chandra's equally shocked expression. "You're all here on purpose?" I asked. "You weren't coerced into leaving?"

"Of course not. We all want children, and when Alpha Kennedy refused to allow us to seek human help with our infertility, a solution was presented to us by Dr. Marcus Ferguson. He told us about this clinic, said the treatments were free because they were all still experimental. We're his test subjects so other werewolves don't face this same problem in the future."

"Alice, the only reason you guys were infertile in the first place is because someone here placed a magical cube in your home that caused it. They made the problem so they could trick you into coming here to fix it."

"You're lying." Alice crossed her arms, the very picture of obstinacy. Freaking werewolves. "They really are helping us. Two of the volunteer couples have already conceived."

"Yeah, because you guys aren't exposed to the magic whammy anymore. And how do you think we found you in the middle of nowhere? We used those cubes to trace its magic signature back to here. We're in cars right outside in the parking lot."

"Dr. Ferguson is going to give us children. And then he'll help us apply to the government to form our own Pack. One where human medicine is allowed."

"About that." I glanced at Chandra, who seemed more than willing to let me speak. She had her hands full keeping the communications channel open. "We spoke to your goddess Danu. She's okay with Packs using human medicine, and we've told Alpha Kennedy, who has agreed. And before you say we're lying again, Rosalind was with us. She heard the words with her own ears."

Alice frowned. "How did you find our goddess? What are you?"

I hated that question more than almost any other. "I'm a Para-Marshal doing her job. Twenty-eight werewolves from two Packs are considered missing, and it's our job to find you and bring you home."

"No. You can't tell anyone you found us. They'll take us away, and we'll never conceive. Please. My heart is already torn open from the three children I lost. Don't take this from me, too."

Bless it all. "They. Made. You. Infertile."

"I don't believe you. Alpha Kennedy would make you say anything to see us retrieved so we can be punished for our deceit."

She didn't want to believe me, so the least I could do was gather a little more information. "Were you the first person approached by Dr. Ferguson about these experimental treatments?"

"Yes. He understood my grief, and when he told me what he could do, I agreed to be his voice."

"You got all the other couples on board?"

"Yes. And now because of me, two of those couples will have a child of their own. Thanks to Dr. Ferguson."

"Did it never occur to you that Dr. Ferguson tricked you into being his mouthpiece? How do you know he isn't the one who had your children killed?"

She snarled at me, and I took a step back, even though I was pretty sure she couldn't physically touch me. This was all in our heads, after all. Right?

"Please, Chandra, leave me alone," Alice said with rage in her voice. "Let us live our lives as we see fit."

A blaze of blue zapped between us and Alice, and

then I was back in the car blinking at the headrest. Chandra was rubbing her temples and muttering.

"That didn't go well," I said. I relayed the conversation.

"It's her grief that is stoking her stubbornness," Chandra said. "She lost the three children I helped her bear, and now all of her hopes and dreams for offspring are riding on this place. She won't accept that, while it's possible she and Raymond are naturally infertile, the other couples were intentionally magicked. They were targeted."

"Do you think this Dr. Ferguson knew about the Andersons?" Jaxon asked. "About their previous inability to conceive, using Chandra to finally have kids, and then losing them? Their loss and grief, and maybe he targeted them first?"

"Alice pretty much confirmed he did, so yes, I do. Without knowing this Dr. Ferguson, I'm speculating on his motives, but grief is a powerful emotion. And they were the first couple reported missing."

"I think this guy's motives are pretty clear," I said. "He wants willing werewolf patients to experiment on, and he's got them. Now we have to find and expose the lie in what he's selling them."

"Wouldn't it be easier to kidnap them and take them back to their Packs?" Novak asked.

"Maybe, but we can't do that. They'll resent us, not to mention they could fight back and hurt themselves, or us. We don't need hostages, we need to expose the truth. Because if this place is experimenting on werewolves, and if it's funded by this Damian guy, then you know well and good they aren't stopping at fertility experiments."

"Agreed," Chandra said. "We need to discover the full extent of what they're doing here and why, before we take any decisive action against them."

Everyone agreed.

A familiar Jeep entered the lot and pulled in next to us. We were now a little bit obvious as a group, facing the town's busiest street—not that I'd noticed more than a dozen cars passing us since we arrived—so we agreed to find a shadier spot to plan our next step. Jaxon found an abandoned grain silo about a half mile outside of town. The interior smelled like dirt and old things, but it gave us shade for Tennyson and Kathleen, and we could talk more easily.

Tennyson lurked near a far wall, keeping his distance from me. I guess twenty-odd hours hadn't fixed whatever he'd felt after tasting my blood, and that was okay by me.

Mom hung on the edges of our circle, and I had half a mind to insist she take her rental and leave, so she'd be safe. But Mom could have taken her keys and left on her own initiative. Instead, she was listening— and then I realized why. The magical signature. The witches who killed her parents. She now had a very personal stake in how this went down.

Which made me want her to leave even more.

Jaxon was already typing away on his phone. "Okay, they have a vague website for DM Clinic. Slogan about making the world a better place, but no clear offering of services. No photos other than a shot of the building's exterior. No email address, just a telephone number."

"Gimme," I said. The line rang three times before a machine picked up. "Thank you for calling DM Clinic. We are not accepting new patients at this time. Please visit our website for more information."

"Dummy line," Novak said. "Whole thing's a front, probably so the town doesn't get suspicious."

"As long as the place pays their local taxes, I imagine the town council doesn't give a shit what they're up to behind closed doors. Jaxon, what about the doctor and dentist next door? Are they legit?"

"One sec." Jaxon tapped away at his phone. "They seem to be. Pictures of the docs and smiling patients. Probably needed legit businesses to move in to keep up the front."

"Yeah, well, I want to know if those front doors even open." I winked at Jaxon, curious to see how we'd play off each other in an undercover gig. "Wanna pretend to be a couple with fertility issues?"

He grinned.

We took Mom's rental to the clinic with Novak stuffed in the back in case we needed quick backup. Before we went in, Jaxon called Chandra's phone so they could listen in on an open line—ear mikes would have been too obvious. I'd also fetched a bug from the Jeep, which I hoped to plant somewhere inside.

The heavily tinted front door did, in fact, open. The lobby reminded me of a doctor's office, with a small waiting area with two chairs and a fake plant, a glass partition, and a single door leading elsewhere. Impersonal and boring. The glass partition was likewise tinted, and next to it was a button that said Ring for Service.

Jaxon pushed it.

I absently scanned the room for any obvious cameras or recording devices and found none. The distant hum of magic remained present, probably whatever protective ward kept their dirty business under wraps. Even Jaxon seemed agitated by it, if the scratching at the skin patch on the back of his neck was any indication.

I knew about skin-walkers simply from being informed. The ability is passed from parent to child, but not all children become full walkers. At ten years old, they perform a ceremony in which their animal spirit either shows itself or not. If it does, the child kills the animal, drinks some of its blood out of respect, and then a small piece of the animal—skin, feather, et cetera—is permanently adhered to the back of the child's neck. In the old days, they'd take the entire skin as a symbol to wear, but it's a lot harder for an eagle skin-walker to get away with wearing a whole cape of eagle feathers in broad daylight.

The glass partition finally slid open, and a middle-aged man in a lab coat appeared. He gave us both a quick once-over, then fixed on an apologetic frown. "I'm sorry, but we aren't accepting any new patients right now."

"Oh, are you sure?" I asked with my best pout. "We heard from a friend of a friend, who's a cousin of mine, that you guys are doing cutting-edge research in infertility."

"Our research is intensely private and by invitation only, I'm afraid. I hope you folks didn't travel too far to see us."

"We just drove in from Wichita, is all."

"I'm sorry you came all the way out for nothing."

"Is there nothing we can do?" Jaxon said, with a touch of desperation in his voice. "I don't suppose we could leave our personal information behind? Maybe we can get an invitation one day, if we can't find another facility to help us?"

"Sure, sure," the man said. He handed Jaxon a clipboard and a pen, then glanced past us. He paused and said, "Excuse me—" And then he literally froze.

I turned the same instant I felt Tennyson behind me. His eyes glowed blue as he held the receptionist in a gazelock. "Feel free to explore a bit," Tennyson said. "This one will not notice a thing."

"Thanks," I replied. Leaving a bug here didn't make a lot of sense, since it didn't look like the room was ever used, but I planted it under an armchair anyway.

The door was, as expected, locked. And it was metal, so I couldn't pass through it and see what was on the other side. But the far wall, which held a weird brown-and-white abstract painting, drew me toward it. Something sparked and pulsed there. I put my palm against it, only for the palm to pass right through on a zap of magic.

A glamour.

Curious, I pushed my face through the veil and was presented with a wide elevator, the big kind you usually saw in hospitals so they could fit two gurneys side by side. Nothing else, just the elevator, and a corridor that angled to my left, probably to the room where the receptionist was currently standing frozen.

No one was around, and I didn't see any cameras, so I stepped completely through the glamour. Studied the elevator. It had a swipe-lock of some sort.

"Shiloh, what?" Jaxon appeared next to me, and we both turned. The illusion was one-way, because I could still see Tennyson and the lobby. "Weird place for a glamour, isn't it?"

"Yeah. Then again, if all the werewolves came here of their own free will, then they'd need the official-looking check-in setup. Maybe this gives Dr. Ferguson or whoever a way to spy on the new arrivals."

"No idea. Wouldn't the werewolves notice the glamour once they're here waiting for the elevator?"

"How do I know? I didn't build this place." I checked the other walls, which were all solid. Then I took the left corridor to find a fairly empty office space. A computer that wasn't on, some file folders full of empty papers. Not a single useful thing, except the key card on the receptionist's belt.

I snatched that and took it back to the elevator.

"Shi, what are you doing?"

"I'm not gonna ride it, I just want to look inside." I swiped the card, and the doors immediately slid back. Jaxon's hand slid to his holstered weapon.

The car was empty. Jaxon put his arm across it to keep it open. I stepped in and snapped a picture of the floor buttons. Five floors, all designated with a combination of symbols that made no sense to me. Even odder, all the floors seemed to go down, not up. The walls were perfectly smooth, not a single hiding spot for another bug, bless it.

"We should not linger," Tennyson said, his voice carrying through the veil easily.

"He's right," Jaxon added.

I gaped at him. "Did you just say Tennyson is right?"

"Don't read into it." He grabbed my wrist and gently pulled me out of the elevator. Its door slid shut. "Come on."

We exited as discreetly as possible, and Tennyson—who'd apparently used his super-speed to run after us, instead of simply asking to tag along—got a ride back to the silo. After explaining what we observed and passing my picture of the elevator panel around,

Gideon said, "Werewolves are not sensitive to glamours. That's likely why they didn't notice the one-way wall you observed."

You learn something new every day.

"I didn't see any obvious security devices," Jaxon said. "But they've got magical wards, so it's hard to know if we were noticed behind the glamour or not. No one attacked, but we were also holding up the only elevator."

"Anyone have thoughts on those floor symbols?" I asked, pointing toward Chandra, who currently had my phone. "By the looks of it, this place is bigger than we assumed, and they're doing more than just fertility studies."

"It's reminiscent of a witch language," Chandra said. She gave the phone to my mom. "I am unable to read it."

Mom's eyebrows furrowed. "It's an ancient language based in Gaelic symbols. The Chicago witch coven is Irish in origin."

"Can you read it?" I asked.

"No, it's far older than I am, sweetheart."

Tennyson slid up to my mom's right and peered down. Mom's internal struggle to stay still played out all over her face. "I've seen some of these symbols in Brighid's home in the past."

"Brighid isn't going to get pissy with us if we go after her witches, is she?" I asked.

"No, Brighid is selfish with her power and knowledge, and while she created the moon witch line, she has no others under her protection. If my history is correct, the Gaelic line was created by Cailleach at the start of the human rule of this world. They are one of the oldest and most powerful."

"Fantastic." I threw both hands up. "Why can't we ever hunt weak entities anymore? We used to get easy jobs, and now we're going after necromancers and super-ancient witch covens."

Tennyson quirked an eyebrow at me.

"I would kill to have K.I.M. and her handy insta-info capabilities right about now."

"I'm texting myself the photo," Mom said. "I may know someone who can translate it."

"So how do we get inside to snoop?" Jaxon asked. "The front door obviously didn't work."

"Maybe we can get the werewolves to spy for us," I replied. "If we can convince them they're part of a larger plan, maybe they'll help us."

"Alice was unconvinced," Chandra said.

"I know, but can you use her to find the minds of the other female wolves? Maybe set up a conference call or something in our minds?"

"I can attempt it, but my last try was quite fuzzy. I'm not sure I'm powerful enough to manage it with their wards up."

"A drop of my blood would boost your power," Tennyson said.

Mom took two wide strides to her left, away.

I glared, irrationally irritated at the idea of anyone

else drinking his blood—which, you know, gross. And why? The fading bloodlust never seemed to go fully away, and it probably had to do with a combination of my djinn nature and his close proximity. I knew what pulsed in his veins. I'd tasted it, been drunk on it.

And very, very unstable on it.

"He's not wrong," Kathleen said with a bland tone. "Vampire blood is powerful in its own right, but she's less likely to develop a bloodlust if she drinks mine."

"The power boost would be half," Tennyson replied.

"I'd prefer not to drink anyone's blood," Chandra said, "but if I do, I'd prefer it still have some human in it."

Tennyson shrugged, seemingly unoffended.

"Hey," I said to Kathleen, "how come you never offered your blood to boost our powers in the past?"

She slow-blinked at me. "You never asked."

Sweet Iblis, I really wanted to smack her.

"Okay, let's give it a try," Chandra said. "Elspeth, would you like to join us? Hearing from a neutral party may help."

"I'd prefer to sit this one out, thank you," Mom replied. "What about Gideon? Someone they're familiar with?"

"All right. Gideon?"

"I'm in," he said.

"It will be easier if you step closer to me. You, too, Shiloh."

We three huddled in a circle, with Kathleen on the fringes. She descended her fangs and punctured a finger. Held the welling blood out to Chandra. Chandra glanced at me, her trepidation shining in her dark eyes. "No moon witch to my knowledge has ever drunk from a dhampir or vampire," she said.

"Here's to new experiences," I replied. I don't know how supportive my smile was, but I tried.

Chandra held my gaze another beat, and then sucked on Kathleen's fingertip.

Something powerful slammed into me and I hit my ass on the hard ground, followed by my head. Dizzy and discombobulated, I blinked up and swore I saw the night sky and a full moon shining down on me through the hole-filled silo roof.

But that wasn't possible.

Right?

CHAPTER 11

"Uh, guys?" I struggled to sit up, because damn, that had been a blast of magic I hadn't expected. Everyone had been hit, including Tennyson, and only Chandra remained standing. She stared straight up, hands by her hips, fingers splayed. Energy crackled around her, like an electric wire flopping on the ground. I'd been knocked a few feet away, and I instantly crawled over to my mom.

She was on her side and holding her head in both hands. "Mom? Are you hurt?"

"My head." Mom moaned. "Anyone sensitive to magic within a hundred miles will have felt that outburst."

I helped her sit up, concerned by how gray her complexion was, even in the silo's gloom. "Did you hit your head?"

"Not really, it's just the feedback. Ugh."

"Okay, sit tight."

Everyone else was struggling to their feet—no, not everyone. All that was left of Gideon was his pile of clothes.

Great, we had a werewolf running around town on a magically induced shift.

Tennyson's eyes glowed green with desire, and Novak had a boner. Even Jaxon seemed to struggle not to give in to his skin and shift.

"That was unexpected," Kathleen said.

"No shit. Chandra?" I followed her gaze upward, thankful to see regular sunshine streaming down and not the moon, because that would have been bad. Her ebony skin glowed with an ethereal light that cast a literal fucking shadow on the ground, and she stared straight up, lips slightly parted. "Chandra, can you hear me?"

The silo disappeared, leaving our entire group—minus Gideon—in the swirling mists with Chandra at our epicenter. One by one, young werewolf couples popped into the . . . *room* wasn't the right word. Meh, chat room, whatever.

Some of them tried to back away, but they couldn't actually go anywhere. It wasn't as if you could walk around in here. It really was like an online chat room or group text, but with faces instead of words. Kathleen's blood had given Chandra the power to get into the mind of every single missing werewolf, male and female, including the Andersons. The mists seemed both cramped and unending, and it was kind of spooky.

"Chandra," Alice said. She clung to a man with ashy brown hair who had to be her mate, Raymond. "Agent Harrison, what's going on? What is this?"

"Think of it as a private chat room," I replied, since Chandra was a bit overwhelmed by magic at the moment. "No one on the outside can hear anything you guys say in here. It's completely safe."

"Did we leave the clinic?" a young woman asked.

"No, this is happening entirely in our heads." I pointed at Chandra, who seemed to be coming around a bit. "She's a moon witch and this sort of telepathy with other females is one of her powers. We're here because we've been working with Alpha Kennedy to find you."

"If he knows we're here, we'll be executed for using human medicine," a man said.

"No, you won't. I know this will be hard to believe, but I, Chandra, and Alpha's Second, Rosalind, spoke to your goddess Danu." Several people gasped. "She has no problem with the Packs using human medicine. All she wants is for her wolves to be happy and healthy and enjoy their lives. We've told Alpha Kennedy all this, and he's willing to compromise, especially since your infertility was caused by magic."

"What do you mean?" the same man asked, so I designated him Harry, simply because I'd never be able to remember everyone's names. Twelve perfect strangers stared at me from their huddle with the Andersons.

"Your homes contained magical wards," Mom said, somehow moving closer even though her legs never actually moved. "They have now been contained, but before that, I used their magical signature to track you all to this clinic's location here in Gabriel."

"You're a witch, too?"

"I am not. However, I do have certain sensitivities to magic."

"Those same wards were found in four other homes where young couples were having trouble conceiving," I continued. "Whoever created those wards has also created some sort of glamour that hides the true nature of your research facility from the outside world."

"They explained that to us," Raymond Anderson said. "The townsfolk would freak if they knew werewolves were here, so they keep us hidden. We aren't prisoners. We're all here of our own free will."

"Are you? Dr. Ferguson played on your grief over your three late children to get you to come here, right? Promising you the moon and the same to these other couples?"

Raymond didn't speak.

"They're helping us," the first woman to speak said, so she became CC—Chatty Cathy. "My mate and I are pregnant."

"So you believe they spontaneously discovered how to cure werewolf infertility in the two weeks you've been here?" I asked, grateful the others had allowed me to take point here. I was probably less threatening to them than an incubus or Master vampire. "Or maybe it worked because the magic whammy isn't under your bed anymore, preventing you from conceiving the old-fashioned way."

Alice looked furious, but she didn't speak against me. The couples looked at each other, as if silently asking if they believed me or not.

"Please listen to her," Chandra said. Her skin still gleamed, but she looked less like a human glow stick. "All we want is to help you return home safely."

"We chose to be here," Raymond replied.

"Then you can also choose to leave."

"I want to go home," a very young lady said. She couldn't have been more than nineteen or twenty, and she clung to her mate like she'd fall over without him. "I miss my parents and my friends."

"But what about kids?" her mate asked.

"I believe Marshal Harrison. I want to go home. They should let us go home, right?"

"In theory," I said.

"You promise on your life that Alpha Kennedy won't punish us for leaving?" her mate said to me.

"Alpha Kennedy is more interested in seeing his Pack whole again, and in bringing to justice the person who violated his lands by delivering those wards."

He squinted at me, but said nothing.

"You said you're a Marshal," Harry spoke up.

"Why are US Marshals butting their noses into Pack business?"

"We're part of the Para-Marshal division," I said, then introduced Chandra, Jaxon, Novak and—begrudgingly—Kathleen. I pointed to my mom. "She's a civilian giving us a hand, and he's"—I indicated Tennyson, who lurked in the back—"helping. He's also the reason we learned about your disappearances, because vampires had gone missing, too, and Tennyson asked"—*asked, ha ha, yeah, right*—"for our help locating them. And now he's helping us find you."

"Alpha Kennedy doesn't trust outsiders."

"No, he doesn't, and at first he was simply tolerating us, until we talked to Danu and discovered the wards. Then he realized this whole thing was bigger than just his Pack. Other Packs have been infiltrated and wards installed in their homes, too."

"There are other couples here from the Florida Pack. Why aren't they here talking to you?"

"My magic is tricky," Chandra replied. "The only reason you men are here is because of your female mates, and I only found them through Alice. None of you are friendly enough with the Florida wolves for me to add more minds. I'm already somewhat overwhelmed."

Guess the power boost didn't last long, because at that moment Tennyson, Jaxon, and Novak disappeared.

"But why would anyone do this?" another young

male asked. "Why make us infertile, and then offer us a solution to the problem?"

"Docile patients," I replied. "As werewolves, you're faster and stronger than almost any human. Unwilling patients would require a lot of restraint in order to do their experiments, so why have your test subject fighting you when you can find a way to make them come to you willingly?"

"You think they're experimenting on us?"

"They most certainly are," Kathleen said, adding to the conversation for the first time. "I work for the Para-Marshals service, but I also serve as an agent for an employer searching for a man called Damian. Is that name familiar to anyone?"

A lot of no's went around. Someone mentioned a Pack neighbor who'd named their most recent son Damian, which was incredibly not useful in that moment.

"Who is this Damian?" Raymond asked.

"His exact origins are unknown, but he's believed to be experimenting on Paras. Splicing DNA, creating his own hybrids. He funded another man's attempt to use a necromancer against a vampire Master in order to take over his entire Line to use against humans."

"Against humans?"

"Yes. It is believed his end goal is to wipe out all human and humanoid life, and to return this planet to the powerful beings who once walked it before the dawn of man."

One of the girls started to cry.

"You truly believe this?" Alice asked. "That some-one went to great lengths simply to get twenty-eight werewolves here for willing experimentation."

"Yes," I said. So did the other women in my group.

Multiple couples stated they wanted to go home at that point.

"You cannot all try to leave at once," Chandra said. "It will draw suspicion and put you all in danger. For now, one pair must request to go home. Test the waters and see what they say. Report back to Alice. Because we have been in physical contact before, if she cries out for me, I will hear her. We can continue to com-municate telepathically and work together to get you all home safely."

"We'll do it." The first couple to say they wanted to go home put their hands up.

"Good luck, and remember, no one else knows what was said here. So keep this secret close and do not show fear to your keepers. We are here in Gabriel, and we will not abandon you." Chandra made some sort of gesture, maybe the moon witch sign for good-bye.

The silo interior winked back into existence, and I swayed a bit. Someone caught my elbow, and I didn't miss the crackle of Tennyson's power beside me. I wasn't used to being in my own head for so long, and with so many other people.

Jaxon stood in front of me, and he bared his teeth

at Tennyson, who released my elbow and took a long step backward. "You okay, Shi?" Jaxon asked.

"Yeah, just a little dizzy coming out of it." Chandra was sitting and rubbing her temples. "Chandra?"

"I simply need a moment," she replied. "That blood . . . it felt like the biggest sugar rush of all time, and now I'm crashing."

"Got it."

"That was an unusual experience," Kathleen said. "Not only the blood exchange, but also the mind meld, for lack of a better term."

"Yeah, it was weird," Jaxon agreed, "but some of us missed the ending. Did you get through to them?"

I gave the three men a quick highlights reel. "Now we wait for them to contact Chandra with the results."

"It's risky."

"It is, but it's a calculated risk. If they ask to leave and are denied, it reinforces the fact that they're actually prisoners of the people running the place."

"Has anyone seen Gideon?" Mom asked.

"No," Novak replied. "The vampire said he could try tracking him once the sun goes down."

"Great," I said. "We're down a werewolf, and we kind of picked an uncomfortable spot to wait on the other wolves to return our brain call."

"Someone is approaching," Kathleen said.

I turned toward the silo's entrance, hoping to see Gideon. Instead, two men walked in, one of them in law enforcement uniform, the other in a dress shirt and tie.

"Gabriel police," the first man said. "May I ask what you're doing trespassing on Mr. Oakley's property?"

I approached the men with Jaxon on my six and showed off my badge. "US Para-Marshal Harrison. This is Marshal Dearborn."

"Officer Joe Murphy. This is Mayor Don Oakley, owner of this here property."

"Pleasure, and I apologize for trespassing. I didn't notice any private property postings."

"That's because we're a small town and people know better," Mayor Oakley replied with a gentle laugh. "Don't get too many outsiders in Gabriel, especially not of your caliber. What brings the Para-Marshals and friends here?"

"We are tracking a runaway werewolf." Thank you Gideon for the perfect excuse.

Both men started looking all around them, as if the werewolf was waiting in the shadows to pounce. And to be honest, I wasn't sure if he was, because I'd never seen magic force a werewolf shift before. Should have thought to ask one of the couples before the group chat ended.

"There's an awful lot of you for one werewolf," Officer Murphy said with an audible tremor in his voice. "Is he that dangerous?"

"He can be if he's cornered or frightened, so if you

happen to spot him, do not approach or attempt to capture. Give me a call." Jaxon gave the man a card.

"Will do. Should we let the town know?"

"I wouldn't," I replied. "You don't want folks to panic. We're hoping to find him and leave with as little fuss as possible."

"What if we just tell folks to be on the lookout for a big stray dog we're looking to pick up alive and un-harmed?" Mayor Oakley said. "It'll keep folks indoors if they think their kids are at risk and less likely to shoot first."

"That sounds like a good compromise, thank you."

"Sure thing. My family's been in this town for gen-erations, way back before farming got too hard out here. We protect our own."

"I can appreciate that." So much. I protected my own, too.

"Grain silo isn't much of a place to set up base," Officer Murphy said. "We've got an empty office up at the municipal building. Police department's only two of us, so we don't need all the rooms anymore."

"That would be wonderful, Officer, thank you." An office space was a way better spot to hang out than the silo.

I left Gideon's clothes behind, hopeful he'd return, shift back and dress, as well as a note about where we were heading. Tennyson wasn't happy about moving, but he could deal. I was tired of the dusty stink of the silo. Our two vehicles followed the police car back to town and down to the municipal building I'd noticed on our first drive through. I also side-eyed DM Clinic as we passed.

Both the mayor and cop led us into the unused office, which had a desk and chair, two empty bookcases, and a nice street view of the brick medical building we were investigating.

Perfect.

"Do you know anything about DM across the street?" I asked.

"No, they keep to themselves," Mayor Oakley replied. "I'll admit, I was surprised when they came here asking to erect their building, but the construction brought a boost of income to the area, and they leased two spaces to locals."

"They've never given me any trouble," Officer Murphy added. "They pay their taxes and do whatever it is that clinic is for."

"No one's ever asked what they do?"

Murphy shrugged. "Said fertility research mostly. As long as they aren't in there cooking up meth, I don't ask."

They're cooking up something so much worse than meth.

"Why the interest?" Oakley asked.

"No real reason," I replied. "The building stood out to me, that's all. You seem somewhat remote for medical research. And please don't let us keep you from your other responsibilities. We appreciate the office space."

"Not a problem. It's not every day a man gets to meet a real Para-Marshal. Only usually hear about you folk on the news, like that vampire . . . thing . . ." Oakley really seemed to see Tennyson for the first time, who stood in the darkest corner of the room, his hood pushed slightly back.

Kathleen closed the window blinds.

"We best be getting back to work," Murphy said, and the pair of men backed out of the room.

"Their fear is amusing," Tennyson said.

"I'm glad they're finally gone," Chandra said. "On the ride over, I heard from Belle and Andrew, the couple who tried to check out of the clinic as a test."

"And?" I asked.

"Belle said her request to leave was denied, because Dr. Ferguson insisted she hadn't given the process enough time."

"Did he say when she would be allowed to go home?"

"No. But Belle also told me the staff seemed agitated and on alert because of a magic surge someone felt right before we contacted everyone. My surge."

"So they know we're here?"

"She isn't certain, and asking questions of the staff would look suspicious. But she said all the wolves are paying closer attention now, and the California Pack is working on convincing the Floridians of what's going on."

"That's a good move," Jaxon said. "We need them all on our side if we're going to get them out of that clinic."

"The question now is, how do we do that?" I asked. "We have no idea what the interior looks like other than it has five levels. We don't know staffing, security, or what else might be there as a voluntary test subject. Or even involuntary. And we have to find Gideon before they do. The last thing we need to worry about is a hostage."

"Technically, they've already got twenty-eight."

I shot him a look. "Mom, anything from your friend about those symbols?"

"Not yet," she said. "Chandra, are you absolutely certain no one else could have listened in on our group mind chat?"

Chandra frowned. "I'm reasonably certain. To my knowledge, no one has ever breached such a communication. Why?"

"Nervous, I suppose." Mom repeated a tiny bit of what we'd talked about in the car earlier—how her parents died, the familiarity of the magic in the cube wards, and her desire to remain hidden from the wrath of those witches.

"We'll do everything we can to keep you safe, Elspeth," Jaxon said, reaffirming his earlier promise.

"I know. But one of the women who murdered my parents could be across the street in that building." Anger overrode some of her fear, and I saw my mom's endless courage peek out. If she could go toe to toe with a powerful earth djinn, she could do anything. Even face down the witches who killed her parents. My grandparents.

"You're one of us," Novak said to Mom. "And like that other guy said, we protect our own."

"You're just saying that because I made you chili."

Novak grinned. "It was blessed fine chili."

"Spare me your sentimentality," Kathleen said. "We need a plan stronger than sitting on our rear ends waiting for one of your female wolves to contact you again."

"How come our side is doing all the work here?" I asked her. "What's your employer contributing besides your sour disposition? Can she help at all?"

"I have not had a chance to update her on our progress. Now that I have news, I'll report in and inquire of any additional information she may have on DM Clinic."

"Thank you."

Kathleen left the room, ostensibly to find a private place to make her call. I didn't like her going off alone, but I needed the input of all my people right now. If she double-crossed me again, I'd put the nearest wooden object right through her heart.

"We need to get inside that facility somehow,"

Jaxon said. "Problem is none of us can just turn invisible at will. Chandra's telepathy only goes so far. My stag doesn't do us any good unless I let myself get captured—"

"Not happening," I said, surprising myself with how quickly I'd shot that idea down.

"I could theoretically seduce someone into getting information," Novak said. "But I would need to actually meet an employee."

My mind jumped to the middle-aged receptionist. I met Jaxon's eyes and saw the same humor there. Novak preferred women, but he was an equal-opportunity seducer. Except the fallen demon was also starting to develop a conscience, because he no longer enjoyed getting straight guys or lesbians to sleep with him. And a middle-aged guy in Kansas? Probably straight.

"What?" Novak said, clearly suspicious of us both.

"Nothing," I said. "The clinic had a receptionist, but he struck me as the kind of person who sits in a booth for his paycheck and doesn't ask questions, so he probably wouldn't know anything."

"Hmm."

"Mom?"

She shook her head. "Other than calling on your father and asking him to pop in to look around, I honestly don't have any ideas."

"Yeah, let's not get Dad involved again. The only reason he checked in last time was because I nearly died from that spider bite. We aren't quite there yet."

"Yet? Watch your words, young lady."

Novak snickered, probably over the "young lady" part.

"There is an alternative no one has put on the table yet," Tennyson said.

"Which is what?" Jaxon asked.

"Shiloh, of course, and her three wishes. Bind her and we have all the power we need."

Jaxon growled once before he charged.

CHAPTER 12

Novak grabbed Jaxon by the arm before he got any-where close to swinging on Tennyson, and he herded him to the other side of the small office space. "Down boy," Novak said.

"No fucking way is he binding her again," Jaxon replied.

"I did not say *I* should bind her," Tennyson said calmly. "We were already bound once, so I am uncer-tain if it's possible to do it twice. But my point remains: with her powers at someone's disposal, breaking into the clinic will be, as you might say, a piece of cake."

"Big flaw in that plan," I said. "No one besides you and I know the binding words, and neither one of us can speak them out loud."

Tennyson's lips quirked, and a second later, Jaxon shouted something indecipherable and clutched at his temples. "Motherfucker!" Jaxon stabbed a finger at Tennyson. "Get out of my head."

I gaped at Tennyson. "You can still talk to him?"

"We've shared blood, remember? I simply choose to ignore him, as I find skin-walkers uninteresting, and he has clearly shown his dislike of me."

"So you can tell Jaxon the words, he speaks them, and I'm bound to him for three wishes?"

"Precisely."

It wasn't an altogether awful idea, but giving power over me to someone I barely knew? And yet trusted, all the same, because we *did* have history. I'd seen it in his own mind, and even though my own new memories of him were as slippery as gelatin, I believed we'd known each other once. Maybe even loved each other.

"I don't suppose I could use a wish to get your memory back?" Jaxon asked.

"I doubt that will work because of rule number one," I replied. "I can't alter the physical state of a human body, and for all intents and purposes, those memories were removed and I don't know where they went. I can't change back what's been done to me. I don't know if anyone can."

The small flare of hope in his eyes dimmed and that sucked. Including Tennyson, I've only been bound four other times in my life, and all of those were unwillingly. As a half djinn, I wasn't summoned the normal ways djinn showed themselves to human wishers. Unsummoned djinn can only be bound if someone knows what we are, and also knows the binding words, which no djinn can speak out loud. Those words are highly guarded in the magic community and sold for huge sums.

A bound djinn in the wrong hands can do a lot of damage. But in the right hands . . .

Before Tennyson and his telepathy, I'd never had a way to utilize my djinn magic to help our team. I'd relied on my intelligence, physical training, and ability to take a beating. Now, though, what Tennyson was suggesting made more and more sense.

"Can't you just write the words down?" Jaxon asked. "His voice in my head hurts."

"No way," Mom said. "Once those words are on paper, you cannot guarantee they'll never be seen by another's eyes. Not even if you burn the ashes and bury them in a field."

"Why not?"

"Because words carry power, and few words carry as great a power as the ability to bind a djinn to three wishes. The right magic user knows how to source these things, and I will not allow that to happen. The more people who know what Shiloh can do, the greater danger she's in."

"Agreed," Tennyson said. "The words are not many, and your headache will subside."

Tennyson's subtle way of saying, *Man up.*

"You sure you want to do this?" Jaxon asked me.

He shouldered past Novak to stand in front of me, then put his hands on my shoulders. Fixed those wide, worried hazel eyes on me, and a warm feeling swooped through my belly. Warm and sweet and it was all him. His kind, caring and protective self. No wonder I fell for him once before.

It made it easy to forget I had a maybe-boyfriend out there somewhere, who refused to return my call.

It's been days. Focus on the mission.

"I need to do this," I said. "But we also need to plan out exactly what those wishes will be for, because rule number two says the power expenditure of wishes two and three can't go over that of wish one."

"Got it. Smart rule, actually."

"It is. My dad's told me some stories about wishers who don't believe what he is, so their first wish is super-lame, like turning an armchair into a toilet. Then it limits the other two wishes to party tricks."

"Sucks to be that idiot."

"Well, when the world is led to believe the whole genie-in-a-bottle myth, when a good-looking guy-next-door says he's a djinn, a lot of people are skeptical."

"Some of us need access to the clinic without being detected," Chandra said. "That absolutely needs to be a wish. Is that something you can do?"

"Yes, we just have to word it right and specify a period of time for the wish, so we aren't, you know, invisible forever."

"Yeah, that would suck," Novak said.

"Would I be able to wish for the twenty-eight werewolves to be teleported here?" Jaxon asked.

"I'm not sure," I replied. "It would certainly make all this easier, but there's already magic at play here, and I can't be sure my powers will override theirs."

"It's no fun if it's not a challenge, right?"

"For once, I'd love no fun and a lot more easy."

"Me too," Novak said. He flexed both hands into fists. "But I'm ready for some not-easy, as long as it gets the job done."

"Okay, so we know one of the wishes is to get inside and not be seen." I really wanted a whiteboard to write all this out, but the office was pretty bare. I did, however, find a notepad and pencil in one of the desk drawers, so score. "Thoughts on the other two wishes?"

"What about being able to see past the glamour they've cast on the building?" Jaxon asked. "Show us what's really there and not what they want us to see?"

I scribbled that down. "Possible. It's dangerous to try and break the glamour completely, because we don't want these people to retaliate against this town. Likewise, we don't want to scare people by a brand-new building or whatever appearing out of the blue."

"Good point. We just need to be able to see what we're dealing with, not blow their whole cover right away."

"You've been plotting, I see," Kathleen said as she strode back into the office.

"Staring at each other in silence got boring," I replied. "What's your boss offering?"

"Aerial support. She will have two Chinook helicopters waiting just outside town limits, prepared to help us remove the werewolves quickly and efficiently. They will be in position within two hours."

Okay, that was kind of impressive, considering Chinooks were military-grade helicopters. So far, we hadn't considered how we were getting the werewolves home, and this solved that problem.

"Not bad," Jaxon said.

Kathleen quirked an eyebrow at him. I filled her in on the wish thing and what we'd come up with so far. "You are brave to bind yourself again," she said.

"Yeah, well, it may be the only way we get a look inside this facility. Mom, what's your impression of this glamour? More powerful than making a few of us invisible?"

"Definitely." She cut her eyes at the closed blinds. "Even from this distance, its power crawls over my skin like insects. I don't like you going anywhere near it again, but I understand this is your calling, and I won't try to stop you."

"Can't we start with the first two wishes and go from there?" Novak asked. "We might need it as backup once we get inside and see what we're really dealing with."

Everyone looked at me. I shrugged. "I'm okay with that, but can we start after lunch? I'm starving."

The town didn't have fast food, but they did have

a diner. Mom and Jaxon walked down there together, and after they called me with a menu in front of them, we all ordered food. Well, everyone except Tennyson, but he looked strong and not in need of blood.

And it didn't occur to me I'd ordered eggs with a rare steak until Jaxon handed me the foam carton. I glanced at Tennyson, who was watching me intently, as always. But I didn't find his stare as creepy as I had in the past. He reminded me a teacher puzzling over a student he wasn't sure how to reach.

While we ate, we discussed who was going to go invisible and break in with me and Jaxon. Mom was staying here, obviously. Chandra had to go, because she was in contact with the werewolves via her powers. One more person to snoop made sense, but we also needed people to stay here in case anything happened.

"Question," I said to Tennyson. "For your gazelock to work, does the person have to see your eyes, or can you do it simply by looking into theirs?"

Tennyson tilted his head as he considered my query. "As long as I can maintain contact with their eyes and mind, they do not necessarily have to see mine."

"Then I vote you come with us." Jaxon groaned, and I held up a hand. "Hear me out. If we have questions, he can be useful in getting others to talk to us. Plus he's got vampire senses and he's fast."

"As am I," Kathleen said.

"But you can't gazelock. Plus, I need you and Novak to guard my mother."

Novak grunted. "I don't like you going off with the vampire."

"Duly noted, but this is our plan. Understood?"

He nodded his assent, but didn't look happy about it.

"I agree with the plan," Chandra said. "We four go in, establish what is truly happening here, and we look for potential escape routes if the werewolves are not allowed to leave freely."

"All right," Jaxon replied. "You ready to do this, Shi?"

"As I'll ever be. Um, do you guys mind giving the three of us space? I'd rather you didn't all hear the binding words."

"Of course," Mom replied. She left with Chandra, Kathleen and Novak. While I trusted everyone except Kathleen to hear to the words and not use them against me, I didn't want to make a big deal out of it. Kicking them all out was easier.

"I'll whisper," Jaxon said with a wink.

"Thank you." Even with a wall and door between us, Kathleen had good ears.

"Are we prepared?" Tennyson asked, mostly to Jaxon.

"Let's do this," he said.

We stood in a circle near the desk. Jaxon flinched and clenched his hands while Tennyson fed him the words, and then Jaxon spoke in the softest whisper possible. "Shiloh Harrison, child of Iblis, I bind thy magic as my servant three times over, and bind myself according to thy terms."

A tremor tingled down my spine and spread goose bumps across my shoulders and ribs. Warmth filled my chest as magic tingled between us like bolts of static electricity. Those bolts materialized into the impression of a rope, thin as a toothpick and made of glimmering gold. It ran from my mind to Jaxon's, an invisible rope I couldn't actually see, but sensed. The tether binding my magic to Jaxon's wishes.

Compared to the tether I'd shared with Tennyson, this one was softer, less powerful. Jaxon touched magic in his own way, but he wasn't as powerful a user as Tennyson, which changed how we connected.

Something else crackled along our tether, though. Not magic or power, but emotion. Strong, positive emotion, rather than negativity or anger. This wasn't the binding of a magic user seeking to cause harm or make selfish wishes. I'd bound to a man who cared about me and others. And I had complete trust in what he'd wish for.

"Did it work?" Tennyson asked. "I sensed a shift in the room. However—"

"It worked," Jaxon replied. His eyes never left mine as they filled with wonder. "I can feel you, Shi. Am I supposed to feel you, too?"

"I don't know," I said. "The tether is usually one-way, but it's also always been with a stranger. Not someone whose mind I looked into and saw myself."

"Pardon me?" Tennyson asked.

Oh yeah, I hadn't shared my newest party trick. "I

have a bit of undiscovered telepathy of my own, possibly from my mom and her parents. Back on the road, after I telecommunicated with you, I tried it on Jaxon. I couldn't hear his thoughts, but I got flashes of memories of us on a beach together. It was what he was thinking about in that moment."

"Fascinating. You are full of surprises, aren't you, young djinn?"

"Apparently, and I'd like to keep it on the downlow for now. It might come in handy later."

"Like if Kathleen flips sides again?" Jaxon whispered.

"Exactly." I opened the office door. "Coast is clear. The binding worked."

Mom came inside first and looked me over, as if something had happened in the past five minutes. "You're going to give me extra gray hairs today, aren't you?"

"Not on purpose. Okay, so the first thing we need to do is make everyone here immune to the glamour."

"What about Gideon?" Chandra asked. "He isn't here with us, but shouldn't he receive the same ability?"

"Since I don't know if he's man or beast, it might not take, but yeah, I can try."

"I should have asked this sooner," Jaxon said, "but do I just start with 'I w-i-s-h' and go from there?"

"Exactly." I wrote the best, most precise wording I could manage at short notice, then handed the paper to him. "Go for it."

Jaxon held up the paper with a slightly trembling hand. "I wish for the following people to be immune to the magic of the Gaelic witch whose wards protect a research facility in this town, Gabriel, Kansas, for the duration of our exposure to it: Shiloh Harrison, Jaxon Dearborn, Chandra Goodfellow, Elspeth Juno, Woodrow Tennyson, Kathleen Allard, the demon Novak, and the California werewolf Gideon. This is my first wish."

The tether between us snapped taut as power flowed between us, the binding words triggering the magic I carried with me everywhere. Magic only accessible by bound wishers or dark magic users. The air in the room sparkled and seemed to solidify for a split second, before shattering in white glitter no one else seemed to notice. The others blinked and rubbed at their eyes, and I caught on a moment later when my own eyes started to sting.

"Is this normal?" Novak asked. "Fucking heaven."

"It might be a reaction from the magic you're opposing," Mom replied. "Give it a moment. Shiloh's power should win."

"Before it burns my corneas?"

My eyes were tearing up from the stinging sensation, and even Tennyson appeared irritated by the reaction. Magic still spilled out of me, possibly battling the strength of the witch's wards, determined to grant this wish to my wisher.

And then my ears popped, the stinging went away,

and I smiled because I knew. "Your wish is granted," I said.

Chandra pulled down the blinds with one finger. "It worked. Take a look."

I did the same. Across the street, the two leased offices hadn't changed in appearance. The third office, which had previously been a single-story brick facade, was now a five-story brick building that had other glittering stones stuck in the bricks on every floor, spaced out in a pattern of some kind.

"Does anyone recognize that?" I asked. It was similar to those on the elevator, but not identical.

"It's the symbol of the goddess Cailleach," Mom said. "She protects this place."

"Well, shit, that's not good."

"We're going up against a goddess?" Chandra asked. "That's a bit out of our wheelhouse, isn't it?"

"Not necessarily against her," Mom replied, and I swore she looked kind of green. "Her own unending magic fuels that of the witches who serve her. Putting Cailleach's symbol here is meant not only to shield it from human eyes, but also to act as a warning against anyone who might interfere."

"Like us?" I said.

"Yes. It's possible Cailleach has never even touched this mortal plane, so it's highly unlikely she'll notice our presence or that the wards have been breached. The witch who set them, on the other hand? She'll have felt a change to her spell, but she may or may not act on it."

"If she's being paid to continue watching this place," Chandra said, "she may come see what's gone wrong, but if it was a single casting, she may not."

"Correct."

Color me impressed. Mom has a lot more magic knowledge crammed into her head than I ever gave her credit for.

"Time for wish number two?" Jaxon asked.

"Yeah," I said. "This should be a lot easier, considering how hard I had to fight for wish one." I wrote this one out for him, too.

"I wish for the following people, in our current physical state, to become invisible to all living eyes, noses, and recording technology for the exact span of two hours before that invisibility returns to normal: Shiloh Harrison, Jaxon Dearborn, Woodrow Tennyson, and Chandra Goodfellow. This is my second wish."

The tether pulled taut again, and a burst of gold sparkles jumped out, moving in little cyclones to surround the four of us individually. No one else seemed to see this, because they simply stood there. I watched the cyclone expand to completely cover Jaxon's body— and then he was gone. So was Chandra and Tennyson. Even my wish tether to Jaxon was gone.

I looked down and realized my mistake.

"Guys?" Novak asked.

"Shit on toast," I said. "Jaxon, can you see me?"

"No," he said directly in front of me.

"I messed up the fucking wish."

"How?" Mom asked.

"Because I can't even see myself, much less my other invisible teammates."

This was going to be a serious issue.

CHAPTER 13

"**W**hat do you mean, you guys can't see each other?" Novak asked. "At all?"

"No, bless it all." I turned and bumped into someone. The swirl of fabric told me Tennyson. "I forgot to factor that into the wording of the wish. All living eyes *includes our own*. Fuck."

"I can partially see the three of you," Tennyson said.

"You can?"

"Yes. Do not forget, vampires exist on a plane between life and death. Perhaps this is what gives me partial sight."

"But no one else can see me, Jaxon, or Chandra, right?" Yes's went all around the office. "Okay, well, at least that bit worked."

"Yeah, but how are we gonna move around without crashing into each other?" Jaxon asked. "If we cause a commotion, someone's gonna get suspicious."

"You said you'd be invisible in your current physical state," Mom said. "Would we be able to see something if your physical state changed?"

"Maybe," I said. "What should I do?"

"Try drawing a big X on your palm. If your hand is closed or against your leg, no one can see it, but if you need to signal each other, you'll see an X in the air."

"Worth a shot." I picked up the pen, noting surprised and amused looks on various visible faces. I couldn't see my own hands, anyway, so the pen floating in mid-air made me chuckle. "This is so weird."

Even weirder was the black ink appearing like, well, magic, approximately where my left palm should be.

"Holy cow, that's creepy," Chandra said.

"Everyone can see the X?" I turned my hand to face the room; everyone said yes. I closed my palm. "Now?" All no's. "Okay, it's weird, but it'll help us keep visual track of each other."

"And if someone else sees an X floating in the air," Jaxon added, "they'll just think they're seeing things and disregard it."

"Hopefully. It's just so weird not being able to see even myself."

"I get it."

"Do not fear," Tennyson said. "I shall do my best to prevent you three from walking into each other during our mission."

The word *mission* from him just sounded weird, like he was being ironic, instead of totally serious.

"Alrighty then," I said. "You guys ready to go snooping? And don't nod, because I can't see you."

Crossing the street felt a lot like lining up for the school bus when I was a kid. Tennyson led us, since he could actually see us a bit, and we used the buddy method of walking hand in hand. I held his with my left and Jaxon's with my right, and he held on to Chandra. I faintly heard our footsteps and the swish of fabric as we moved, but feeling pressure on both hands, not seeing them at all?

Kind of a mind-fuck. I did not like being invisible. At. All.

Novak had gone ahead, head ducked over a piece of paper with the building's address on it. He held the front door open long enough for our quartet to slip inside, while pretending to puzzle over the paper. He was supposed to play it all off like he'd written the suite number down wrong, so in case there were security cameras at all, they wouldn't pick up on the door opening and closing on its own.

The glamoured wall between us and the elevator was gone, and we walked right through it as Novak rang the buzzer for service. A moment later, the elevator doors dinged open, and the same middle-aged man stepped out. He walked around to the desk, while Tennyson led us into the elevator. The doors shut, but it didn't go anywhere, and we didn't want to arouse suspicion by pushing a button.

Fortunately, we'd talked this bit out before leaving the office, so we didn't have to talk too much where it was deadly quiet.

Are you nervous? Tennyson asked.

A little. I don't like not knowing what to expect.

If all my centuries of life have taught me anything of value, it is that the unexpected can often be the most rewarding experience of all.

Something in his tone gave me the impression he was smirking at me.

The doors slid open, and the receptionist got in, muttering about idiot out-of-towners. We'd spread out with our backs to the rear wall of the car, but he still got uncomfortably close in the large space. He hit the first button on top, and the car rose to the next level. Butterflies erupted in my stomach, and I must have swallowed a bit too hard, because the guy's head snapped to the left.

No one could see or smell us, but they could still hear us, and I silently screamed at myself for not focusing on more senses than just the eyes when I wrote the wish.

Sweet Iblis, please, no one get hiccups.

The doors slid open. The receptionist got out first, and then Tennyson slipped our chain through the doors before they closed. The hospital-like corridor was quiet, and the man went directly into a small office across from the elevator. He sat in a recliner, put his feet up, and unpaused whatever show he was watching. The room also had a mini-fridge, microwave, overflowing garbage can, and computer monitor showing the lobby, angled toward the sliding glass window.

So this guy's literal job was to sit around and occasionally fend off nosy people?

Cushy.

Tennyson squeezed my hand twice—the agreed-upon signal that we were going to keep moving from a stopped position—so I passed it to Jaxon. After a pause, Tennyson pulled me down the corridor.

And I say it was hospital-like, because it had the wide hallways, linoleum floors, and numbered doors every few yards. But it also didn't seem to be occupied. Some of the rooms had beds, others only the electric panels on the walls where equipment would one day go, but none had occupants.

"Guess they aren't using this one," Jaxon whispered.

"Makes sense," I replied. "They wouldn't want their random security/front desk guy getting an eyeful of their goings-on."

"Agreed," Tennyson said. "Let us attempt to find stairs before risking the elevator again."

We didn't find stairs, which was definitely a building code violation. But it was also smart on the bad guys' part, because it left the elevator as the only way in or out—an elevator you needed a key card to access.

"Can you gazelock the desk clerk while I rob him of his key card?" I asked Tennyson.

"Certainly."

So we went back to the little office and did just that. The guy was mesmerized long enough for us to get back onto the elevator. I chose the symbol that looked the most like it could be a dog or wolf, which was third from the top.

"Should we split up and search?" Chandra asked. "Go in pairs?"

"Yes," I said. "Explore and return to the elevator in thirty minutes." After a split second's hesitation— and because I didn't need the argument—I released Jaxon's hand.

"Shi—" he started.

"Go with it." We didn't have time to discuss the pairing choices, because the doors slid open to a much more active corridor than two floors down.

Our foursome kind of collided a bit on the way out the elevator doors, but we managed to do it without making noise. Not being able to see myself was discombobulating enough without knowing three other invisible bodies were out there moving around. The hall was the same size and shape as the other, but people were actually moving around up here. Not only a few folks in white lab coats, but also men and women in everyday garb, and it didn't take long before I recognized faces.

The werewolves.

Tennyson squeezed my hand twice before leading the way. I stuck close behind, and his cloak occasionally brushed my legs. It took a bit of dodging, but we wove our way into the bustle. Everyone seemed free to move about, as we'd been told, but I sensed an air of tension in the werewolves, probably thanks to our interference. Being told you were volunteers and then being denied the ability to leave could shake up even the bravest person.

Werewolves didn't take well to captivity.

We passed a bit too close to a female patient, and her head snapped to the side. I swore she looked right at me, which wasn't possible. She shouldn't be able to see or smell me—but werewolves had sensitive ears, too. My shoes didn't squeak and my clothes didn't make much noise, but it wasn't as if I could stop breathing or slow my heartbeat.

Being a vampire like Tennyson occasionally had perks.

A very familiar voice drew us toward one of the rooms. Alice and Raymond Anderson were speaking with a Floridian couple in hushed tones, so we inched into the room. Raymond looked in our direction briefly, then returned to the intense conversation. I caught enough to know they were discussing leaving the clinic. Alice mentioned Chandra's name, and I nearly spoke up. But a disembodied voice would probably cause a ruckus that might bring doctors or guards down on us, and Tennyson and I needed to remain undetected.

More and more of the werewolves appear to be in favor of leaving, Tennyson said.

Good news for us. Now we need to a plan to get them out.

We need to acquire more information about this facility.

No kidding.

Curious about something, I focused on Alice and pushed into her mind the same way I had with Jaxon this morning. I didn't know her well, but we'd spoken and I knew a few things about her. If I could reach her mind . . . there. An image of three toddlers, all under the age of five, with bright, smiling faces. Raymond and Alice wrangling them in a professional photography studio, the family in cute, matching outfits. No words or sense of emotion, only their joyful quintet.

I pulled back, and in that same moment, Alice looked at me. Not directly in the eye, but exactly where I stood near the door, Tennyson's hand cool in mine. She stood, and I held my breath. Instead of my position, Alice poked her head out the door.

"Something wrong?" the other female asked.

"I've got the strangest sense of being watched," Alice said.

"I got that sense, too," Raymond added. "But I don't smell anyone nearby except us."

"It's bizarre." Alice was close enough to touch me

if she moved six inches to her left. "Then again, everything about today has been bizarre."

Tell me about it.

Inside my head, Tennyson chuckled.

Once they resumed their conversation, I double-squeezed Tennyson's hand so we could keep moving. We circled the entire floor and found only werewolves and the occasional person in a lab coat. No obvious guards anywhere, and only a few security cameras that I could easily spot. We waited by the elevator, and Tennyson brain-shared when Jaxon and Chandra joined us.

We should wait and follow one of the lab coats, I said.

Agreed.

Jaxon's flinch indicated Tennyson shared the information, and the softest sound was probably Jaxon whispering it to Chandra. With Tennyson's guidance, I found Jaxon's hand again; he squeezed tight.

We waited a little longer than I would have preferred, considering we only had a little over an hour of invisibility left. Should have asked for longer than two hours, but it was too late now. Finally, a dark-haired woman with a small metal tray approached the elevator. The tray held four labeled blood samples.

Score.

She swiped her key card, and the elevator dinged open. After she entered the car, Tennyson led us inside, sticking close to the walls. She went down one to the floor we'd skipped. It had the same basic shape, but instead of rooms, the corridor held a series of both open labs and secured metal doors that reminded me of solitary confinement cells.

We trailed the lady to one of the labs, where she handed over the samples to someone else, before returning to the elevator. Five people were working in the large lab, which looked like the set of an apocalyptic movie right before the deadly virus was accidentally released on the unsuspecting populace.

In other words, it was creepy as hell. I'd hated chemistry in school, so I didn't know a beaker from a Bunsen burner, but all the familiar equipment was there, along with computers, dry-erase boards covered in numbers and weird words I didn't recognize, and a refrigerator full of blood samples and other things.

No one here was really talking, though, and we couldn't access a computer with so many eyes in the room. We moved past the first lab to one of the sealed doors. It had a window with a cover you pulled back to peer inside. My hands were full, but the cover slid very slowly open, thanks to Tennyson. He made a startled noise that didn't bode well for whatever was inside, and when he gave my hand a single squeeze, I nudged him aside to look.

On a torn mattress on the floor, a creature lay moaning softly. And when I say creature, it's because I wasn't entirely sure what I saw at first. A man's bare torso was really the only easily human part of him. His muscled arms ended in furry, clawed hands, and his legs were basically those of a brown wolf. No visible dick, just a brown thatch of fur covering his groin. And his head was . . . grotesque. Human nose and mouth, but the rest of him was pointed ears and wolf fur.

An experiment. Either a werewolf trapped during a shift, or a man turned werewolf. The former was awful, but the latter was downright horrifying.

This is insane.

Agreed. Let your friends look, but we must keep moving.

I tugged Jaxon toward the little window. His hand gave a startled jerk. I knew when Chandra looked, because she couldn't hold in a startled gasp. Inside the room, the creature growled. The window cover slid shut.

Three more rooms in a row contained similar creatures in varying stages of transformation, all of them men. We passed another lab with half a dozen scientists—doctors? researchers? Whatever. Again, a lot of quiet and not much information. More cells and hybrids.

Our invisible time was quickly winding down when he finally hit pay dirt. Nearly back to the elevator was a propped-open door that said "Morgue." The interior looked like any city morgue, only the refrigerated lockers were bigger, and in the far corner, two women were performing an autopsy, while a tall man in a lab coat watched. The dead body was mostly human, but both arms and legs were furry, clawed, and wolf-like.

They'd split the man's chest open.

". . . most successful so far for what we want," the

man said. "I want to know why he fell over and died in the middle of an exam."

"That's what we're looking at," a woman replied. She had bright auburn hair, so she got designated Red. "His heart is incredibly enlarged, so it's likely the stress of the protocol ended in heart failure."

"So we need to adjust the protocol to account for that."

"Yes, Dr. Ferguson."

Son of a bitch. That was the guy in charge of the fertility treatments.

Another man entered the morgue, and our group had to shift quickly out of the way to avoid a collision. "Dr. Ferguson," he said. "Sorry to interrupt, but I thought you'd be interested to know that there's a group of Para-Marshals in town."

Ferguson looked sharply up, his weathered face pinched in a frown. "Are they responsible for the power surge earlier?"

"I believe so. According to Office Murphy, they're here chasing down a rogue werewolf, and they've taken over an office in the municipal building. There was a report made of a large dog-like creature on the east side of town, so that's likely true."

"Perhaps, but too many unusual things have happened already today. A random couple wanting treatment from us, that magical surge, Para-Marshals, and now one of our werewolf volunteers wants to go home? No. Have those Marshals watched, Hiller."

"Yes, sir," Hiller replied. "Already on it. So far, they haven't left the municipal building. Oh, and they have a vampire with them."

"A vampire?" Red asked. She's paused in the process of removing and weighing a kidney. "In Gabriel?"

I could practically see Tennyson's smirk.

"That's unusual," Ferguson said. "I don't like it. We're too close to perfecting our protocol. I won't allow interference in our plans. I don't care who they are. If any of them comes near this building again, kill them."

"Yes, sir," Hiller said.

Guess we got under his skin.

Time grows short, Tennyson said. *We must allow ourselves time to leave the building unnoticed.*

Yup.

After Hiller left, we backed out of the morgue as quietly as possible. Even though we'd only searched three out of five floors, I'd seen enough to know the place was bad fucking news, and whoever this Damian person was—and DM Clinic, really?—he was twisted. We waited as long as we could for someone to use the elevator, but we were already cutting it close, so when no one came, I swiped the keycard when no one else was in the corridor.

It took a minute to arrive, and then we were headed down. With no time to return the keycard—hey, it might be useful later—we went right to the ground floor, opened the main door as little as possible, and left. Tennyson led us directly across the street to the municipal building. Banged open the door to our office, and we'd only just released each other's hands when the power of Jaxon's wish shattered.

I blinked my own body back into focus, before looking around. Yup, all of us were there, and we all appeared to be intact.

"That was a mind-fuck I don't want to do ever again," Jaxon said.

"Agreed," Chandra replied. "Being invisible to my own body was highly disconcerting."

"It was fucking weird," I agreed, "but we got the information we needed."

"Which is?" Kathleen asked. She was clearly agitated and bored, even though she could have spent the last two hours looking for Gideon, instead of moping around the office with my mother.

Wait.

"Where's Novak?" I asked.

"Looking for your missing werewolf," Kathleen said.

"But that Hiller guy said none of us had left the building."

"Who?"

Our quartet—okay, so mostly me and Jaxon, but the others chimed in a little—detailed our surveillance, ending with the morgue conversation.

"My God," Mom said. "They're creating made werewolves?"

"Yup, and everything Ferguson said confirmed it," I replied. "They call it a protocol, and apparently, he's nearly perfected it."

The danger in creating a serum to turn adult men into forced wolves was staggering, no matter who possessed the technology. The only way to force someone into being a werewolf required a painful bite from a shifted, born wolf and a near-death bleed-out by the human. The transformation was also incredibly painful, and few survived the change. It was an ineffective way to create a shifter army for anyone, but this?

This was some serious shit.

"Ferguson is also highly suspicious right now," Jaxon added. "Especially of us being here, so we need to make a better show of actually looking for Gideon before dark."

"We also need to figure out if this place has a motel," I said, "because there's not really enough room for us to sleep on the floor in here."

"I can take care of that while you continue your discussion," Mom said. "I need a bit of air, anyway."

"Be careful."

"I always am," she said, throwing my words back at me.

Seriously, Mom?

"So Damian is creating another army for himself," Kathleen said after Mom left. "Just as he paid for the necromancer to steal a vampire Line and bend it to his will, he wants werewolves who are obedient to him."

"Pretty much. And it's all been happening under our damned noses."

"Bumfuck, Kansas, isn't exactly on our radar, Shi," Jaxon said. "They're remote for a reason."

"It just doesn't seem possible no one knew what was going on here."

"Damian has a long reach," Kathleen said. "Let us not assume no one else knows about this facility."

"Like who?"

"Such an army is attractive not only to the private sector, but also the more public."

I was at a loss, but Chandra helped out with, "Such as the US government?"

"Precisely."

"Wait," I said. "You think the government is sponsoring this research?"

"It isn't entirely beyond the scope of believability. Can you imagine the United States equipped with an elite unit of soldiers as fast, strong, and deadly as werewolves? Able to shift and move on land at ten times the speed of the best human SEAL? Generally immune to conventional weapons? No opposing country would challenge us ever again."

"Maybe before we start accusing our government of supporting this," Jaxon said, "we get some proof first."

Kathleen's pursed lips suggested she knew more than she was letting on, but getting information out of her was like getting blood from a rock, and it wasn't really the point right now: getting the were-wolves out was.

"So they know we're here," I said. "And they seem to believe we're here looking for a rogue wolf, but they're suspicious because of the timing of Jaxon and me showing up at their facility and one couple asking to leave. So we need to keep up that front while we dig for more answers."

"But how do we dig?" Jaxon asked. "I've only got one wish left. I mean, I could make some of us invisible again so we can snoop some more—"

"Not yet. Chandra, can you communicate what we learned to Alice and the others? Not the hybrids, specifically, but reinforce that the scientists there are up to no good, and to be ready to make their move."

"What move?" Chandra asked.

"That is the million-dollar question right now."

And I had no freaking clue what the answer would be. But I fully expected bloodshed. These researchers had a goal in mind, but so did I: tear that blessed building down brick by fucking brick. No matter what.

CHAPTER 14

Novak returned before Mom with news that he'd found evidence of several dead rabbits on the outskirts of town, likely werewolf kills, but he hadn't been able to track Gideon. It gave Tennyson a starting point, though, when the sun finally set, and we filled Novak in on everything he'd missed. He was up to speed when Mom returned with three motel room keys to a rundown place I'd apparently missed on the drive into town.

She'd also gotten a response about the elevator glyphs in the meantime, and she didn't look happy about it as she brought it up on a tablet. "They're Gaelic, as I suspected, based on the protective ward from Cailleach," she said. "But they've been modified using American symbols, as well. This one is an eagle's talon, this one a quiver of arrows."

The more I stared, the more easily I saw the symbols twisted up in the original Gaelic. "Do you know what they mean, though?"

"No, it's some sort of code that obviously has meaning to the people who work in that building." She looked me dead in the eyes, her expression grave. "Shiloh, the eagle talon, the arrows, the olive branch, this six-sided star, the circle . . ."

"Oh my God," Jaxon said. He looked like he wanted to hurl.

"Okay, what does all that mean?" I asked. "I mean, the eagle is all over American stuff, so are you saying the government is somehow involve in this?"

"Not just the government." Jaxon pulled out his badge and held it next to the tablet. "They're all symbols in the Marshals Service badge."

"They're what?" Chandra asked.

"Look."

I looked. Really looked, and the more I studied the badge and the tablet, the more easily I saw it. The individual symbols buried within the Gaelic representations on the elevator buttons added up to the whole of the US Marshals badge emblem. "You have got to be shitting me."

"Your Marshals Service is involved in this?" Tennyson asked.

"Evidence sure points that way," Jaxon replied with open disgust in his voice. "Fuck."

"But the Marshals are overseen by the Department

of Justice," I said. "So we're saying the federal government is involved in private experimentation using werewolf DNA?" The only person in the room who didn't appear shocked at all was Kathleen. "Let me guess. Your employer already suspected as much?"

"Yes," she replied. "Why do you think Lars and I were placed within the Para-Marshals? And Weller's arrest last week for his part with the necromancer only confirmed our suspicions."

"When were you going to tell us?"

"When I had more concrete evidence, which I now have, thanks to your mother and her sources." She flashed my mom a creepy smile. "You should have been an investigator, Ms. Juno."

"I prefer my quiet life and my garden," Mom replied. "And believe me, I am eager to get home."

I was eager for Mom to get home and out of harm's way, too, because shit just got super-serious, and I didn't want her involved in this anymore. "Mom, maybe you should take your rental car and head back to Wichita. Get a flight home."

"I will soon, sweetheart."

"But—"

"I can still be of use here. I want to help." There was something about how she said it, though, that made me suspicious, but I didn't want to get into a fight with my mom in front of everyone, so I just nodded tersely.

"So, what do we do now?" Novak asked. "We're out here unofficially, and if Ferguson or one of his people reports us to the brass, we'll get called back to headquarters. Debriefed again on what we're actually doing out here, and what do we do? Lie? Say we know you're conducting illegal experiments in the middle of corn country?"

"I don't know," I replied. "This Damian person is apparently working with the DOJ to create their own Paras. First controlling vampires, and now a werewolf army."

"Do you think the men in those cages were military volunteers?" Jaxon asked.

"It's possible. What human parts we saw were definitely fit and muscular, so they could be army, navy, et cetera."

"This doesn't truly surprise any of you, does it?" Tennyson said. "Your government was quite happy to accept help from werewolves in the 1940s to stop a world war, but in the last forty years or so, you've shunned them. Shunned vampires, as well. You fear what you cannot understand or control, but instead of learning to coexist, you seek ways to more effectively contain or destroy us, as you've done with other races throughout your history."

Anger built behind his words, and by the time Tennyson stopped, his eyes glowed red. And some of that anger, somehow, trickled over to me, that vinegar odor poking at my own temper. I pushed back against that blood connection, because I did not need to get upset and release the Quarrel on my friends.

Well, allies. Kathleen had yet to re-earn her friend status. I'd also never tested the Quarrel on a dhampir and wasn't sure how much it would affect her human half.

"I hate to admit this," Jaxon said, "but I agree with the vampire. The only thing that really surprises me is it took us six years to figure it out. I mean, what was the fucking point of the Para-Marshals all this time?"

"A diversion," Tennyson said. "The public faces of peaceful coexistence with Paras in the form of private policing, while your own organization invests in ways to rid yourselves of the problem entirely."

"And allows the government to keep track of all the Paras in the meantime," Novak said.

But something about that didn't quite add up for me. "You don't seriously think the DOJ wants to exterminate all of you, do you?" I asked.

"Perhaps the DOJ doesn't want extermination," Kathleen said, "but Damian does. Working with the Marshals is a compromise to get what he wants, and it's likely he'll turn on his government handlers once he's achieved his goal."

"He gets his werewolf army and we get zip?"

"Precisely."

"Wonderful." I let out a long, frustrated breath. "So wait, if the government is funding this, then what's Damian contributing?"

"Protection," Mom replied. "Kathleen, are you certain this Damian is a man, and not potentially a follower of Cailleach? A witch?"

Kathleen slow-blinked in her version of surprise. "I am uncertain of Damian's true identity or gender. We only know he or she is quite powerful, has magical resources at his or her disposal, and has influence within the government. This is likely why he's been able to sway the DOJ to his side."

"Or her side."

"Mom, what are you implying?" I asked. "That Damian is one of the witches who killed your parents?"

"It's possible. It explains the wards on Pack lands, Cailleach's mark on the building, and the magic I sense all around us." To Kathleen she said, "You've never actually met Damian, correct?"

"Correct," she replied. "Neither has my employer, and the one agent we sent to smoke Damian out once returned in many small pieces. We've kept our distance since."

"So at this point, we have no way of knowing if Damian is a witch or otherwise," I said. "What's our next step? Do we contact Agent Keene and tell him we know about this place? We know and they shouldn't trust Damian because he'll double-cross them once the research is complete?"

"My first loyalty is not to the Para-Marshals, and yours shouldn't be, either. None of your loyalty should." Kathleen squared her shoulders. "None of us are fully human, and the Marshals seek to protect humanity, while going behind our backs to find ways to destroy Paras. To make us submit and be controlled by their whims, not our own, when we are clearly more powerful. Our service to them has been a joke."

I wanted to rebut her statements, but I couldn't. She was right. While I was raised as a human, I was still half-djinn and not fully of this world. Even Chandra and my mother, who were both still technically human, were magic-touched, so they were unique. They were part of the larger tapestry of the universe that the average human never got to see or experience.

I did want to believe that our service as Para-Marshals had meant something in the grand scheme of things, because I'd believed in us. I went into this with Julius because I wanted to be part of something bigger than myself; I wanted to help people. Help Paras. To make a fucking difference, bless it all. And we had. Tennyson being here was proof of that. Yet . . .

Torn and angry, I stalked out of the room, down the short corridor to the main entrance, and then out onto the municipal building's narrow porch. It wasn't big enough to pace, so I walked to the small parking lot adjacent to the building and paced there, weaving in between the parked cop cruiser and a Ford pickup that had seen better days.

I hated what we'd discovered, but I wasn't sorry I knew now. Knew the very same people who'd given me a job were secretly trying to find a way to shackle me and my friends.

"Shiloh?"

Jaxon's voice was not unwelcome, but it didn't stop

my pacing. He inserted himself in front of me, his own hazel eyes sparking with anger and confusion, same as mine probably were.

"It wasn't all for nothing," he said.

I blinked hard. "How did you know I was thinking that?"

"I know you, remember?"

"Remember? Very funny."

He winked. "Sorry. It's hard to remember you don't recall all the things I know and don't know. All the conversations we've had over beer and pizza. The time we lay in bed after making love and you told me how you never felt like you had a place in the world until you, me, and Julius founded the Para-Marshals units. That being part of our team gave you focus and a home, and now you're wondering if it was all a lie. If any of it mattered and it does. All of it matters."

He brushed his thumb across my chin, those words caressing not only my mind but my wounded spirit. Beautiful, meaningful words that broke something loose deep inside me, and I pulled him close and kissed him. A hard, bruising kiss he returned in kind. I grabbed his jacket, and he spun us until my back hit the side of the pickup, and hot damn he tasted good. Like mint and spice and a deeper male flavor I couldn't seem to get enough of.

Maybe we hadn't been together in years, but the attraction was still there—and if the half-hard dick rubbing against my belly was any indication, Jaxon felt it too.

Sweet Iblis, this is wonderful.

More powerful than anything I'd felt with another man, I wanted to find a quiet place to learn more. To relearn a man my body told me I knew in wicked and wonderful ways. A man who looked at me like I was the most important person on the planet. A man—

—who tore his mouth from mine.

"What—"

Jaxon shook his head, lips kiss-bruised, cheeks bright red. "Shi, we can't."

"Yes, we can."

"You've got a boyfriend."

Well shit, that was still technically true, and thank goddess Jaxon had a level head, because I wasn't a cheater. Although wasn't kissing another man cheating? Ugh. I really should have negotiated time to track down Vincent to talk before I took this job. But I'd reached out and Vincent hadn't. Didn't that mean something?

"You're right," I said. "I'm sorry, I shouldn't have kissed you."

"It's okay. I enjoyed the hell out of it, but we can't go there. Not while you're figuring things out with Vincent."

"I know. Thank you for stopping, because . . . that was some kiss."

He tilted his head a few degrees, lips quirked in a half smile. "It sure was. Don't suppose it was familiar at all?"

"In some ways, yes, I guess. I mean, my body kind of knew things would be amazing if we got naked together, but I don't consciously remember why. I guess that's what attraction is, right?"

"Yeah, and attraction was never the issue with us."

"Right. Thank you, also, for what you said. About it all mattering. I had no idea who I was or what I wanted until I met Julius. And you, too, apparently. With Julius gone, you're the only one who remembers the earliest days, except I don't remember you being there." I let out a long, sad breath. "My Para-Marshals service has been everything to me, and I'm scared it's all falling apart."

Jaxon took one of my hands and squeezed. "Maybe the Para-Marshals aren't your destiny. Maybe it's the people you met because of it, and there's something even bigger waiting for you. Something better."

"I hope so." I rested my head against his shoulder, amazed at how good it felt to lean on someone else for a change. To not have to be in charge and put together for a few minutes. "I needed this."

"Always happy to help."

"I still have no idea what to do next."

"Shiloh?" Mom yelled from the other side of the lot. "Um, your vampire is causing an argument."

I raised my head. "He's not my vampire. Why do people keep saying that?"

Jaxon chuckled and released my hand. "Come on, let's go see what's up."

We strode into the building on Mom's heels and back into the office, where Tennyson appeared to be squared off against Kathleen, Chandra, and Novak. No one was baring fangs, but the tension was palpable.

"What'd I miss?" I asked.

"I have always been perfectly clear that my first priority is to my line," Tennyson said, his eyes red headlights. "My line and I are perfectly content to be left alone, but if any of my kind are kidnapped and experimented on by humans again, I will retaliate. I made that perfectly clear to your human authorities after the necromancer incident."

"Okay. What's that got to do with what's happening right now?"

"He wants to tell the Dame and Homme Alphas where their wolves are and why," Chandra said.

"We've discovered the location of their people as we said we would," Tennyson replied. "It is our duty to inform them of what we know."

"Are you nuts?" I asked, alarmed at the idea and the very, very bad consequences. "You want to tell Alpha Kennedy his werewolves are being used for DNA splicing experiments in a secret lab in Kansas? Then what? We can't have every Pack in the country descending on this place to rip it to pieces in retaliation. It'll play right into Damian's hands and prove the Packs are out of control and need to be destroyed."

"That's what we're trying to tell him," Novak said. "Only you said it better."

"Look, Tennyson, I know you sympathize with the Alphas, because you know what it feels like when your family goes missing. All we're asking for is time to get a handle on the situation before we get the Packs further involved."

Tennyson simply stared at me.

"We need to shut down this lab," Kathleen said. "It is dangerous and dabbling in things best left alone. We also have no idea what they are doing in there beyond creating their own werewolves."

"She's right," I replied. "We will involve the Packs, but not yet. Please, Tennyson, just a little more time."

"I have no loyalty to the Para-Marshals," Tennyson said after a beat. "However, I do consider you a friend, Shiloh, so I will do as you ask."

"Thank you."

"I'll reach out to my other unit teammates," Chandra said. "They're loyal to the Para-Marshals, but they won't take well to them developing weapons out of Paras. Perhaps they can do some additional digging for us while we suss out the situation here."

"I like that plan."

"All right, I'll make the calls in the car so I don't disturb the think tank."

"Some of us should continue looking for Gideon," I said once Chandra left. "They know we're here, so we need to put on a show. Mom, I really think you should leave town before things get any crazier."

"All right," Mom said. "If you think that's best."

"I do. This isn't your fight, and I don't want you here if shit hits the fan. Literal or paranormal shit."

"You're right, Shi," Jaxon said. "Elspeth should go before it gets any more dangerous. I'll go out with Novak and keep searching for Gideon."

"Thank you. I'll go out with Chandra when she's done on the phone."

"What do you want me to do?" Kathleen asked.

I pinned her with a hard stare. "You aren't part of the team anymore. Do whatever you think will be helpful."

She slow-blinked.

We left Tennyson and Kathleen behind in the office space to do whatever; Tennyson probably wouldn't come out again until the sun set, so he could move about more freely. He wouldn't explode into a pile of ashes if a beam of sun hit him, but it would scorch his skin black, and that wasn't a good look on him. Novak and Jaxon set off to the east, the pair of them amusing physical opposites in every way, but both men fully capable of defending himself (I had to trust that was true for Jaxon, since he was a Para-Marshal and all).

We got anything that was ours out of my mom's rental, and I hugged her for a long time by the driver's side door. "You be careful, daughter," Mom said. "May Mother Earth protect you."

"I'll be careful, I promise. And if your resources find anything else of value?"

"I'll forward it to you immediately. I love you."

"Love you, too, Mom."

I always hated parting from her, because my mother was the embodiment of inner peace. She made me feel safe in an unsafe world, but knowing she was driving away from a dangerous situation made it hurt less. I watched the taillights make their way down the road, until the car disappeared on the horizon.

Chandra finished her calls a few minutes later, and I filled her in on what was up. "Letting your mom go was a good call," she said. "She did what we asked her to do, so there was no sense in continuing to expose her to danger."

"Exactly. Ready to go hunt a werewolf?"

We went in the opposite direction of the boys. I nearly called Jaxon and asked him to use his last wish to locate Gideon, but we might need that wish later on down the road. Besides, how difficult would it be to find one werewolf in a town of less than eight hundred people?

Harder than I imagined.

We searched until dusk and found more clues, including paw prints, but not the young werewolf himself. His clothes at the silo hadn't been disturbed, and I saw no sign he'd even returned. The longer he remained missing, the more I worried someone besides us had found him first. And I really didn't want to report that to Alpha Kennedy.

Hey, thanks for letting us borrow a werewolf, but he's gone missing, too. Sorry.

Not happening.

When our quartet reassembled at the office, it was empty, so we hit the town's small diner for dinner. We got a lot of looks, which annoyed the hell out of me, but our group had two black faces in a sea of very white. Add that to the general xenophobia of a small town, and we were always going to offend some of Gabriel's sensibilities. The waitress was prompt and polite, though, so I ignored it in favor of a big platter of fried chicken.

Halfway through the meal, though, the hairs on the back of neck prickled. I rolled my shoulders, as if stretching out a crick, as an excuse to look around. The diner had a long, eat-in counter, and a man in a denim jacket and baseball cap caught my attention. Something about him seemed out of place, and it wasn't the ancient coat or loser ball team on the cap.

Curious, I pushed my mind toward him. It might not work, because we'd never had a conversation, or been in proximity in any meaningful way, but what was the harm in trying? I silently asked who he was and who he worked for, hoping to see something, like I'd seen into Jaxon's and Alice's minds.

Nothing.

Maybe I was too far away.

I wiped my fingers on a napkin, then stood. "Be right back." I strolled over to the counter, grateful the stool next to my target was empty. Without looking directly at him, I leaned forward and flagged down a server. "Can I get some extra napkins for my table?"

"Sure thing." She handed me a small stack from a bin on her side of the counter. "Here you go, hon."

"Thanks bunches." I turned to go and "accidentally" brushed my elbow against his shoulder. "Hey, sorry."

"Barely felt it," the man said in a monotone voice.

When I returned to my seat, Novak frowned and said, "We have plenty of napkins."

"I know, but the guy with the out-of-date jean jacket?" I said in a hushed voice. "There's something about him that's got me on edge. I tried to do that mind-peek thing."

"The what thing?"

Oh, right. I still hadn't disclosed my newly discovered ability to Novak and Chandra. We hadn't had a chance away from Kathleen until now, so I told them what I'd done to Jaxon in the car. I also admitted to seeing into Alice's mind during our invisible field trip. "Anyway, I couldn't get anything on him," I continued, "so I thought if I touched him, or got close, I'd be able to sense something."

"And?"

"Dude, I just sat down. I haven't tried again yet."

"Give her a minute, Novak," Jaxon said.

Novak squinted at him. "She really saw into your head?"

"Yeah. She saw some memories of us, because that's what I was thinking about."

"Huh."

I picked up a chicken leg and took a bite, while pushing my thoughts toward the man again. The image of a large brown wolf, muzzled and caged, flashed in my mind, along with the word "menace." "Oh no," I said as I dropped the chicken leg. "I think he captured Gideon."

CHAPTER 15

"**W**hy do you think he has Gideon?" Jaxon asked.

"Because he's thinking about a caged wolf and thinks he's a menace," I replied. "Who else could it be?"

"You think he's working for DM?"

"Almost positive he works for them and he's here to keep an eye on us. Someone dial my phone."

"What? Why?"

Instead of asking questions, Novak discreetly palmed his phone in his lap.

"I'm going to take a call and go outside to answer it," I replied. "Maybe he'll follow me."

"Oh yeah, draw out the bad guy," Jaxon said. "Great plan."

"Deal with it."

My phone rang, and I made a small show of excusing myself to go outside and answer the call. All I got on the other end was diner noise, and Jaxon distantly complaining about my hero complex. The latter made me smile, and I thought back to that intense kiss in the parking lot. I was insanely attracted to the guy, but a relationship with a coworker I barely knew was a very bad idea. It hadn't worked once before, apparently, so why would I think it could work now?

It couldn't, and besides, I had a boyfriend.

Maybe.

The sidewalk in front of the diner was quiet, and I could easily give Vincent a second call. Talk about things and see where we stood. This needed an in-person conversation, though, and I couldn't keep getting distracted by my love life. Not with so many lives at stake. We had no idea what forces we were actually up against, the numbers DM Clinic had, or what they knew about us. So I faked having a conversation on the now-dead line and kept half my attention on the diner door. The place had street parking and no attached lot, so I hung around just beyond the light of the wide front windows.

Denim Jacket didn't let me down.

After only a few minutes of talking to myself, he left the diner and strolled in my direction, hands in his pants pockets. I gave no indication I saw him coming and giggled at my silent phone for good measure, then said good-bye. Giving him the chance he needed to make a move.

Hired muscle is so predictable.

He acted as if he was going to walk past, and then at the last second he lunged at me. I allowed him to twist my left arm up and behind my back. My phone clattered to the sidewalk. Something hard pressed into my ribs. "I've got a gun on you," he hissed into my ear. "Walk. To the alley."

"Don't hurt me," I replied with just enough fear to sell it. Idiot didn't know I was letting him abduct me. Or that I could break his hold on me faster than he could pull that trigger.

We walked into a narrow alley between the diner and the building next door, and it cast us in shadow. A few feet down, he stopped us. "Who are you?" he asked.

"You grabbed me," I replied. "Who do you think I am?"

"Trouble, you and your friends, and I don't need trouble in my town."

"Your town? You don't look like the cop I talked to this morning, so try again, Barney Fife."

"Mouthy bitch." The gun pressed harder into my ribs and he pushed me face-first against the brick diner wall. Now he was testing my patience. "How about you answer my question? Who are you?"

"Someone you're about to regret calling a bitch." I tensed, prepared to dislodge the guy's hold on me, but a rush of air was followed by a thud, and Barney Fife was gone. The distant glow of red and cloying scent of vinegar clued me into Tennyson's presence before I could turn and spot him.

He held the guy against the opposite building by the neck, Barney's feet about a foot off the ground. "Do not touch what's mine," Tennyson said.

Okay, we really needed to have a conversation about ownership, and soon.

"Do you feel better now that you've gotten that out of your system?" I asked him. "I didn't actually need rescuing."

"I acknowledge that you are quite capable of defending yourself. However, my response was instinctive and immediate. We have shared blood, so we are connected."

The bad guy made a noise of disgust, and Tennyson's grip tightened. "Who are you guys?" he garbled out.

"People who now hold your life in their hands," Tennyson replied. "You will answer her questions, beginning with your name."

"Hugh Warner." His voice was gone a bit distant as he fell into Tennyson's gazelock.

"Who do you work for?" I asked. Having an overprotective vampire in my back pocket was turning out to be pretty blessed useful.

"I'm field security for DM Clinic."

"What's 'field security' mean?"

"Means I blend into the town, keep my ears open for any suspicions about the clinic and what they do. And I keep it safe from unwanted outsiders, such as yourselves."

Huh. "So you're an informant."

Hugh blinked once. "Yes."

"Did you recently capture a rogue werewolf?"

"Yes."

Okay, now we were getting someplace useful. "What did you do with the werewolf?"

"I turned him over to my supervisor at DM."

"A guy named Hiller?"

"Yes."

Great. The bad guys had our werewolf. And I had more questions, but doing this in the open was dangerous. Someone could walk by the mouth of that alley at any moment and see us. "Tennyson, take him and meet me back at the motel. I'm getting the others."

"As you wish," he replied. The pair was gone in a flutter of black cloak.

Oh, to run as fast as a vampire Master.

My friends were settling the bill when I returned, and they'd had the rest of my meal boxed up. I told them what was up once we were packed in the car.

"So this guy kidnapped Gideon and gave him to DM," Jaxon said. "Good instincts on this one, Shi."

"Yeah," Novak said. "This new power of yours is coming in handy. Any others you feel coming online?"

"Not so far, but Iblis knows what might happen in the future," I replied.

"Maybe you need another boost of vampire blood."

"No!" Jaxon and I said at the same time.

Tennyson and Hugh were in the center of the three

rooms Mom had rented for us earlier in the day. It was hard to believe we'd only come into Gabriel this morning and not a week ago; so much had happened in less than twelve hours. Hugh sat in the room's only chair, Tennyson across from him on one of the two double beds. Tennyson's eyes were normal, so he wasn't gazelocking Hugh anymore.

"Mr. Warner has agreed to cooperate with the rest of your interrogation," Tennyson said.

"Excellent," I replied. And now that there were five of us against one, Hugh looked a bit green. And scared. "Where did we leave off? Oh yeah, I want my werewolf back."

"I can't get him for you, I'm sorry," Hugh said. "I don't have that kind of internal clearance. I don't even know where in the building he's being held."

"Do you have access to their computer systems?"

"No. Like I said, I'm field security. I rarely go inside that building, and even then, it's usually only the first floor."

"The first floor is a glamour, so anything you think you see is probably bullshit, anyway."

"Glamour?"

"Yeah. When you look at that building, how many stories do you see?"

He looked at me like I was deranged. "One."

"It's five stories high, Mr. Warner. There's a magical ward protecting it from outside eyes, so no one really knows what's going on in there."

"It's a fertility clinic that's secretly helping were-wolves fix their infertility problems."

Novak snorted, and the harsh sound made Hugh flinch.

"It's so much more than that," Jaxon said. "And we're here to shut it down."

"If it's protected by magic, how do you see past it?" Hugh asked.

"Trade secret," I replied. "What we know and do is not important to you right now. You being allowed to live beyond this moment is what should be important to you." I'd never murder someone in cold blood, but he didn't know that.

"You . . . you can't kill me." Hugh didn't seem too certain of that, though. "I mean, aren't you Para-Marshals?"

I jacked my thumb at Tennyson. "He's not."

Tennyson played his part perfectly by baring gleaming white fangs; Hugh paled.

"Look, I don't know what you want me to tell you," Hugh said. "I'm not part of any inner circles, and I don't know anything about what else the researchers may or may not do in that clinic, I swear."

"How do you get inside?" Jaxon asked.

"There's a door on the rear of the building. Every-one's got a unique key card and pass code."

"Tennyson," I said. "Mind doing a quick recon for us?"

"Certainly." Tennyson rose and was gone in a rush of air.

"Who comes and goes on a regular basis from that clinic?" I asked.

"Dunno, the researchers, I guess. But I never see them around town, so I don't really know where they live. The receptionist, Petey, he's an in-towner, though. I know that."

"If no one regularly comes and goes," Chandra said, "it's possible they live in that building, possibly on one of the two floors we didn't get to see."

"That makes sense," Jaxon replied. "No need to explain all the people working in such a small clinic, and no need for those researchers to interact with townsfolk and draw suspicion."

I nodded, because it was the best explanation. "Do you know how many people DM employs?"

Hugh shook his head. "Not really. I mean, Mr. Hiller once casually mentioned how important security was, because three dozen jobs depended on it, so I guess between thirty and forty."

Thirty to forty people with some truly fucked-up morals, if they enjoyed experimenting on other species. "Other than the twenty-eight werewolves currently seeking treatment, who else is there voluntarily?"

"I don't know. It's not my job to know this shit."

"Plausible deniability," Jaxon said. "You can't spill what you don't know."

Tennyson breezed back into the motel room. "The depth of the building to the naked eye is the same as what the townspeople see from the glamour. I found a rear door and locking mechanism that matches his description."

"Perfect." I held my hand out to Hugh. "Key card and pass code."

Hugh squawked.

I put my hands on the arms of his chairs and leaned in. "Let me be perfectly clear about something, Mr. Warner. As of this moment, you have quit working for DM and are now planning the fastest, most efficient means of driving out of town tonight. If you do not, my vampire friend over there will drain you to the point of near death, and then leave you like that in the middle of a cornfield many miles from here, to live or die as your body sees fit. Do we understand each other?"

Hugh had gone pasty white, and I worried I'd overdone it, but he nodded. "I understand," he whispered.

"Good." I stood up straighter. "Key card and pass code."

Hugh fumbled for his wallet and produced a piece of plastic the size of a credit card. All black, with the DM Clinic logo, and a magnetic stripe on the back. "Pass code is 4576."

"What's directly inside the door?"

"An elevator. You need the card for that, too."

Just like the other elevator. "What else?"

"A hallway to some meeting rooms. I've been in one or two when Mr. Hiller called a meeting."

"When you turned over the werewolf, did you go into the elevator or visit another floor?"

"No. I've only ever been on the first floor, I swear."

The guy had given us some good intel, but he didn't know anything that could really help us get our werewolves out safely.

"Anyone else have a relevant question?" I asked.

"How did you get paid?" Jaxon said. "Cash, check, debit?"

Hugh swallowed hard. "Cash. I'm on a fixed retirement income, so it's money under the table."

"Of course it is," I said. This Damian guy was too freaking smart to leave a paper trail. "I'm guessing he pays Petey in cash?"

"Probably. We don't really chat, you know? He watches TV all day, while I just keep an eye on things out here."

"Are you the one who told Hiller we were in town?" Jaxon asked.

"Yes. I'm friendly with Officer Murphy, and we got to talking right after he found you guys in the silo, talking about a rogue werewolf. When I told Hiller about it, he told me to capture the werewolf first, if I could."

"You didn't think to ask why?"

"I'm not paid to ask questions."

That had become abundantly clear.

"What about the building's security?" Novak asked. "Cameras? Alarm systems? Anything you can tell us?"

"There's a visible external camera in back near the rear door. Uh, I've never noticed an alarm system, but they gotta have master controls somewhere in the building if we need key cards to get inside. I don't know where, though."

I glanced at Tennyson; his slight head-tilt confirmed the exterior camera. And we were running out of use for this guy. He was an employee with likely no real value to DM, so keeping him as leverage wasn't realistic. Besides, we were the good guys, and unlawful imprisonment wasn't really my style.

"Okay, you're free to go," I said to Hugh. "However, the vampire over there will continue watching you, so if you call anyone, or speak to anyone on the street, or do anything except go home, pack up some stuff, and drive out of town for good, you'll end up in that cornfield. Or worse."

Tennyson approached Hugh's chair with enough menace in his expression I was almost scared of him. He leaned down and whispered something into Hugh's ear. I couldn't hear the words, but whatever Tennyson said, Hugh's jeans darkened at the crotch.

That was some impressive threat to make a grown man piss himself.

The pair left the room, and I have no idea if Tennyson actually followed the guy, or if he simply hung around on the porch for a while, but he didn't come back right away.

"Okay, that was both useful and pointless," Jaxon said. "We know a little bit more, but I don't see how it's going to really help us."

"Knowing there are two entry points is helpful, though," Chandra said. "And we now have access to the building's rear entrance."

"True."

"But what can we actually do with that information?" I asked. "There could be thirty to forty potential hostiles in there, not to mention their experiments. Yes, the werewolves are on our side, but what if their floor goes into some kind of lockdown mode and they can't get out of their rooms?"

"They likely have those kinds of backup protocols in place," Chandra said. "After all, one couple asked to leave and were denied, and two dozen agitated werewolves is trouble waiting to happen."

"Agreed." My phone chose that moment to ring. Rosalind. "Oh great." I really wanted to let the call go to voice mail, but she'd entrusted one of her people to us, and we'd lost him. She deserved to know some of what we'd learned today. *Some.* "This is Shiloh Harrison," I said after putting the call on speaker.

"It's Rosalind, Second of the California Pack," she replied. As if I didn't know all that. "Alpha Kennedy is eager for an update on our missing Pack members."

Might as well start with the only real good news I had. "We have tracked down the exact location of your missing werewolves, and we've confirmed that the people who lured them out here did so by manipulating the Andersons, and placing those wards in various homes to cause unnatural infertility."

"Have you made arrests of these people?"

Seriously? "No, because things are pretty complicated." I explained the glamour around the building, and our unsuccessful exploration of three floors—leaving out the whole wishing thing, and Rosalind didn't seem to care how we became invisible, only what we learned—as well as what we'd learned from Hugh Warner—leaving out Gideon's abduction. "One of the couples asked to leave and they were denied, so it's unlikely the person in charge will react well to a sudden uprising and demand for departure."

"I agree. My people are prisoners in this clinic, and that cannot stand. Tell me your exact location, Marshal Harrison. I will bring the full power of my Pack down on those people if they will not release mine."

"Bad idea for many reasons, most of all public perception of a werewolf attack against what appears to be a perfectly legitimate business. We can't shatter this particular glamour right now. Attacking the clinic plays right into their hands. These people want to prove werewolves are dangerous to humans, so please, let us handle this."

"I dislike your logic, but I agree with it. Does Gideon agree?"

"Yup."

"May he answer for himself?"

"He's not in the room at the moment." I made a mental note to collect his stuff from the silo and have "Gideon" send Rosalind a text. Deceitful, but if I could keep his kidnapping a secret for a while longer, it boded well for the next time Rosalind and I met face-to-face. Maybe she wouldn't try to break mine.

"What is your plan to retrieve my wolves?" Rosalind asked.

"We're working on it." I purposely left out the whole "the US Marshals service and maybe even the Department of Justice is in on these experiments" part of our discovery. I needed to keep her and the Alpha's trust in my team to get this done without risking an all-out attack on the clinic by pissed-off werewolves.

"It sounds as if you've made great strides toward a solution. Please, continue to update us on your progress."

"I will, thank you." I ended the call and flopped onto one of the beds. "That went better than I expected."

"Are you sure lying about Gideon was a good idea?" Jaxon asked.

"I didn't lie. He's not in the room, is he?"

"Has anyone heard from Kathleen recently?" Chandra asked. "It's been several hours since we parted ways."

"Nope."

Jaxon tried to call her. "Voice mail."

I texted her asking for an update, and I got one back almost instantly—except it was a new text from my mom. Safe in a hotel in Wichita. Flight home in the morning.

I replied with a few emojis, then told the team.

"Question," Jaxon said. "Can I use my last wish with you to summon another djinn?"

"Um." I sat up as I tried puzzling that one out. It took a lot of power to summon a djinn who wasn't already attracted to your emotional state. "I'm not sure, but why? Trying to get more wishes?"

"Trying to get more eyeballs. Last week, remember when Novak and Kathleen's helicopter went down? Your dad was able to teleport to the location without being seen by rescuers and tell us their bodies weren't inside."

"He did?" Novak asked.

"Yeah, it's how we knew you'd been taken by someone. Weller tried using you guys against us by pretending to have murdered Kathleen over the phone to get our cooperation."

"So you want my dad to spy on the clinic for us?" I asked.

"Yes."

"No, and for the same reason as before. Without knowing the limits of the magic user we're facing here, I don't want a djinn as powerful as my dad anywhere near this place. Djinn and magic users generally repel each other, anyway, because djinn are born with their magic inside them, while most magic users and abusers draw magic from external sources."

"So he might not be able to see through the glamour and get through the wards?"

"That, and if this magic user is powerful enough, or if they somehow know the binding words, they could find a way to bind my dad to them, and then we'd be not only up shit creek, we'd be tumbling over a shit waterfall."

Jaxon nodded his understanding. "Okay. Just a thought. We need to toss out every possibility we've got and see what sticks."

"I know, but getting him involved is just too dangerous."

"You know he'd risk it for you."

"Which is exactly why I don't want to call for him."

"How about one of your siblings?"

I gave him a sharp look. "You know about them?"

"Of course."

Oh yeah, memory loss. I must have really been into this guy if we'd talked about my extended family. "I've never met any of them. They'd have no reason to help, and I don't know how to call them, anyway. Plus, I think the power expenditure of wishing for another djinn will be too high to work as your third wish."

"Damn."

"Why don't we just call the blessed CIA or something?" Novak asked. "The werewolves are being held against their will, and no way is whatever they're doing to those men legal."

"I honestly don't trust the government right now," I replied. "Not if the Marshals Service is involved. Who knows who else is funneling money and resources to Damian and his people? And local law enforcement doesn't have enough resources or experience to deal with a Para issue like this."

"And we did technically do a warrantless search earlier," Jaxon added. "So how do we explain how we know about the other experiments?"

Novak grumped. We all wanted the shut this clinic down, but we had to be smart about it, not barrel in with guns blazing, metaphorically or not.

We were getting nowhere, and all the iced tea I'd guzzled during dinner needed to come out, so I excused myself to the bathroom to release it. As I washed my hands, I studied myself in the mirror. I honestly couldn't tell if I looked confident and put-together, or stressed and worried. Everyone was deferring to my lead, and I still wasn't used to having that sort of power.

I didn't look like a raving lunatic, though, so I counted that as a win and returned to the main room. Tennyson was back, and the power that always seemed to snap and crackle around him was super-charged.

Oh crap. "Tell me you didn't feed off Hugh Warner," I said.

"I did not feed off Hugh Warner," Tennyson replied. "I did, however, find a handsome young man in need of sexual release. He was quite eager to offer up a small amount of blood in return."

"You had sex while we're trying to figure out how to shut down this clinic?"

"I needed to feed in order to maintain my strength. It is so much easier to seduce a blood donation with an orgasm than to take without permission."

As a big fan of informed consent, I couldn't fault him that logic. I also let him know what I'd told Rosalind and about Kathleen's continued silence.

"I am pleased to hear the Packs have been given some information, and while I do not condone your misinformation about Gideon, I understand your reasons."

"Gee, thanks."

We ended up sort of breaking the meeting there, because we were going in circles in terms of what do to. Right now, the werewolves were safe and not in immediate danger—something Chandra confirmed after a quick brain-chat with Alice, who had also not seen a glimpse of Gideon on their floor—so we could take time and think. Or not think. Sometimes the most obvious solution to a problem came when I stopped trying to force it.

Tennyson retired to one of the rooms, while Chandra and Novak gleefully took another. When the wall-banging began a few minutes later, I turned the TV on as a distraction for me and Jaxon. Then I retreated to one of the beds and texted Vincent. Mom had given me his number, and it was far beyond time I reached out again.

Me: I've been thinking about you a lot lately. I really want to talk.

Jaxon found a cooking competition show and we settled on one bed, not touching, to watch. I kept checking my phone, and after nearly forty minutes, Vincent pinged back.

Sweet Iblis, yes, he's finally communicating with me.

Vincent: You kept a huge thing from me for months. Not sure there's much left to say.

With my heart in my throat, I replied, I had to protect you from that part of my life. It's dangerous. I'm so sorry you were hurt. You didn't deserve it.

Vincent: No, I didn't. But you were hurt, too. Are you okay?

I really wanted to hear his voice, but this was better than nothing. Physically, I'm fine. Everything has changed, though, and I don't know how to fix it.

Vincent: Maybe there's no fixing this.

I shifted to sit with my legs dangling off the side of the bed so Jaxon couldn't see my face, or the hurt I couldn't hide. Vincent and I had been on the cusp of a "let's get serious" conversation a week ago, and now he wanted to break up? I thought hard before I responded. Can't we at least talk on the phone first? I can try to explain why I hid who I am?

> **Vincent:** Now is a bad time. In New Jersey visiting my parents. Your world scares me, Shi. I'm sorry.

My throat closed and I blinked back hot tears. I wasn't going to cry over a guy, bless it, but I cared about Vincent, and I hated that he was breaking up with me— not only via text, but without an actual conversation about what had happened. No chance to plead my case, no chance to offer a sincere apology.

Through blurry eyes, I typed, I'm sorry, too. I wanted us to have something. Maybe I wanted it too much. Please take care of yourself.

When no reply came after several minutes of staring at my dark phone, I dropped it on the floor and curled up on my side. Head on the flat motel pillow. I hated crying, so I tried to let the emotions work through me on their own, but Jaxon had to get all concerned.

"Shi? What's wrong?" A warm hand squeezed my shoulder as the bed moved beneath us. "Hey?"

"I think Vincent is dumping me." My voice was

raspy, and I hated the weakness, but every part of me knew Jaxon wouldn't judge me.

He climbed off the bed to retrieve my phone, and I stared at the wallpaper while he looked at my messages. The bed dipped again as he settled behind me. "I'm so sorry."

"I lied to him."

"You had good reason. You were protecting him."

"I was protecting myself, too." I sat up, stupidly angry at Jaxon for trying to make me feel better. And even more, I hated the sympathetic look on his face, because it made it more difficult not to cry. "I pretended to be human, I pretended to be a regular Marshal, because I was afraid he'd look at me like so many other people do when they can't figure out what I am. A freak. I've only ever felt at home with the Para-Marshals, and we're falling apart. It's all falling apart, Jaxon."

I sobbed once, and then all I knew was the heat of his arms around me, the broadness of his chest against mine, the strength with which he held me close. I pressed my face into his neck and forced the tears back, unwilling to lose it in front of someone I'd only known a few days—except my body knew him. Knew we'd once been close, knew he'd take care of me, knew he wasn't a stranger.

Maybe I couldn't trust my memory about Jaxon, but I trusted myself. Our mouths came together in the same moment I reached for his belt buckle. He found the hem of my shirt, and we moved with a practiced ease at once familiar and completely new. Few words passed between us as we kissed and touched and gradually shed clothes. I didn't want to think, didn't want to worry or wonder or plan. All I wanted was to feel.

And I felt plenty as we pulled the covers back and I pushed Jaxon onto his back. Climbed on top and welcomed him into my body. He held my hips in a sure grip that didn't direct or control, and I leaned down to kiss him again. Everything about his kisses was comforting and sure, and I needed more.

A tiny part of my mind warned me this was a bad idea—getting involved with a coworker for the second time was a recipe for disaster—but I told my better angels to go fuck themselves. My demons got to live it up tonight, and live it up we did. Several hours and two orgasms later, I collapsed into bed, exhausted and sated.

I had no idea what tomorrow would bring, but for a little while tonight, I was content and at peace, and I slept safely in Jaxon's arms.

CHAPTER 16

Loud knocking on the motel room door startled me and Jaxon right out of bed and onto our feet. I reached for my firearm, which was on the floor by my jeans. Jaxon was nearly to the door with his own gun out when he realized he was naked, so I threw his boxers at him, which had ended up on my side of the bed. I simplified things and wrapped the bed's coverlet around me.

Jaxon checked the window first, then opened the door a crack. "Officer Murphy, it's a bit early, isn't it?"

"Sorry to disturb you folks, but it's important," Murphy replied.

"Sure, just give me a second to put a shirt on. You caught me still in bed."

"Certainly."

He shut the door and snagged his shirt off the floor. I took the moment to collect my clothes and duck into the bathroom to get dressed, leaving the door half-shut so I could listen.

"Come in, please," Jaxon said. "Should I get the rest of my team?"

"I don't believe that will be necessary," Murphy replied. "But I do need to speak to the male vampire in your group."

"Tennyson? Why?"

I ran my fingers through my messy hair as I joined Jaxon and Murphy. Murphy gave my rumpled appearance a once-over I did not care for, and then winked at Jaxon. "Mixing business with pleasure?"

Jaxon grunted. "Why do you need to speak with Tennyson? He's a civilian, not a Marshal."

"Because half an hour ago, a man named Hugh Warner was found dead in his truck by highway patrol, less than two miles outside of town. Drained of blood."

Crap on a cracker.

"Did they find bite marks on his body?" I asked.

"No, but what else can drain a body of blood other than a vampire?"

"You'd be genuinely surprised to hear the answer to that, Officer. I'll get Tennyson."

"I appreciate it."

Instead of shocking the cop by using the telepathic link, I walked next door and knocked. Tennyson answered quickly. His nostrils flared as he very clearly scented me, and his eyebrows went up, but he didn't comment.

"Officer Murphy has questions," I said. "Hugh Warner was found dead outside of town."

"Intriguing." He followed me back to my room.

Murphy shrank a bit, because anyone with two eyes could tell Tennyson was old and powerful, and yeah, intimidating when he focused on you.

"How may I assist you, Officer?" Tennyson asked.

"Just need to know your whereabouts last night between six and midnight," Murphy replied in a less than steady voice.

"I was in several places last night, including physical proximity to Mr. Warner, as well as a young man whose name I believe was Ross. I did not, however, leave town limits at any time between those hours. In fact, as of around seven-thirty or so, I did not leave my room next door until just now."

Murphy scribbled notes on a small pad, his fingers shaking a bit. Probably wasn't every day a cop from the middle of nowhere had to question a Master vampire.

"Why do you suspect I killed Mr. Warner?" Tennyson asked, as bored as if he was ordering a cup of coffee.

"Body was drained of blood," Murphy replied. "Seems suspicious that less than twenty-four hours after you drop into town, one of my people ends up dead."

"I understand your suspicions, but they are unfounded, I assure you. I've lived long enough to know how to feed without killing. I am here in Gabriel to assist my companions, not murder your townsfolk."

"I believe you, but you gotta know I had to ask."

"Of course. You are doing your duty as a protector of this town. I expect nothing less than your best work, and I am happy to cooperate, as I have nothing to hide."

Other than chasing the guy out of town on some unknown threat, but none of us were about to bring that up. Hopefully, once Murphy started chatting with the neighbors, no one else mentioned it, either, but I trusted Tennyson had been discreet in tailing Hugh to his home.

"Well, I appreciate the cooperation," Murphy said. "You folks gonna be in town much longer?"

"At least another day or two," I replied. "We're still looking for that rogue werewolf, and we have a new lead to investigate today."

"Good luck with that. Haven't had any reports to the station about a stray dog or rogue wolf, but if I do, I'll pass it along."

"I appreciate it, Officer."

Once Murphy left, Jaxon called Novak to pass the bad news along to him and Chandra. I ignored Tennyson's curious look and went into the bathroom with fresh clothes, and then took a shower. Not that it would help if Novak came into the room anytime soon. He'd know Jaxon and I had had sex, and under the hot shower spray, I wasn't entirely sure how I felt about it. Not Novak knowing, but me and Jaxon.

At the time, it had been exactly what I'd needed. Physical comfort to help ease the pain of Vincent's rejection. A little bit of certainty in an uncertain situation. I absolutely didn't regret the sex, I simply wasn't sure what it meant going forward. I'd known Jaxon for what? Three? Four days? And maybe it didn't have to mean anything. Maybe it was just sex between friends and that was it.

Yeah. Right.

When I left the bathroom dried and dressed, Novak was smirking at me from the unused bed, hands behind his head as he reclined against the pillows. Tennyson lurked in the corner. "Don't start," I said to Novak.

"Did I say anything?" he retorted.

"I can hear you in your head, and I know you, so don't start. Where are Jaxon and Chandra?"

"At the diner getting coffee and shit to go. Can't really talk about the case in a crowd of people."

"True." The other bed was still messy, so I made it before sitting down to zip up my boots. "Kathleen?"

"Still nothing."

I growled softly under my breath, annoyed at her continued absence, when her inclusion in this trip at all had been based on her promising to stay close and keep us informed of everything she knew. This disappearing act worried me, and not only because she'd already betrayed us once. We were also within a hundred yards of a place capable of restraining more than two dozen werewolves at once. Who was to say they couldn't easily capture a dhampir, as well?

The door opened. I tensed, but it was just Jaxon and Chandra with a tray of takeout coffee and a bag of baked goods. "The lady who waited on us said they make the best bear claws in the county," Chandra said.

I was starving, so I grabbed a coffee and a bear claw. Jaxon, I noted, sat on the opposite bed, which was gentlemanly. We hadn't had a chance to talk about last night, and doing so in front of our friends—especially Novak—was not happening.

"Someone must have been watching Warner," Jaxon said.

"Or his place was bugged," Chandra added. "Either way, someone found out he blabbed. Or suspected he blabbed, so they removed him as a problem."

"So Dr. Ferguson and his people must know we aren't just here for the rogue werewolf."

I washed a bite of bear claw down with too-hot coffee. "I'm getting to the point where I want to just walk in the front door, ring the bell, and demand they give us Gideon back."

"That receptionist will deny he's there," Novak said.

"And he probably believes that, if he's as out of the loop as Warner was on what really happens in that building. He doesn't strike me as the kind of guy who'd resist too hard if we walked through the glamour wall and used Warner's key card."

"If it's still active, now that its owner is dead."

Good point.

My phone rang. Mom's name popped up on the screen, which was odd, since it was barely after seven in the morning. Maybe she had an early flight home. "Hey, Mom, what's up?"

"Hello, Shiloh," a strange male voice said.

I dropped my coffee in my lap and barely felt the burn over the icy pit in my stomach. "Who is this?"

Jaxon was in front of me in an instant with deadly fire in his eyes. With a shaking finger, I turned the call over to speaker.

"I'm someone who's very eager to meet you, young lady," the stranger said. His voice was deep and heavy, as if coming from a dark pit, and it sent shivers down my spine.

"Why do you have my mom's phone?"

"She was not eager to part with it, but a few broken fingers persuaded her."

"You son of a bitch." Instant rage blasted through me, and I tried to rein it in before it set off the Quarrel. "I will kill you for touching her."

The asshole had the nerve to laugh. "You'll be doing no such thing, young one. I have something you want, and I'm willing to trade you in kind."

"What do you have exactly?" Someone had put a

towel in my lap, and I wrapped my free hand around it so I didn't accidentally lash out and punch someone.

"I have your mother, a beautiful woman named Elspeth Ann Juno. I also have in my possession a young, fiery werewolf named Gideon who was delivered to me yesterday afternoon by a mutual acquaintance who is no longer among us."

Chandra, I noticed, had her phone out and was recording this conversation.

Smart lady.

"Seems like you've been busy collecting people who don't belong to you," I said.

"And they are all in reasonably fine condition, if somewhat angry about their current accommodations."

"Broken fingers is reasonably fine?" I squashed down another rush of rage, because me getting pissed off and losing control would help no one. Especially not my mother.

"She's since learned it's smarter to cooperate than resist, and I hope you will realize that, too, so no one else is unreasonably harmed."

"I like that idea. No more harm. Why don't you let my mom and Gideon go, and while you're at it, you let the twenty-eight werewolves you're experimenting on return to their home Packs. That way we don't have to tear your clinic down brick by brick."

The man laughed again. "You seem to think you have any true bargaining power here, and you don't. I know your numbers and your collective abilities, and they are small. Not even your vampire Master could so much as scratch me if I didn't allow it."

"You think a lot of yourself. Do you have a name, or should I just call you Pretentious Asshole?"

"You may call me Damian for now, but soon you will call me Master."

I laughed out loud, but it was a bitter sound. "The fuck I will ever call anyone Master."

"You will if you don't want thirty deaths on your conscience, young djinn."

Oh no. No, no, no.

I looked into Jaxon's wide, startled eyes. Damian knew what I was, and that was bad. Capital B-A-D, bad.

"I'm listening," I said.

"You will come to me of your own free will, and you will bind your magic to me as my servant for the rest of your days, and in exchange I will release Gideon and Elspeth without any further damage."

I clapped a hand over my mouth as my stomach heaved. This was my absolute worst nightmare come true. Someone with power knew what I was and potentially had the ability to bind me to him, not only for three wishes, but forever. I'd be a magical slave to his whims. I managed not to throw up and asked, "And if I don't agree?"

"Then I will drop the infertility act and turn all of the werewolves over for medical experimentation and certain death in likely painful ways, and your mother's death will last for weeks. I can be quite creative when I'm upset."

Thirty lives in exchange for mine. Thirty lives in exchange for an existence of slavery and torture, because Damian was evil. He'd force me to use my magic for horrible purposes, and I'd live a long life of abject despair, because my djinn blood meant a longer life than the average human.

Thirty lives.

"I realize this is a very emotional decision," Damian said. "So you have until sunset tonight to enter the DM Clinic lobby of your own free will. Think it over, Shiloh. Your mother is counting on you."

As soon as he hung up, I dropped my head into my hands and screamed. Screamed in fury, in fear, and in absolute hatred of the man who was forcing me to make this decision. To willingly choose my greatest fear to save the lives of others. Jaxon held me, but it wasn't enough to calm the storm raging inside me.

"You must calm yourself, Shiloh, you are distressing your teammates."

Tennyson's oddly soothing voice floated in my mind, and unexpectedly helped lower my rage levels. I clung to that bizarre sense of peace, uncertain where it was coming from, but grateful for it nonetheless. It took time before I could pull away from Jaxon and even out my breathing.

"Can I wish for you to teleport your mom to safety?" Jaxon asked.

"Doesn't matter," I said, unsurprised at how hoarse my voice was. "He'd still have Gideon and the other werewolves as leverage. We might still need that wish for something, because we have until sunset to find another option. Besides, there's a tiny chance that having an open tether to you via one last wish could interfere with what he has planned."

"Makes sense."

"You cannot go to him," Tennyson said. "He will exploit everything that makes you unique and turn you into a slave."

I jerked to my feet and got into his face. "You think I don't know that? This is my biggest fucking fear come to life, Tennyson! I fucking know!"

His eyes flashed crimson, and I didn't protest when someone pulled me back a few steps. Jaxon turned me around, his hazel eyes both loving and furious. "We'll find another way, Shi. You cannot go to him."

"What if there is no other way? We can't openly attack the clinic now, because he has hostages he won't hesitate hurting, or killing in retaliation. Find me another way, and I'll take it, Jaxon, but I can't let thirty innocent people die for me."

"I know. Chandra?"

"I'll let Alice know what's going on," she said. "They deserve to know they've become expendable pawns."

"Make sure they know to stay calm and don't act suspicious, or the place might lock everyone down."

"I will." Chandra left, probably next door where she could concentrate.

"Now are you willing to get your dad involved?" Jaxon asked.

"Absolutely not," I replied. "He can't use his power to interfere, and if he found out what's going on, he'd volunteer to go in my place, and that is an epically bad idea. An earth djinn bound to three wishes is bad enough, but to someone who is ostensibly powerful enough to force a permanent binding? Not happening. He can't get involved, Jaxon."

"Okay, I understand. I'm just throwing out options here."

"My dad is not an option. I don't want to make this trade, but I will, so let's try to come up with feasible alternatives to me becoming a forever slave to dark magic."

"Dark magic?" Tennyson said.

"I heard it in his voice. When people dabble in dark magic it changes them, physically, mentally, emotionally. Whoever this Damian is, he isn't doing this for the powers of good and balance. He's doing this for evil and we have to stop him."

"We fucking will stop him," Novak said, speaking up for the first time since the phone call. His expression was stony, determined. "We protect our own, Shiloh."

"Thank you."

"I'd let you hug me, but you're covered in coffee."

I rasped out a sound not quite laughter and went to get fresh clothes. I had one clean shirt left to go with yesterday's jeans, but at least they weren't coffee-soaked. After I changed, I sat on the closed toilet seat and rocked, allowing my body to work through some of the emotions still rocketing around inside. I was pissed at the situation, but I was also furious with myself for getting Mom involved in the first place. I'd sent her away, instead of keeping her close, and Damian's people had gotten to her. She was in danger, with possible broken fingers, because of me, and if the only way to fix that was to trade myself for her?

In a fucking heartbeat.

Someone knocked. "Shi? You okay?" Jaxon.

"I'm decent." Not okay, no, but I was dressed.

He came inside but didn't shut the door. "Novak went next door to make some phone calls. Trying to raise Kathleen and maybe get us some backup."

"Tennyson?"

"Gone, too. Said he had to check in with Drayden about something."

"Maybe Drayden will show up with a couple hundred of his friends."

"Maybe." He squatted in front of me and brushed a stray lock of hair off my cheek. I usually kept my hair braided so it didn't get in my way, but I hadn't fixed it since yesterday. "Is it okay to admit I'm terrified right now?"

"Yes. So am I, but I think you know that."

"I do." His lightly Southern accent had deepened with his frayed emotions. "I have loved you since the moment we met, Shiloh Harrison, but I fell in love with you because of how big your heart is. You wanted to help Paras in need so badly. You wanted to make a difference in their lives. In our lives, and you did. You still do. I cannot imagine my life without you by my side, as my partner or my lover. We *will* find a way out of this."

My eyes watered, and I blinked hard against those tears. "Did I ever tell you why I'm scared to be bound to wishing?"

He tilted his head, but didn't say yes or no. Part of me wondered if I'd already told him this story once upon a time, but I needed to tell it again.

"Before Tennyson bound me last week, I'd only been bound to the Rules of Wishing four other times. Three were because I'd agreed to help the wisher, but the fourth was . . . forced upon me by a man named Kress. He was a Wish Collector."

"A what?"

"Magic users who abuse their power to collect wishes. They can sense when a tether is made between a wisher and a djinn. The powerful ones can trace the tether back to its source, if the tether remains in place long enough, and kill the original wisher with a spell that shifts the bond to him or her. They take control of the djinn's power until the bond is broken by killing the collector, killing the djinn, or the collector breaking one of the Rules of Wishing."

"Kress did that? Collected from your other wisher?"

I nodded, more angry tears stinging my eyes. "The woman who'd bound me needed my help, but Kress tracked the tether, and he killed her in a horribly painful way that I couldn't stop. I watched a beautiful soul named Jenny die because of my magic. And somehow, because I was not fully djinn, Kress was able to circumvent the Rules. He made me do horrible things to people. A rival skidded out on black ice and became paralyzed for life. A woman who'd scorned him was left broken and battered by others, because he wished it so. An entire building burned to the ground, leaving hundreds homeless, so he could buy the property for redevelopment.

"This is what I'm terrified of, Jaxon. Of another evil man forcing me to hurt others. To hurt Paras, or the people I care about." I cupped his cheeks in my palms. "I don't know what I'd do if he forced me to hurt you, or Novak, or Chandra. And maybe I don't remember our past, but I do believe we had one, and that I once loved you with my whole heart. And that a piece of me still loves you."

His eyes went liquid. "I never stopped loving you. I just had to put those feelings away for a long time. I'd rather just be friends than have to leave the team, or you."

"Our timing sucks."

"Yeah, it does. But we had last night, and hope is not lost."

"No."

He frowned. "This Damian character isn't going to kill me to take over the tether, is he?"

"No, if he was a Wish Collector, he'd have done it by now. He wouldn't have to bargain with me to get my cooperation. He's using some other form of magic, so if he succeeds, you guys need to do everything you possibly can to find a way to break his hold on me."

"Believe me, we will. How did you break your tether to Kress?"

"My dad found out, and since he couldn't directly interfere, he called in a favor with another Para. He had Kress killed."

"Just killed?"

My lips twitched. "Kress may have literally been drawn and quartered, and his body buried in the woods somewhere in Canada."

"I knew I liked your dad for a reason. So we find a way to kill Damian. Easy enough."

Not so easy until we knew the limits of Damian's strength and the true source of his power.

"So wait," Jaxon said, "how old were you when this thing with Kress happened?"

"Seventeen."

"Fuck me, that young? You went through all that when you were a teenager?"

"Yup. It was the most traumatic experience of my life, and it was years before I let another person bind me to the Rules. Not until after I'd joined the Para-Marshals and gained some confidence in myself again."

"You seemed pretty cocky the day we met."

"That day I had backup in the form of an ex-Army Ranger and a pissy werewolf. If my dad hadn't been kidnapped, I may never have found my courage."

"I don't believe that. Not for a second."

"That's just because you know me."

"Yeah, I do. You were always meant to be a hero, Shiloh Harrison. And a leader."

"If you say it's my destiny, I'll smack you."

He brushed his lips lightly over mine. "You said it, not me."

"Thank you for this. Listening. Supporting me."

"It's what we've always done for each other. Hey, you want to see one of my favorite memories of you?"

I tilted my head, but saw no humor or teasing in his expression. "Okay." I pushed my thoughts toward him, easily stealing into his mind. A series of images flashed one after another. Our headquarters. The living room. Jaxon on the couch with his left leg in a cast. Smiling at someone. Me in a chair nearby reading a book out loud. Both of us laughing at a funny part.

"I broke my leg from a fall off a building during a case," Jaxon said. "I hated being stuck at home while you guys went out and worked. But every time you were home, you tried to entertain me. You read me books, we played cards. But it was that specific day, that specific book, when I truly understood how blessed I was that you'd found me, befriended me, and had given me the brief opportunity to love you."

I sniffled and wiped my eyes, overwhelmed by the force of emotion in his voice and thoughts, and I eased back out of his mind. "Thank you for that. It's a beautiful memory."

"You're welcome."

Jaxon stood and offered me his hand, then gently pulled me to my feet and into a warm, all-encompassing hug. I had ten hours of daylight looming ahead of me that felt like both an eternity until sunset, and not enough time to do everything that needed to be done. I wasn't ready to give up and go with Damian, but I also didn't see a viable alternative yet.

All I could do was hope my friends came through with a plan, or I'd soon be walking into a fate worse than death.

A fate that would cause me to welcome death with open arms.

CHAPTER 17

By the time lunch rolled around and my stomach growled, I could tell my friends were hiding things from me. Tennyson, in particular, was being crazy secretive and taking a lot of private phone calls. I'd tried brain-speak to get him to divulge something, but he started blocking me, and the impact of hitting that mental brick wall eventually made me stop.

And if I got close enough to someone to peek into their mind, all I got were thoughts of rainbows and bubbles and other bullshit. Not cool. I didn't like being out of the loop, and I made my feelings known over a lunch of burgers and fries from the diner.

They were probably going to miss our business when we eventually pulled up stakes.

"We're trying to protect all of us by keeping our plan quiet," Jaxon said. "If it doesn't go down how we hope it will, and if you get tethered to Damian, he might be able to get access to our plans before we enact them."

"Well, when you get all logical about it," I groused, still not happy. This was my fucking future, and I deserved a say. But Jaxon was right. Damian could gain access to my thoughts, so the less I was involved in this plan, the better.

"I agree with Jaxon," Kathleen said, her voice a jolting surprise. She stood in the open motel room door, her face flat as always. "It's best you be kept in the dark about certain things."

"Except maybe not the rest of us," Novak said. "Where in heaven have you been?"

"Speaking with my employer and ensuring aid in our effort to destroy this clinic and its research."

I narrowed my eyes at her. "Destroy the research, huh? Are you sure your mystery employer doesn't want it for herself?"

"I assure you she does not. She believes in the old ways and in leaving creatures as they are. However, she does have quite a bit of useful technology at her disposal."

"Like those helicopters you mentioned that are supposedly waiting for us?"

"Precisely."

"Do I get a hint?"

"No. However, I would like to speak privately with the others."

"Fine." I collected my food and took it to the room Tennyson had used last night, unsurprised to find it empty. He was off somewhere, hopefully preparing some sort of interference in tonight's main event.

And now that I was alone again, my thoughts turned to things left undone. I didn't really have anyone to say good-bye to, other than the people one room over. I'd say whatever I could to my mom when I saw her at sunset. My dad . . . no, he'd want to get involved, and that was too dangerous. Besides, I know he loves me, and he knows I love him.

I pulled out my phone and hovered a finger over the dial button on Vincent's information. I owed him more than a breakup via text. I wanted to talk to him one last time, to hear his rich, accented voice. To picture his handsome face smiling at me once more. Maybe it was selfish, but I called anyway.

It rang for a long time, until the line picked up with a lot of noise in the background. "I didn't expect to hear from you again," Vincent said.

"I had to call. I hated leaving things the way we did. You deserve more than that from me. Where are you, anyway?"

"Chuck E. Cheese's for my niece's birthday."

"You have a niece?" My stomach curled in on itself as I realized the wealth of information I truly had never learned about Vincent's family and life outside of work. We hung out and we had great sex, but things hadn't gotten much beyond surface stuff. And while I think we both wanted that in the end, I'd probably lost the chance to really get to know Vincent Ortiz, and that sucked.

"Yeah, she's turning six. Isabella."

"It's a lovely name. Can you tell her happy birthday from a friend of her uncle?"

"Sure." The noise stopped, replaced by the rasp of wind, so he must have gone outside. "So you're a Para, huh?"

"Yes. Did anyone tell you what I am?"

"Said it's classified information."

Yeah, right. If the Marshals were involved in Damian's clinic, more people had that information than I knew. "My mother is a magic-touched human, but my father is an earth djinn. I inherited some of his ability to grant wishes and use magic."

Vincent sputtered. "Your dad is a genie? Are you serious?"

"Perfectly. And I don't share that information easily, because there's no one else like me in the world, and my powers have been used against me in the past."

"Nine months, though, Shiloh. I get you were protecting the half-genie thing, but you could have told me at least that you were a Para-Marshal."

"I'd like to say I would have, if we'd actually gotten serious. But I blew that, didn't I? By lying to you for so long about what I do. Who I am."

"I've been lied to before. Four years ago. She lied and then she took me for everything I had, including my own construction firm. I lost it all because I trusted and fell in love, and I never thought I could do that again until I met you."

This time, I didn't try to stop my tears from falling, fueled by the depth of his wounds and my own keen sense of loss. I'd lived my life and never stopped to think what my lying could do to Vincent, or that he'd be this wounded if/when he learned the truth. "I'm so sorry. I didn't know."

"You shouldn't have to know about someone's shitty past to be honest with them. I probably could have handled you being a Para-Marshal, but you didn't give me a chance to be honest with you in return."

Probably could have handled.

"What about me being half-human?" I asked, while staring at a creepy oil painting of two kids in a field that looked more like snakes than grass. This motel decorator had issues.

"I don't know. I'm not a fan of the Paras, but they've never hurt me directly."

And there it was—the indirect racism. Lumping all of us under one umbrella and assuming we acted, reacted, and believed in the exact same ways, simply because of the past actions of others. But at least we were finally being honest with each other.

"I'll take that as a no, then," I said, then released a long breath. "You deserve a safe, happy life, Vincent.

I hope you find a woman who can give you that. I really do."

"Thank you. Shiloh, is something going on? You sound strange."

"There's a lot going on, actually, which is why I had to call you. I couldn't leave things like we left them last night. I had to talk to you one last time."

"One last time? Are you in some kind of trouble? Do you need help?"

I smiled at the protectiveness in his voice and wiped away a few more errant tears. "I am surrounded by people trying to help me, but I may have come face-to-face with an enemy I can't defeat."

"Are you sick? Is it cancer?"

"No, goddess, nothing like that. Someone is trying to use my own powers against me, and they have the leverage to do it. Hopefully, it doesn't come to that, but I just can't say for sure if I'm going to win this fight. And I'd regret it every day for the rest of my life if I wasn't able to talk to you. For us to at least make peace with each other. Say good-bye."

"No good-byes, hell no." He swore a blue streak in Spanish, which made me smile. "Maybe we aren't together anymore, but I still care about you. Tell me how to help."

"You can't. You're a mortal man, and this is a magical battle. Promise me, no matter what, you'll live the best life you can."

"Shiloh—"

"Promise. Me."

He let out a soft, sad sound. "I promise. You make me a promise, though."

"I'll try."

"Fight. You fight with every fiber of your being, and when you win, you call me and let me know. Maybe once we're both back in Maryland, we can get together and have a celebratory drink."

I closed my eyes and breathed a few times before I could manage a watery, "I promise to fight. It's in my djinn nature to fight and rebel, so no problem there."

"And the drink?"

"As long as you're paying, I'm in."

"Good. And, uh, good luck with this bad guy. You deserve a safe and happy life, too, Shiloh."

"Thank you." I wanted to keep the conversation going, to stay on the phone with the last remnant of my old life, and forget what I was about to face. But I couldn't, and staying on the line wasn't fair to Vincent. "Enjoy the birthday party, okay? Don't eat too much pizza."

"Be safe."

"I'll do my best. Until next time?"

"Yeah, until next time."

I hung up and sank onto the edge of one bed, my cooling lunch no longer appealing to me, despite still being a little hungry. Maybe I should head over to the diner with the company credit card and gorge myself on my favorite foods. Nachos and cheese fries and a big slice of cheesecake. The DOJ owed me at least a final meal, considering their apparent duplicity.

And goddess knew what my life would be like under Damian's thumb.

No, I couldn't think like that. I had to believe we'd find another way. Or if we couldn't, and I did end up tethered to Damian, that my friends would do everything they could to get me back. I'd only been tethered to Kress for nine days, before my father intervened. I couldn't imagine a lifetime of that sort of pain and misery.

I'd sooner find a way to kill myself.

Bored with staring at the walls—and needing to distract myself from such morbid thoughts—I played with my tele-picture ability a little. I'd already looked into Jaxon's head, and maybe if I wasn't in the room they'd let their guard down. I didn't want in on the plans for obvious reasons, so I'd have to be careful.

Curious if it would work with everyone or only certain species, I tried to push my way into Novak's mind. At first, I didn't see anything, only had an odd sense of darkness. And then a rapid slide show of naked men and women flashed into my mind, and I shut that feed off fast.

Sweet Iblis, he truly did think about sex nonstop. I mean, okay, he's an incubus, but good grief. And it was an effective way to keep me out of his head and away from their plans. No more mind surfing for me right now.

The motel room door swung open, and I expected Jaxon, but I got Tennyson instead. He swept inside and shut the door, cutting off the scant bit of direct sunlight and casting him in a backlit shadow. It was hard to believe that a little over a week ago, I'd been intimidated and a little scared of him and his powers, and now I barely blinked when he entered a room.

He'd saved my life more than once, and I didn't know how to properly thank him for it.

"You are apart from your team," he said as he lowered the cloak's hood, showing off that many-colored hair that fascinated me so much.

"Kathleen came back and they're discussing strategy. Apparently, I'm a liability if Damian does manage to bind me."

"An intelligent maneuver on their part. However, you seem distressed."

I snorted hard through my nose. "I am far beyond distressed at this point, Tennyson. I genuinely do not know if we can beat Damian tonight, and I hate it. I hate not knowing who I'm going up against. At least when I faced down the necromancer, I was aware of his plan for you, you know?"

"I understand." He surprised me by sitting beside me and unsnapping his cloak. I rarely saw him without it. Black linen pants and a matching shirt hugged his tall, lean frame, and despite lacking muscled bulk, his entire body radiated power and strength. I soaked a bit of that in, because I needed the comfort it offered without any actual physical contact. "Would it soothe your fear any if I informed you that Drayden is currently seeking a powerful ally to assist us tonight?"

"Depends on the ally."

"Danu deserves to know her children are being held against their will and that they are being exploited in the name of science."

That perked me up a bit. "You think Danu will come here and help?"

"It's possible."

"But back in Portland, she said she could only offer information, not directly help us."

"Goddesses say many things out of impatience, young djinn, and at the time, Danu had no reason to believe her children were being harmed. Discovering they are in danger may force her hand, especially as Cailleach is her rival."

"They're rivals?"

"Ah yes. Since the first spark of life on this world, they have fought over the British Isles. Cailleach was jealous of Danu's ability to turn wolves into men and she sought to destroy the wolvish residents of Ossory Island by imbuing men with magic. But instead of following Cailleach, those men used the magic gifts for their own purposes, and it is often believed they became the first dark magic users in Europe."

"Cailleach didn't stop them?"

"She was too focused on her battle with Danu to care, but by then the Ossory wolves had spread across

Europe. You see, as you experienced during our visit with Brighid, time moves differently here than it does on the astral plane where the old gods and goddesses still live. Centuries passed in the blink of an eye, so Cailleach created the Gaelic witch line in her own image, but because the world was changing and so few still worshipped Cailleach, her power was diminished, and the witches were not powerful enough to hunt down and destroy Danu's children."

"So Cailleach is still jealous of Danu, but Danu doesn't give a shit because she's stronger and would rather play video games than be worshipped by people who clearly still believe in her?"

"Correct."

"Do you think Danu coming will lure Cailleach here? I don't want to turn this no-stoplight town into a magical OK Corral with goddesses going at each other."

"I do not know Cailleach, and I do not know if she's on this plane or elsewhere, or if she still protects her own. The ward on the clinic wall suggests she does, but we will not know unless she makes an appearance."

"Well, let's hope she doesn't. I mean, I'm all for Danu helping us free her wolves, but . . . yeah."

"I understand. It is in your nature to protect the people of this town, despite them meaning nothing to you personally."

"That's part of being in law enforcement. You put yourself out there and protect the innocent, whether it's a jogger from a mugger, or an ancient evil trying to take over the mind and body of your friend." I met his eyes, which sparkled with flecks of green. My nose tingled from the warm, sweet scent I always associated with his positive emotions. "No matter what happens tonight, thank you."

"It's been my pleasure, Shiloh." His lips twitched, and he touched his side where he'd had flesh scooped out by that blessed melon baller during the necromancer's ceremony. "Mostly."

I chuckled, the first time I'd really laughed in ages. "I feel you on that. Are you healing?"

"The flesh is no longer raw. However, vampires do not regenerate, per se. I will always carry the scars of that day on my body."

"I'm sorry."

"It is what it is. I did what I had to do for my line's safety, and I have no regrets."

"That makes one of us."

"We all make mistakes, young djinn, and you will make many more over the course of your natural life. But wallowing in those mistakes helps no one, least of all yourself. You are young, you are strong, and you possess the vast stubbornness of any earth djinn in existence. You will overcome this."

Overwhelmed by his unwavering belief in me, I did something I never thought I'd do—I threw my arms around Tennyson's shoulders and hugged him. Really hugged him, his slender body cool against mine. His own arms draped loosely around my waist and he pressed his cheek to mine.

"You do your people proud," he whispered. "Human and djinn alike."

"Careful there, Tennyson, your humanity is showing."

He made a soft, not-quite-chuckle noise, then gently pulled out of my impulsive hug. "Perhaps I have not completely forgotten what it's like to be human. You remind me of all the things vampires forget over time, such as compassion and sacrifice. Thank you for that."

"You're welcome."

Of course, Jaxon chose that tender moment to walk in. His eyes narrowed at the sight of us sitting so close together, but he didn't comment directly. "Can I have Shiloh for a little while?" he asked.

"Certainly." Tennyson stood and put his cloak back on in a swirl of black fabric. He stopped next to Jaxon on his way out the door. "Love her while you're able, skin-walker, for no one can predict how tonight will end."

He left Jaxon gaping after him, both eyebrows raised.

"You guys have a plan?" I asked.

"Bare bones, but yeah, we've got a plan." Jaxon shut the door, then took Tennyson's place beside me on the bed. "He bring back anything useful?"

I told him about Danu's potential appearance, as

well as a bit of the backstory between Danu and Cailleach.

Jaxon groaned when I finished. "Great, that's all we need. I can see the headline: Small-Town Destroyed in Supernatural Grudge Match."

"Danu may or may not even come, and Tennyson doesn't know where Cailleach is right now."

"Don't you ever think it's weird that Tennyson not only knows so many goddesses, but also how to find them?"

"Yeah, I think it's weird, and believe me, if we survive tonight, I plan on getting that story out of him. You know his sparkly hair? When Danu shifts, her wolf has the same hair. Fur. Whatever."

"Huh."

I nudged Jaxon's shoulder with mine. "You know, there's something else I've been wondering about."

"Such as?"

"I've been told your skin is a deer—"

"Seven-point stag, thank you very much."

"Fine, a seven-point stag. I've been told that."

"But you've never seen it that you remember."

I nodded, encouraged when Jaxon's expression went thoughtful, instead of being annoyed by my unasked question. Or sad, as he often got when reminded my only slippery memories of him were about four days old. He stood and moved to the largest open area of the somewhat small room. His lips moved as he spoke words I couldn't hear, and a sense of magic filled the room. Strong, but displaced, and instead of shifting like a werewolf, the air around Jaxon shimmered, and then flashed gold. I blinked his new shape into focus.

And even with one set of antlers half-regrown, he was stunning.

I stood, and at five-eight, I'm fairly average-to-tall for a woman, and his shoulder was the same height as mine. The size of a small horse, with shiny brown fur, and those gorgeous antlers. The side that hadn't been torn off during the vampire fight stood up from his majestic head a good two feet, and the side still healing was already eight inches or so high. He was a tad unbalanced, but didn't seem to notice.

He watched me with too-human eyes as I gently rubbed his flanks, then down his forehead. He nuzzled my palm with his nose, and I smiled. Rested my own forehead against his and existed in the simple beauty of his skin form.

"I'm so sorry you were hurt because of me."

He made a noise of protest, then stamped one hoof.

"Yeah, well, I feel responsible. I dragged our team into Tennyson's mess, and you got hurt. You could have died."

The sound he made in his throat sounded a lot like, "So could you."

"Thank you for showing me, Jaxon. Truly."

I stepped back, and the air shimmered again as he changed from skin to man in a burst of magic.

"You know, you rode me once," he said.

"Oh yeah?" I waggled my eyebrows, because I'd ridden him just last night, and thank Iblis I had that wonderful memory of him to take with me.

He snorted laughter. "No, I mean my skin. It was during a job you and I were assigned to. You were stabbed in the leg by a fairy blade, so you couldn't walk. The only way for us to get away was you riding my stag."

"Wow. I've never even ridden a horse, but I rode a gorgeous stag and forgot it."

Jaxon tapped the side of his head, so I pushed into his thoughts—which was becoming easier and easier with him. I saw myself limping, clutching a bleeding calf. Him looking back at his own flank while I climbed aboard. Tearing through the woods astride him.

"This mental picture-share thing is pretty handy," I said.

"I want you to have all the memories you can of us. Even when we weren't a couple, we were a great team."

"I know." I touched my chest directly over my heart. "In here."

With hours yet until sunset, and my own fate currently out of my hands, Jaxon and I curled up together on one of the beds, and I watched the interconnected parts of our life play out in his mind. Each new memory of his replaced what had been taken from me, and I memorized each one as best as I could.

Because if Damian won, I needed all the happy memories I could get to take with me into a life of torment as his slave.

According to the weather app on my phone, sunset was officially at 7:10 p.m., so around six my nerves got the best of me, and I ended up pacing the long porch that connected all eight of the motel's rooms. I couldn't sit still—not only because of what Damian wanted from me, but also because I didn't have the first fucking clue what my team was planning.

And being the team leader on the outside of things? It sucked ass in a big way.

But I also trusted my people to do their best and make a plan that got every innocent life out of DM Clinic safely and with the least amount of drama.

Then again, if Danu and Cailleach showed up, drama was going to reach epic levels. It made me glad most of the other pantheons stayed out of earth business and let us be, but some of the Western European and a few African deities still liked it here, especially with Paras exposed to the masses, so to speak.

And if government agencies around the world— Paras were all over the globe, not just in the States— continued to look for ways to control or destroy Paras completely, some of those deities might decide to come out of retirement and fight back. The last thing this world needed was a multi-plane battle between not only rival deities, but also Paras versus humans.

We had to find a way to keep the peace, starting with destroying this clinic and its nightmarish research in less than an hour . . .

By six thirty, my stomach was rumbling for food, but I was scared anything I tried to eat I'd just barf back up.

I hate barfing.

Chandra tried reassuring me that they had my back and their plan would get the werewolves out safely, but it didn't help. Novak tried, too, and I just ended up hugging him, because I didn't know what else to say—until we understood the extent of Damian's power, they could not guarantee I would stay free of his control, let alone save the werewolves.

Kathleen disappeared and reappeared in the motel several times, and she always gave me a steady nod of support, which I appreciated. But the slow setting of the sun on the distant horizon felt like the light going down on my freedom. A few minutes before seven, I dragged Jaxon into the bathroom and hugged him tight. I memorized the firm shape of his body, his unique scent, and sound of his breathing.

"I won't let him take you," Jaxon whispered. "You have my solemn vow."

"You can't make that promise, but thank you."

"I love you, Shiloh."

The words were both new and familiar, and I felt the truth of them in my very core. Maybe my mind had been altered, but my soul had not, and I knew deep down in the part of me that instinctively trusted Jaxon that I loved him back. Probably had for a long time. "Me too," I whispered.

We shared one last kiss before parting. It was time.

Chandra and Tennyson were gone, but Kathleen and Novak were waiting for us with earbuds for everyone. We did a quick sound check and could all hear each other. With a deep, steadying breath, we began walking down the main street toward DM Clinic. Damian hadn't said to come alone, or no weapons, so we all had our service weapons, and Novak had a small arsenal of blades hidden under his coat.

The sight of the brick building with its glowing protection symbol made my insides quiver, but I kept my head high and my spine straight. I could do this. Not show my terror as I faced my greatest fear—imprisonment. More than physical imprisonment, which all djinn fear, it was the imprisonment of my magic that scared me the most. I knew how my abilities could be abused. And unlike full-blood djinn, my human side allows me to feel compassion and regret for all those hurt by the wishes I had no choice but to grant. My future was one of punishment on top of torture.

I was glad I hadn't eaten.

The dark glass door of the clinic drew near. My friends followed me in flanking positions, and we probably got odd looks from any townsfolk watching from the diner or their front porches, but I didn't care. I had one goal right now, and that was to save Mom and Gideon from Damian.

Everything else was details.

I opened the door and strode inside, exuding more confidence than I actually felt, buoyed by the support of my companions. On the other side of the lobby, just past where a regular person would see a wall, stood three familiar faces and one perfect stranger. Hiller stood with Mom and Gideon both kneeling in front of him. They were both gagged and wore silver collars, and Hiller blatantly had a control box of some kind in his hands. Mom stared straight ahead, her shoulders back, and instead of fear, her entire expression was one of undisguised fury. Her left hand was splinted and bandaged, and that tweaked my temper.

Next to her, Gideon looked out of it, as if he'd been drugged in addition to collared. They both appeared otherwise unharmed, so I stopped walking with about ten feet between us and studied the man who had to be Damian.

Damian was handsome, I had to give him that, with a face any movie star would envy. Dark, almost-black hair and dark eyes. His age was difficult to guess, but I'd ballpark it at late twenties to early thirties. He wore simple slacks and a white button-up shirt. But for all his average man exterior, power engulfed him in a pale blue aura that seemed . . . familiar. Similar to the aura of Cailleach's power that protected this place, but . . . that was impossible.

Unless he was from the line of those dark magic users Cailleach first created to defeat Danu's were-wolves.

And the longer I stared at him, the more I got the sense that we'd met.

Or maybe he looked like someone I'd once met.

"Shiloh Harrison," Damian said in that same deeply powerful voice. "It's an honor to finally meet you."

"Can't say the pleasure is all mine," I replied. "I get a little pissy when people kidnap my mother, so can we skip the pleasantries. Who are you?"

"You know who I am, just as the dhampir behind you knows who I am. She's been hunting me for a long time, haven't you, pet?"

Kathleen growled.

"The infamous Para-Marshals," Damian continued. "Or what's left of them, I suppose. I have to admit, I was hoping you'd bring along Master Tennyson. He is quite the unique vampire, isn't he?"

Someone behind me must have shifted position, because Hiller held up that box. "Stay put until you're told to move," he said. "Those collars have built-in lasers, and with one push of this button, the lasers will behead them both."

Shit.

"What did you do to Gideon?" I asked.

"He wasn't cooperating, so I injected him with a minute amount of silver nitrate. Just enough to make him ill and docile, but it won't kill him."

Not only had I gotten one of the California Pack wolves kidnapped, now he was mildly poisoned. Great. Alpha Kennedy was going to skin me alive.

If we won, that is. Something to look forward to.

"What do you want with me?" I asked Damian.

"Don't be coy, Shiloh," he replied with a smirk I really wanted to punch off his face. "You know why I want you."

"What good are three wishes to you? You're already powerful, I can tell from here." He'd get a lot more than just three wishes if I bound myself to him, but I needed to hear the bastard say it. Confirm my worst fear was his goal so everyone heard him.

"My dear, I have more use of you than three wishes. Once your will is bound to mine, I will have full control of your abilities. You will exist to serve me."

Mom made a distressed noise, but I avoided looking at her. She didn't want me to do this; she didn't have to say it for me to know. But I had to play along for as long as possible, so Chandra and Tennyson could do their thing. Hatch their plan.

Save the day.

"How is such a binding possible?" I asked. "The Rules of Wishing are clear, and I am bound to them, not the wisher."

"Because I'm not binding you through the rules, my dear. We share another unique bond that will allow me, not you, to control your magic. You will merely be a vessel."

Next to me, Jaxon flexed both hands into fists.

"What sort of bond do we share? I've never met you before today."

"We share a bond of blood." Damian grinned, and in it I saw no mirth. Only sinister intent, and it made my blood curdle. "You see, child, I am your grandfather."

CHAPTER 18

I laughed out loud.

My grandfather? This was supposedly a super-criminal mastermind, and he was going with that lame line? But one look at my mother's grave expression and my laughter dried up.

"My grandparents are all dead," I said. "My djinn grandparents died hundreds of years ago, and my mother's parents were murdered when she was a small child. I have no living grandfather."

"Except you do, child," Damian replied, that annoying smirk deepening. "I am your mother's father. Give yourself a moment to feel our connection through her magic. It's there, I assure you."

I didn't want to feel our connection, thank you very much. I didn't want there to be a connection at all. "My mother's father was killed by vengeful witches, daughters of Cailleach. You can't be him."

"They intended to murder me, yes, because I would not accept their bargain. You see, they feared me because of who I truly am, and so they sought to bring me under their thumb. But I saw through their plan, and while my wife was sadly sacrificed that night, I did what I did so that your mother could live. But I had no idea she would one day bring me a gift such as you."

I looked at Mom again, but she wouldn't meet my gaze, which turned my insides to jelly. Was Damian telling the truth? Was he truly her father? How the fuck did he look younger than her?

"I admit," Damian continued, "your mother did an excellent job hiding you from me. The magic you inherited from me was dwarfed by what you inherited from your sire, so I never knew you existed until six years ago. When a human woman unleashed a djinn power in the mountains of Colorado, I had to investigate. And that's when I felt you. My granddaughter. Elspeth's only offspring."

The traveling freak show. Rescuing my dad and Jaxon.

The first time I'd truly used my djinn powers to help other Paras had damned me to this moment.

"You didn't know he survived, did you, Mom?" I asked.

She shook her head and looked up, both cheeks streaked with tears.

Even though she was gagged and couldn't speak, I had to reassure her. "This isn't your fault." To Damian, who had snorted at that, I asked stonily, "How are you still alive? If I'm going to become your magical slave, I deserve that answer." I couldn't be sure, but the sun had to have set by now. We'd been talking for several minutes already, so the plan had to be in motion—or almost there.

"Simple," he replied. "The witches came in numbers, but I had the power, for my line is older than theirs. More ancient."

"More evil?"

He raised one eyebrow. "Evil is in the eye of the beholder, granddaughter. Those witches sought to kill me and take my power, so I, in turn, killed them and took theirs."

I blinked hard. "That's how you have the protection of Cailleach. But how is that possible? You're a man, and her children are all . . . ." Tennyson's story screamed back into the forefront of my thoughts. "Your line was one of her first. One of the men Cailleach gave power to in order to defeat Danu's Ossory wolves."

Damian smiled at me in such a condescending way I wanted to vomit. "I am of that line, yes. Cailleach's original warlocks. We have survived these millennia by keeping to ourselves, but the witches found me. They recognized the origin of my power and were naive enough to believe that their numbers could beat my experience. I'm far older than I look."

"And Cailleach didn't mind you murdering her daughters? She created them because the men she gifted magic to failed her."

"She was unhappy at first, until she realized the depth of my ability to move around in the human world. To influence the powerful from behind the scenes, and to . . . shall we say, push the correct pawns across the chessboard into the desired outcomes. She is bored with the world of men, but she has never lost her desire to see the Ossory wolves and all of their offspring eradicated from the world. That desire gave me her protection here."

"You're researching a way to slaughter all living werewolves?"

"Slaughter. Control," he said with a shrug. "Either way. I have a government contractor who is keen on a means to effectively fight back against a werewolf uprising."

"The US Marshals' Office?"

His eyebrows jumped. "They contacted me five years ago, because they'd heard of my particular set of talents. They don't trust the Packs or the vampire Lines to police themselves, and while your Para-Marshals can handle a rowdy gremlin fight, you are ill-equipped to manage a true battle should those creatures choose not to play nice with humans any longer."

"But the Marshals's Office isn't the only agency you're working for, is it?"

"Your interrogation is amusing, child, but it's growing tedious. I believe I've answered enough questions for the moment. We have a bargain to see to."

"First, I need your word that my friends here, including Gideon and my mother, will be allowed to leave peacefully and without interference from you or local law enforcement. You will not hurt them, and you will not hunt them."

"You're hardly in a position to bargain or make demands." Damian tilted his head. "But I admire your spirit, so let us bargain. I have no interest in your mother or your friends, as long as they cease interfering in my work. If we cross paths again, I promise nothing."

"I don't hear an 'I promise not to hurt them,' Grandpop."

"You have my word that if they leave me in peace, I shall leave them in peace."

"Okay." I met Mom's eyes and mouthed, "I love you."

She blinked hard and more tears trickled down her cheeks. The gag made it impossible for her to return the verbal gesture, but I knew. I've known my entire life how much she loves me.

I looked at Jaxon, whose confidence outweighed my own, before meeting Damian's smirking gaze once more. "How do we do this?"

"Simultaneously," Damian replied. "I will ask you a question, and if you answer in the affirmative, those collars pop off and their lives are spared. Your friends can collect them and go on their way. I will not stop them."

"Will anyone else from this building stop them?"

Damian's eyebrows furrowed. "No. They will not. You have my word."

Your word doesn't mean shit to me, crazypants.

"Then let's do this," I said.

"Excellent. Shiloh Harrison, daughter of Iblis, granter of wishes, will you bond your magic to mine of your own free will, to serve me henceforth, forsaking all others for the rest of your days?"

I inhaled a deep breath, then let it out slowly so I didn't lose my lunch with it. Looked Damian dead in his dark eyes, and said, "I do."

Three things happened at the same time. First, the collars around Mom and Gideon fell away, and Kathleen dashed around me to collect them.

Second, the wish tether binding me to Jaxon flared to life as his voice in my ear began to speak. *My third and final wish is to . . .*

And third, a new tether reached across the space between us from Damian to me, glowing with an oily blackness that terrified me. But as it slunk its way toward me, my ingrained djinn instincts had me saying, "Wish granted," despite not hearing exactly what Jaxon asked for—all my magic knew was it adhered to the Rules.

Damian's black tether altered direction, and I watched in horror as it latched onto Jaxon instead of me. He fell to his knees from the force of the binding as Damian roared in anger. "What did you do?" Damian snarled.

"Jaxon?" I reached for him, but a layer of black magic covered him now, and I jerked away from the electric pulse that zapped my fingers.

Through my earbud, voices shouted orders. Kathleen had both dispatched Hiller and was fleeing the building with my mother, while Gideon shifted. He and Novak attacked Damian at the same time. I was too frozen with shock to do anything other than stare at Jaxon, whose entire body trembled under the terrible force of his bond to Damian. Then the magic around Jaxon pulsed. He let out a distressed scream as his own magic sparkled.

Uh-oh.

Novak growled behind me, and Gideon snarled like a beast possessed. The entire building shuddered as all sorts of magical forces collided at once, and I knew my team was coming through. Liberating the pack wolves and tearing this place apart.

Jaxon's mighty stag form stared at me with crazy eyes, one big foot pawing at the ground like a beast about to charge. With Damian's aid, his deformed antler grew to match the other, and then they grew more, blackening into something even darker, more deadly. He lowered his head to charge.

Strong arms whisked me out of the way as Jaxon charged with a roar. Tennyson's power crackled around us, but he wasn't alone. At least a dozen other vampires swarmed the lobby and entered the fray. Damian was strong, and he was holding his own.

Do not kill the deer, Tennyson said, and I hoped he was broadcasting to all his vampire pals.

"He wasn't supposed to do that." I shoved at Tennyson, who'd taken me all the way outside. "Let me go!"

"You are who Damian wants, so I'm removing you from the immediate situation." He carried me around the side of the building, all the way to the rear, where the unexpected sight of more vampires, and a few werewolves, shifted and not, were swarming the back exit.

Backup was here.

But the clinic wasn't going down easily. Some sort of protective ward had cast the doorway in a glittering pink glow, keeping us out, and also trapping others inside. From the crowd, Rosalind strode toward us with an unexpected guest star: Danu. Danu had lost the emo-Goth look and traded it for full-on biker chick leather. And she looked pissed.

"After all these millennia," Danu said, "Cailleach is still trying to murder my children. She should have stayed off this earth and away from my people."

"Can you get us inside?" I asked.

"Our guiding laws prevent me from interfering directly in the actions of men. However, Cailleach threw down the gauntlet by allowing her symbol to guard this residence, so I'm going to tear it down."

Danu strode toward the pink barrier, put both palms on it, which made the ward sparkle like static, and she said something in a language I'd never heard before. The barrier wavered and burst.

Goddesses were handy in a fight.

"Where's Chandra?" I asked Tennyson.

"She went inside with the first wave," he replied. "A few were able to enter before the barrier appeared."

"Then let's get our friends out of there."

"Indeed."

I led Rosalind, Tennyson, and others inside, where a gremlin stood near the elevator with a joyful look on his face. Gremlins loved to fuck up technology, but despite how they appeared in most movies, they weren't ugly green monsters. They looked more like Keebler elves: short, fat, and kind of innocent—until they opened their mouths and showed off rows of razor-sharp teeth. And this one seemed to have broken into DM's security, giving us free rein of the elevators.

"You guys really did plan this out," I said.

Tennyson smiled.

The elevator dinged, and the car doors slid open. Instead of familiar faces, six men with automatic rifles, and also wearing lab coats, barreled out and opened fire. The noise combined with surprised screams. I lunged for the nearest man, grabbed his rifle by the barrel and punched him right in the nose. He yelped and fell to his knees. A stray bullet struck my hip, but

I ignored the pain and swung that rifle like a club. I took out a second shooter, while Rosalind and Tennyson dispatched the other four.

"Guess these guys do double duty as guards and techies," I said. Between getting shot and Jaxon's sacrifice, my temper was reaching peak nuclear levels. The Quarrel started bubbling up, tempting me to unleash it, and I was very fucking tempted. "Have someone tie them up."

We cleaned out the elevator of bad guys, and then filled it back up with as many of us as would fit, including Danu. Rode up to the werewolf floor, only to find more of those pink wards over every doorway, as well as the elevator exit. Chandra, a man I didn't recognize, and several shifted wolves paced the corridor in front of us.

"This happened a few minutes ago," Chandra said, indicating the wards.

"Well, we expected they'd have security measures in case of emergency," I replied. "Lucky us, we have a key."

"You do?"

Danu shouldered her way forward. "Hello again, daughter of Brighid."

Chandra blinked hard. "Hi."

As before, Danu placed both palms flat against the energy and zapped it out of existence. She stepped out of the elevator, and the werewolves pacing by Chandra went immediately to their haunches, and then flattened their heads to the ground. They knew their goddess.

"Don't be afraid," Danu said. "You came here seeking answers and these humans stole from you. The only vengeance I want is against your captors. Be well, my children."

Her words went over well, because the wolves stood and eagerly filed into the elevator. Danu spread her arms above her head, and a rush of power surrounded her like an orange mist, swirling and swirling into a small cyclone only a few of us seemed able to see. The walls and floors vibrated, as if struck by an earthquake. The cyclone blew out, smashing through the remaining pink barriers on a thunderclap of noise.

"Much better," Danu said smugly. "Cailleach's magic has been neutralized. I always was stronger than her."

"Thank Iblis," I replied.

"Thank *Danu*," Rosalind said.

"Right. Chandra, get the werewolves out of here."

"Where are you going?" she asked.

"The floor where the experiments are being held. They deserve freedom, too."

"Is that wise?" Tennyson asked. "You do not know their state of mind, or if they're a danger to you. And you've been shot."

"It's a flesh wound." I'd had way worse, and my hearty djinn half kept the bullet from penetrating my flesh too deeply. I could still see the bullet, so I plucked it out and dropped it to the floor. "Besides, you're coming with me."

He arched one eyebrow.

I turned to wait for the elevator, only to find what appeared to be doors to a lab. "What the—?"

"It's a hidden elevator," the man with Chandra said. "Believe me, we had the same reaction."

It kind of made sense, since this elevator led to the outside and freedom. And we couldn't exactly get the werewolves out via the regular elevator, because I had no idea what was happening in the lobby between Damian and the others. A flash of grief tried to wear me down, but I couldn't think about Jaxon right now. Mom and Gideon were safe, and I had a fucking job to do.

"Tennyson and I will use the other elevator to check the rest of the floors," I said.

"Take Hanson with you," Chandra said, gesturing at her companion.

"Why? What can he do?" I didn't sense any real magic in him, and he appeared human. But not everyone with abilities had them because they could manipulate the magic coursing through the world and its inhabitants.

"Try to punch me," Hanson said.

Why not? I was in the mood to hit something, so I wound up and aimed for his chin—only to pass right through him. I spun around, and Tennyson caught me before I fell.

"Intriguing," Tennyson said.

"Now you punch me," Hanson told Tennyson.

He looked at me, and I shrugged. Tennyson stepped toward Hanson, and this time, he connected. Hard enough to make Tennyson gasp, but Hanson's head didn't move a centimeter. Tennyson shook out his fist, his eyes sparkling with annoyance.

"I can control the density and vibrational speed of my molecules," Hanson said. "So I can pass through solid objects or stop a speeding car, depending on the situation."

"I like you," I said. "How do you know Chandra?"

"We dated a few years ago."

I can only imagine how that would have gone over if Novak was here. "Cool, let's go."

The other elevator was on the opposite end of this floor, so we ran. The sea of waiting werewolves parted for us to pass. Whatever the gremlin had done to the system, I pushed a button and a few seconds later, the elevator arrived. Two shifted wolves had joined us, as well, and I wasn't sure if they were former residents or Rosalind's backup, and it didn't really matter if they were willing to help.

We went up one floor, and as the doors slid open, braced for a fight. Instead, we walked into a chaotic scene of scientists stabbing away at computer keyboards, while others ran huge magnets over storage systems. A woman noticed us and screamed, which led to others drawing guns on us.

Never a good idea.

We took out the researchers before they could fire a single bullet, leaving them all unconscious and/ or bleeding—the werewolves had a little too much fun—so they couldn't hurt us or escape. I didn't care so much about stopping them from destroying their hard drives, because that information couldn't see the light of day either way. Once this group was contained, we checked the first cell. The half-man, half-wolf inside was convulsing, white foam leaking from his mouth.

"Shit, they've been poisoned," I said.

Tennyson ripped the door off its hinges, while Hanson vibrated through the door of the next cell down. But the test subject was dead before we got to him. A black-furred wolf stepped inside, sniffed, and then gave a mournful whine.

Every single hybrid was dead in his cell, and the horror of it made my stomach turn. "Who are these fucking people?" I asked, mostly to myself as I tipped closer to completely losing my grip on the Quarrel. "First they experiment on other human beings, and then they murder them when they're found out?"

"Cowards who cannot face their enemy head-on," Tennyson said, "so they attempt to cheat."

"And destroy lives in the process," Hanson added. "When Chandra called and told me about this place, I had to come take it apart." He spoke with such passion and anger, I silently wondered how he'd come into his abilities in the first place.

"We need to secure the rest of the floors in this

place," I said. "According to a source, the top floor is where the scientists lived, so anyone who hasn't already tried to leave is probably cowering up there." And they did not deserve to be arrested gently, not after destroying so many lives in the name of science. Or whatever.

I closed my eyes.

"Shiloh, what are you doing?" Tennyson asked.

"I'll get in touch with Chandra and get teams sent out," Hanson said.

"You may wish to hold off on that a moment. And perhaps move farther down the corridor."

"Why?"

A rush of air around me was probably Tennyson whooshing Hanson and the other two wolves out of the way.

Every ounce of rage, fear, horror, and grief rose up from deep within me and spread across my skin in a hot flush. I pushed it up, unleashing the Quarrel on the men and women above me, the enemies I couldn't see but hated nonetheless. As my magic pulsed, I imagined those cowards suddenly turning on each other, fighting each other, beating each other senseless through a fit of unexpected rage.

I definitely felt better afterward, and I turned to face the four people I'd come up here with. The two wolves were flat on their bellies, while Hanson simply gaped at me. "What was *that*?" he asked.

"Special trick of mine," I replied as I strode toward

them. "Now you can call Chandra about picking up the other scientists. They might be a little black and blue, though."

Hanson gave me a funny look, then headed off with the two wolves, already speaking into his earpiece.

"Your power is quite impressive," Tennyson said. "I've never felt such chaotic magic before."

"It's not something I use often, because it can really hurt people, but those bastards deserved it."

"Indeed. What are you going to do now?"

"I'm going back downstairs to face Damian. But first, I need a favor from you."

"Name it."

I swallowed hard, not only because of what I was about to ask, but because of the way my body already craved it simply from his nearness. "I need some of your blood."

Tennyson tilted his head to the side, his blue-speckled eyes searching mine briefly, before he sliced his forefinger open on a fang and held it out to me.

Without hesitation, I took that offered finger into my mouth and sucked.

CHAPTER 19

The first time I drank Tennyson's blood, I did so because I was slowly dying of a magical spider bite, and I didn't have much choice. I'd gone a little bloodlust-crazy and tried to kill my mom, but I'd also had *a lot* of blood that day. The second time I drank because I was, yet again, dying, and I'd come so close to it that I'd spent the post-drink time unconscious, with only a lingering bloodlust in the days since.

This time I wasn't dying, but I also moderated what I took, the bitter liquid coating my tongue and mouth as I drew more out of the puncture wound. The power in Tennyson's blood sizzled down my throat to my stomach, where it radiated from my core to every part of my body. My toes vibrated, my scalp itched, and I felt strong enough to flip a car with a single finger.

And I knew sharing his blood again would change

me a fraction, just as I'd changed after the first two times. We were already telepathically linked, and as I charged my battery on his life force, I pushed my thoughts toward his. Not tangible thoughts, only the whisper of them, and images from Tennyson's mind flashed into my own.

Me as he saw me now, holding his finger between my lips. Me on the stairs at headquarters, sobbing over the deaths of his vampires because he'd wished for me to take over the emotional strain so he could try to track them telepathically. Me dying in his arms in the necromancer's lair as he ripped his wrist open to save my life. Me standing up to Brighid in her own home. I searched, but all I saw was myself.

How did I crowd the thoughts of a vampire so old and with so much history?

Didn't matter. I left his mind and returned to the task at hand. Just when my instincts were edging toward biting so I could get more blood, I yanked myself away. Tennyson's energy crackled around us both as we shared a small amount of space, so close we nearly touched. I met his eyes, which now glowed green, and when I licked my lips to draw the last of the blood in, his gaze dropped.

For one split second, I was positive Woodrow Tennyson, Master of his Line, was about to kiss me.

And I would have let him.

Thankfully, my earbud sparked to life. "Shiloh, where are you?"

Kathleen's voice.

"I'm on the fourth floor with Tennyson, why?" I replied as I took a full step back from him.

"The werewolves have been evacuated and the rest of the floors are being swept. However, a problem still exists in the lobby."

"Yeah, I know, I'm heading there now."

"Copy."

"I'm coming with you," Tennyson said.

"Might not be a good idea," I replied on my way to the elevator. "This is a family fight."

"Family?"

Oh yeah, he hadn't been in the lobby to hear the good news. "Damian is my maternal grandfather. He's related to Cailleach's original wolf killers. Surprise!"

Tennyson's lips parted in the most shocked expression I'd ever seen on the man. "Then the legend of the Ossory wolves is true?"

"Apparently. And now I'm related to it."

I filled him in on the backstory during the elevator ride to the lobby, all the way up to Jaxon's wish. Something hit me then, and I pushed the stop button so the car jerked to a halt. "Did you guys know Jaxon was going to use his wish like that? You were right there to snatch me out of the way."

"He informed me of his intentions, but no one else. He wanted to be certain you were removed from the situation as quickly as possible, so Damian could not exact physical retaliation for his actions."

I pressed both hands into my eyes, overwhelmed with both gratitude for their teamwork and fury for having plotted this particular switcheroo behind my back.

"He loves you, Shiloh. He sacrificed himself for you, because of that love. The memories you bargained away? They were of the person you loved most in the world, and you lost your memories of him."

Regret and grief tried to overcome my anger, but I wouldn't let them. I hadn't lost Jaxon yet, and now was the time to go get him back. I'd deal with the emotional fallout of this conversation later.

"I appreciate you guys trying to save me." I dropped my hands, keeping them in tight fists by my side so I didn't lash out at him. "But don't fucking lie to me again."

"My apologies."

"Good." I pushed the button to resume our trip. "Let's go kick my granddad's mystical ass."

"With pleasure." He dropped his cloak to the floor. His eyes flashed crimson, and the tangy odor of vinegar betrayed his own fury at Damian, who had had his fingers in the necromancer's plot. This was personal for us both.

The elevator doors slid open to a scene of destruction and chaos. The real wall separating the lobby from the receptionist area was smashed in, drywall and broken glass all over. Furniture was broken, and the glass in both the front windows and door were shattered. Half of the exterior wall was blown out, exposing it to the night air. Vampires and werewolves persistently climbed in those holes to launch themselves at Damian, who stood in the center of it all, like a rock star on stage. Except he wasn't greeting his adoring fans, he was knocking all comers back with blasts of black energy from his hands.

Two wolves came at him from opposite sides. Damian blasted one wolf with that black energy, while simultaneously reaching out and grabbing the second wolf by the throat. The beast was as large as Damian himself, but the warlock held the struggling wolf as it was a small child. The wolf clawed at Damian's chest with his back feet, shredding the front of his shirt but leaving no actual mark on Damian's skin.

And then it struggled even more fiercely, trying to get away.

But it had no chance. Damian snapped the wolf's neck without so much as a blink, and threw its lifeless body at an approaching vampire. The psycho hadn't even broken a sweat.

Novak knelt in the corner of the room near an overturned chair. He had scorch marks on his clothes and one bloody-looking burn on his neck, and he seemed to be talking into his earbud. I didn't see Jaxon in the small arena, but over the noise of battle, I could hear his stag's angry screams.

The black tether between him and Damian pulsed faintly and threaded its way out the hole in the wall.

Hopefully, the vampires had corralled Jaxon else-where, because I had to focus on my asshole grand-father.

Damian wasn't looking in our direction, so I pulled my gun and fired every round directly at his back. I didn't see blood, but the impact knocked him to his knees. Tennyson blurred past me, and he had Damian against the wall, a hand around his throat, Damian's feet a foot off the floor. Red light blazed in Damian's face, and Tennyson's fangs grew longer than I'd ever seen them.

Damian broke Tennyson's hold and head-butted the vampire. Tennyson barely flinched. Their move-ments blurred as they fought each other, Damian's physical speed matching Tennyson's blow for blow. They blasted through more drywall, knocked an-other huge chunk out of the exterior wall, and then hit some sort of support beam that made the ceiling crack down the center.

It was the closest I'd ever come to seeing two gods in hand-to-hand combat, and it was breathtaking.

And kind of terrifying.

If someone as strong and old as Tennyson couldn't bring Damian down, we were in serious trouble. I longed to join the fight, to get my own vampire blood-fueled punches in, but they were moving too fast.

Finally, Tennyson did something that gave him the slightest advantage. With a devastating punch, he sent Damian headfirst into the exterior brick wall, and then was on him in a blur. He hauled Damian to his feet in the same position they'd started, his fangs nearly as long as my fingers now.

Uh-oh.

When Tennyson fed off the necromancer, he'd briefly obtained the necrotic magic. If he bit Damian—

Damian shouted when Tennyson pierced his jugular, and I used the distraction to race across the lobby to Novak—which I did crazy-fast, thanks to my earlier O-positive energy drink. And Novak noticed. "I ain't gonna ask," he said. "You got a plan for defeating this guy?"

"Not really, but Tennyson seems to."

Damian roared and with an ear-popping drop in air pressure, some force knocked Tennyson across the room. His body shattered the drywall, and he fell to his knees, clothes and long hair covered in dust. Damian advanced two steps before Tennyson threw both hands forward and a blast of gray power smashed into Damian's chest. It threw Damian right through the last of the standing office drywall, and he crashed into the interior wall just beyond. Tennyson had not only taken power from Damian, he'd physically weakened him, as well.

With my enemy momentarily stunned, I used my newfound speed to bolt across the room to Damian's side, and I smashed the butt of my gun into his nose with all the power coursing through my veins. Then I cut off his scream by hitting him in the temple hard enough to send him sailing sideways to the floor. Tennyson appeared by my side, and he wrestled Damian until Tennyson had Damian's hands trapped behind his back—hands that seemed to be the direct source of his energy bolts that had hurt so many.

Forgoing the gun this time, I punched him in the mouth. "You kidnapped my mother." Another punch. "You blackmailed me and hurt my friends." Third punch split his bottom lip wide open. "You can rot in hell."

Damian roared once and head-butted me. I crashed backward into the remnants of the reception desk, shocked by the power of that impact. Granddad packed a punch.

A circle of shifted wolves and vampires had formed, all watching and waiting as the three of us waged a magical battle. I would have loved to see Danu tag in to the fight, but hey, goddesses had their own priorities, and her wolves were free now. Damian was our problem.

He tried to backward head-butt Tennyson, but Tennyson creatively used the momentum of Damian's action to flip Damian backward in a spectacular move that left Damian facedown on the ground—arms still trapped behind his back—with Tennyson on top of him.

Supernatural wrestling with an audience to boot. Time to get our opponent into a three-count.

Except Damian started laughing, and with both blood and drywall dust smearing his face, it was pretty freaking creepy.

"I'm sorry, does this tickle?" I asked, then kicked him in the mouth.

"I'm merely amused you think you can win here," Damian replied. "You're a foolish child."

Tennyson growled, and his hands started doing that gray-glow thing again. Damian hissed in pain, and the skin around his wrists where Tennyson held him began to sizzle. "I thank you for the power increase," Tennyson said. "How long will it take to burn down to the bone?"

"Drinking my blood may be protecting you from my power, vampire, but it won't last. I'll make your death last for days for stealing from me."

"Better men have tried to kill me and failed."

A clucking sound caught my attention, and I glanced behind me. Novak was a few feet away, and he tossed me his set of butterfly swords. I caught them by the hilt, then snapped them apart.

"How about we end this right now?" I asked as I turned back to the pair of men on the ground. I mimicked using the swords like scissors. "We chop the head off the beast and stop this bullshit."

"Careful you don't awaken a hydra, child," Damian said. "You have no idea what you're truly up against."

For a guy about to lose his head, he was being awfully confident. I glanced at Tennyson, whose stony expression only said *kill*. "I'll take my chances," I replied.

I took a step toward Damian, not eager to kill the man because of all the questions I still had, but ready to see his evil plans stopped once and for all. The ground started to vibrate; tiny bits of debris danced atop the linoleum floor. The air went hazy with magical power, making the hair on my arms stand on end. I lunged in the same moment the world exploded in sharp black light. I flew backward into a warm body, and we both sprawled to the ground. My entire body tingled and jerked, as if I'd been hooked into an electrical current.

Around me, werewolves whined and vampires hissed, but I couldn't freaking see anything. Black light might sound like an oxymoron, but we were not in darkness. The absolute blackness of Damian's power and his soul had filled the room and blinded me to everything else.

A hand closed around my throat, and I'll be blessed if Damian didn't lift me right up off the ground. I didn't have to see him to feel him, his skin sizzling against mine. I couldn't breathe or get my body to do anything other than dangle there and choke and burn.

"You may have won today, but you will be mine one day, Shiloh," he said, his words as heavy and horrifying as this constant blackness. "And I always keep my word."

Through the agony in my throat and the lack of

oxygen in my lungs, I still managed to grind out two words. "Fuck. You."

Tennyson!

I'm sorry I failed you, Shiloh . . .

The pain stopped abruptly as unconsciousness swallowed me up.

I found the pain again the moment I became aware of voices all around me. I was on something moderately soft, thank Iblis, but my throat blazed with heat and my head hurt like a son of a bitch.

"She's coming to." Novak? My brain was kind of muzzy, but it sounded like him.

"Wh-op-n?" I'd meant to ask "What happened?" but my tongue wasn't cooperating.

"Relax, no one is in immediate danger," Novak said. Yeah, definitely him. "You've got a nasty magic burn on your throat that even the vamp's blood isn't healing all that fast, and you took a big blow to the head."

My version of "I did?" didn't come out well, either, but Novak understood.

"Damian must have thrown you headfirst into the bricks, because that's where I found you when all the dark went away."

I finally blinked my eyes open and found myself staring up at a sea of stars. The scene started making more sense. I was outside, on a blanket, with people moving all around me. Novak was sitting beside me and, I suddenly realized, holding one of my hands. He was protective, sure, but he was rarely the one offering comfort.

Oh no. "Who died?" Victory and whole words!

"Two of the werewolves Rosalind brought died of their injuries."

"Our people?" Tennyson's grief-stricken apology in my head roared back. "Tennyson?"

"He's weak, but he's . . . well, I guess he's not technically alive anyway, but he's still undead. Damian used my swords to pin him to the wall through his heart. Shredded it, but the blades weren't silver, so it didn't kill him."

"Thank goodness. Damian got away?"

"Yeah." Novak's already grave expression went even darker. "And . . ."

"What?"

"He's still got Jaxon, Shi. They're both gone."

"What!" I tried to sit up, which was an epically bad idea. My entire body ached, but I couldn't sit on my ass right now. Novak helped me sit up by keeping an arm around my waist. The skin around my neck stung and pulled in weird ways, and I was glad there were no reflective surfaces nearby. If it looked half as awful as it felt . . . ugh.

The new viewpoint also brought the scene into a much sharper clarity. I was on the front lawn of the professional complex, and not only were local and state police present, but so were other people in suits with US Marshals badges around their necks.

Oh great, we've been reported.

The vampires who'd helped didn't seem to be around any longer, and I didn't see Tennyson, but I trusted Novak that he'd survived the fight. And I shoved back a pang of grief-stricken anger at Damian having gotten away with Jaxon. I hadn't been strong enough to break that bond before Damian disappeared with my . . . *lover* wasn't the right word. Best friend?

Close enough.

I did spot Chandra and Hanson speaking animatedly with three Marshals, and no one looked happy. "What did I miss while I was unconscious?"

"The Pack wolves are all currently en route to their proper home states," Novak replied, "thanks to those helicopters Kathleen promised us. Haven't talked to the Dame Alpha of Florida, but Rosalind assured us that Alpha Kennedy is in our debt."

"That's nice." A werewolf Alpha wasn't a bad ally to have. "Vampires?"

"They're gone. One of them took Tennyson someplace to heal."

Polite way of saying he was off to find a couple dozen blood donors. I wanted to thank Tennyson for his help, but it would have to wait. Right now, we had to get this current mess sorted. "Where's my mom?"

"Back at the motel. I called and told her what happened, but made her swear to stay away from the scene until we properly secured it."

"Thank you."

"Family helps family, Shiloh."

The stark emotion in his voice startled me into turning around and really looking at him. The big incubus rarely wore his emotions on his sleeve, or expressed more than anger or boredom. But tonight, instead of a powerful fallen demon, I saw a man who'd survived a battle with his friends, and who had lost one to a powerful warlock. He and Jaxon squabbled like brothers, and that's because they were. Maybe I couldn't remember their relationship, but Novak did, and he was hurting too.

I leaned into him in a sideways hug. "We'll get Jaxon back. That's a promise."

"I know." His arm tightened around my waist briefly. "Didn't know Jaxon was gonna wish himself into your spot. Jerk."

"Apparently, he only told Tennyson so he could swoop in and get me out of the way."

Novak grunted.

"Miss Harrison? Mr. Smith?" The three Marshals Chandra and Hanson had been speaking to approached my blanket, and the shortest of the three had spoken. "US Marshal McGovern."

Novak helped me stand so I could politely greet the newcomers. Must be from a local office, because

I didn't recognize any of them. Hanson and Chandra stood off to the side. Chandra's folded arms and undisguised glare did not endear me to these three at all.

"Shiloh Harrison," I said.

"Novak Smith." He'd needed a last name for the official paperwork, and creativity wasn't exactly Novak's strong suit.

"Miss Goodfellow informed me of your activities of the past few days," McGovern said with a bit of a sneer I didn't care for. "You used government resources for an informal investigation, while under temporary suspension from your positions as Para-Marshals. Is this information accurate?"

Well, when you put it like that . . . "That's correct," I replied. "The investigation into the missing werewolves was tangentially related to our necromancer case last week. Chandra personally knew one of the missing couples, and she asked us for a personal favor while we were all on paid vacation."

"Miss Goodfellow said something very similar. And had you gone about your investigation as civilians, without using government-bought weapons and vehicles, this would be a very different conversation."

I crossed my arms. "I'm sorry, but did anyone tell you what was going on in that clinic? That they were splicing human and werewolf DNA to create hybrid creatures that they then murdered tonight?"

"That clinic is private property, Miss Harrison. The werewolves were there voluntarily."

Seriously? This guy must be one of the compromised Marshals. Great.

"Then why wasn't the couple who asked to leave granted that request? Why did the place have all kinds of magical wards and security if they were volunteers?"

McGovern looked at me like I was a special kind of idiot. "All of the volunteers signed paperwork stating they would remain in the clinic for a minimum of eight weeks, and this particular couple had only been there for two."

"Paperwork no one remembers signing, by the way," Chandra interjected.

"The documents are legal," McGovern said. "What you did here, by interfering in a legal clinical trial, is not."

"Excuse me?" I said. "They were experimenting—"

"You're not hearing me. You trespassed on private property, and then caused several million dollars of damage to said property that the US Marshals' Office is liable for."

Anger blazed through me hot and hard, and I pulled back on the Quarrel I'd already unleashed once tonight, even though I really wouldn't mind siccing it on these three assholes. "The guy in charge of this place kidnapped my mother and demanded I trade myself for her release! He invited me over, so I didn't fucking trespass anywhere."

"Miss Goodfellow reported a similar story, and

yet the person in charge of this facility is Dr. Marcus Ferguson, and he's assured us beyond a shadow of a doubt that he neither kidnapped your mother, nor demanded you come here and interrupt his place of work."

I looked at Chandra, whose exasperated expression said she'd trying telling them about Damian, and they didn't believe her. Or they did, but perhaps they'd known about this place the entire time. Kathleen and Damian had both intimated that the government was interested in his work.

"You're protecting him, aren't you?" I asked, directing my question to all three Marshals. "You're protecting Damian and this place."

"This place is a private business whose work you interrupted," McGovern said. "You're lucky Dr. Ferguson isn't pressing criminal charges against any of you."

I gawked at the guy, so flustered I couldn't find the words to tell him how I felt about Dr. Ferguson and criminal charges.

"What about Jaxon?" Novak asked. "That bastard Damian took our friend with him."

McGovern turned his blank stare to Novak, who still stood just behind me. "According to our records, Jaxon Dearborn returned to his residence in Maryland three days ago. We've found no proof he was ever here in Gabriel."

"You have got to be shitting me!" I threw both

hands in the air. "Isn't there security footage some-where in this town that shows him? Officer Murphy met him when we first got here yesterday. Two days ago, whenever." My sense of time was totally skewed. I didn't even know how long I'd been unconscious.

"We've spoken with local law enforcement, and no one remembers seeing Marshal Dearborn here."

Fucking Damian. He probably whammied the entire goddess-damned town to forget Jaxon had been here, simply to cover up his kidnapping. Be-cause maybe Damian hadn't wanted Jaxon bound to him, but now he had the perfect hostage. And lever-age against me, the person he really wanted by his side.

"What about Rosalind and Gideon?" I asked. "They both interacted with Jaxon this whole fucking time. So did Alpha Kennedy."

I swear McGovern was trying to hide a yawn. "The werewolves were gone when we arrived, and when I attempted to speak to Alpha Kennedy, I was informed the Marshals Service is not welcome on Pack land, they'll deal with the matter internally, and he has no further use for us. Under federal law, I'm required to abide by the Alpha's wishes."

The part about sorting things out internally sounded about right, but the second part sat wrong, and I suspected McGovern was lying about that phone call. Especially when Novak told me ten minutes ago that Kennedy owed us a favor.

But challenging McGovern wouldn't help, so I made a mental note to call Rosalind myself.

It just meant that we were at an impasse—which was almost certainly what McGovern wanted.

"This is insane," Novak said. "A US Marshal has been kidnapped, and you idiots couldn't care less."

"Watch your tone, Mr. Smith," McGovern replied. "You are a civilian speaking to a government agent."

"Civilian?"

"Yes." McGovern carefully looked at Novak and Chandra, and then seemed to take intense pleasure in meeting my eyes when he said, "You're all fired. Turn over your weapons and badges immediately."

"Fired?" I squawked. "What gives you the authority?"

"My boss does, and as I said, you're lucky you are all getting off with simply losing your jobs and not jail time. Guns and badges."

"I want to speak to my own superiors. I don't know you. For all I do know, you're rent-a-cops with stolen badges."

"The order came down from the top, Miss Harrison, and I guarantee you it's legit. You don't have a choice here." He tilted his head, and I saw the trump card before he landed it. "You see, I've been informed that a civilian named Elspeth Juno rented three rooms at the local motel recently, and that she's yet to check out. I'd hate to see her connected to or implicated in the crimes you and your teammates have committed today."

Fuck it all sideways.

Novak growled softly at the implied threat from McGovern. He'd never admit it, but Novak loved my mom, too. And if saving her meant temporarily losing my badge and gun? We'd both do it in a heartbeat.

I considered loosing the Quarrel on those three numbskulls just to see them start beating the crap out of each other, but I was a freaking adult, and I could get fired like one. But as I eased my badge out of my wallet, my chest squeezed with grief over what I was losing. Temporarily, I hoped. The Para-Marshals had been my life for the better part of six years. It had given me direction and purpose when I was lost and floundering. It had given me a family of strays who knew how it felt to be alone in the world.

I handed over that part of my life to Marshal McGovern, whose knowing smirk told me one thing for sure: Damian had set us up to fall. And maybe we had fallen, but we were still strong. We'd pick ourselves back up and continue the fight, with or without the support of the US Marshals behind us. With vampire support, Pack support, and the friendship of at least one goddess, we'd find Jaxon and take Damian down for good.

CHAPTER 20

We picked up Mom at the motel and drove straight out of town. Even if I'd wanted to stay around and try to find some evidence, some trail Damian might have left behind, the Marshals had the place under a tight lock and key now, and if we got caught snooping, we probably *would* see jail time. So would my mother, and I couldn't allow that to happen. Not after everything she'd done for me, protecting me my entire life.

This time, I'd protect her.

Mom's rental car had been hidden in the old silo, of all places, so at least we had that. I didn't care about the other rental, since it had been paid for with our government card. We left town in Mom's car with only our personal belongings. I felt naked without my gun and badge, and I tried to doze as we drove, but the constant itch of my neck healing kept me awake.

Chandra drove, with Novak riding shotgun, me and Mom in back. It felt so strange to have entered Gabriel with so many others and to now leave without them.

I did make that phone call to Rosalind, and she guaranteed me that no one from the Marshals' Office had called with questions. Her wolves were happy to be home, Gideon had been promoted in his position within the Alpha's home, and she reiterated Kennedy's promise that he owed us. That news made all the other losses more bearable.

Kathleen was probably with her own people by now, doing whatever it was they did for her mystery employer. She had come through with backup and the helicopters, though, so . . . Tennyson was off healing, and I hoped to hear from my friend soon.

Jaxon . . . frustrated tears welled up every time I thought of him, stuck with a magical maniac, who was doing goddess knew what to Jaxon right now. My heart ached for him.

Chandra pulled into a hotel on the outskirts of Wichita and got us a room for the night. All they had left was a double, which was fine. I ordered room service, because food would also help with the healing process—and I was coming down off vampire blood again, so the two rare steaks were exactly what I craved.

While I ate, Mom got red-eye flights back to Los Angeles for Chandra, and Philadelphia for the rest of us, and then arranged for rental cars to get us all home. I tried to sleep for the three hours we had before leaving for the airport, but I was too restless from the fight. Or, more likely, from the aftermath. Keyed up when I should have been exhausted. And I was ashamed of myself for losing the fight against Damian, especially with a teammate as powerful as Tennyson and his blood injection.

No one talked about it, though. Not the fight, not being fired, not what's next? We all wallowed in our losses.

When we landed in Philly, I had an unexpected voice mail from McGovern stating we'd be allowed to return to our headquarters in Maryland to collect any personal items we might have left behind. My clothes and toiletries weren't a big loss, but I was grateful for the chance to say good-bye to my second home of the last six years.

Not that I'd ever tell McGovern that, the smug bastard.

I offered to drop Mom off on the way south, but she declined and I was glad. Maybe I was twenty-eight years old but right now, I needed my mom.

And I'd been sad to say good-bye to Chandra, but I had a feeling we'd see each other again soon. She was just as fired as the rest of us, after all, and I considered her a friend. And Novak maybe considered her something more, seeing how long they lingered on their good-bye.

The house was dark and quiet, the usual security shields offline, which was strange—except I realized why the instant I walked into the house.

We'd been ransacked.

The dining table that held K.I.M.'s equipment was empty. Our weapons were gone, our cache of extra phones gone. Even the silver-laced cage we kept in the basement for emergency imprisonments had been dismantled and removed. Anything that remotely belonged to the Marshals' Office had been removed, leaving the house feeling barren and cold.

We hadn't just been fired. We'd been ejected without a parachute.

"Surprised the fuckers didn't change the locks and burn all our clothes," Novak grumped.

"They couldn't," I said. "According to their official report, Jaxon wasn't there, and this is his official residence. He wasn't fired, and it would look suspicious if he was kicked out of his home, if he's still technically on suspension."

"A cover-up."

"Yup."

Uncertain and lost, I wandered upstairs. While Jaxon was the only person who had lived here full-time, we each had preferred bedrooms for the occasional overnight, and I passed mine. Novak didn't technically live here, since he preferred finding a warm bed to share with a willing sex partner whenever we weren't working, but he had a room with extra clothes and things in it, too.

The next room must have been Jaxon's, because even though I didn't know it in my head, my heart said it was as I pushed the door open. Paintings of the forest and streams and wildlife covered the walls, and the room smelled pleasantly of him. I sat on the bed and thought of all the good sex we'd probably had here, while I only had the memory of our motel sex.

I'd traded my memories of him for a way to stop a necromancer whose magic Damian had put into motion, and I was filled with hatred for the warlock. I hated Damian more than I'd ever hated another person in my life. He was evil.

He had to be stopped.

"We'll find him," Novak said from the open doorway. He and Mom stood there together, both of them vivid studies in concern.

"I loved Jaxon once," I said for no reason in particular. "I still love him, and he did what he did because he loves me. I won't give up on him. Not ever." No matter what condition he was in when we found him, I'd stay by Jaxon's side.

"We know he loved you, sweetheart." Mom sat beside me and gathered my hands in her lap. Squeezed them tight. "We all loved him in our own way, and Novak is right. My father took your friend, and I will help you find them."

"Mom, you're not responsible for this. You had no idea he was still alive."

"No, but perhaps if I'd used my own magic more, instead of hiding it away, I'd have sensed him sooner. Stopped him before things got this far, or before he knew who you were."

"We can't change it. I don't blame you for any of this, I swear."

Mom blinked hard several times, leaving tears glistening on her eyelashes. "You have no idea how much I needed to hear you say that."

"How can I blame you for protecting me my whole life?"

"I blame myself. The moment he walked into the room where I was being held, I knew who he was, simply by the energy he exuded. I was so young when he supposedly died that I didn't really remember his face, but I knew him instantly. And before he'd spoken a word, I knew he wanted you."

"He didn't get me, though, thanks to Jaxon." I looked at Novak, who'd come deeper into the room, and he seemed . . . smaller. As if the weight of his own emotions had shrunk him down. "And you. You guys all fought for me, and for the werewolves."

Novak nodded. "If we did anything right, we came through for the werewolves. We set out to find them and set them free, and we did that. We got that win, Shi. Just took a few blows along the way."

He was right. We had completed the mission we'd

set out to do a few days ago, when we agreed to help Chandra locate twenty-eight missing werewolves and return them safely to their Packs. We'd done that. We'd also exposed horrific scientific experimentation and gotten ourselves fired for the effort, but I wouldn't take it back—because now I knew the enemy I was up against.

And not only was my enemy my evil warlock of a grandfather, but also the very establishment I'd once worked for: the US Marshals' Office. An organization that had been the public face of policing Paras for the last forty years, and had only invested in the Para-Marshals for the last six.

Julius had gone to the Marshals with the idea of a small division of people with supernatural or magical abilities, and he'd been made a unit leader. So had Weller, and both of them turned out to be traitors in their own way. I'd believed in the Para-Marshals once, but now all I could see was a smoke screen and a web of lies. And I wasn't self-absorbed enough to think the Para-Marshals had come about simply so Damian could keep an eye on my movements, but maybe . . .

The entire thing had just blown up in their faces.

Ours too.

"We can't do anything to fix it right now," I said. "We all need to sleep and recharge, so we can think logically and not react emotionally."

Novak's eyebrows rose. "Who are you, and where's my friend Shiloh?"

I blew a raspberry at him.

"Mature, as always," Kathleen said from the doorway. Appearing as if out of thin air, like usual.

Novak snarled at her. "Where've you been?"

"Tying up loose ends. Do you now believe what I've said about how the government is not to be trusted?"

"Yes, we do," I replied. "Seeing as we all got fired tonight and no one in charge gives a shit Jaxon was kidnapped."

"I give a shit. Jaxon was my teammate here, and I consider him an ally. As such, my employer has a gift of good faith, as well as an offer for each of you."

I stood, curious and wary all at once. "What kind of offer?"

"Come see your gift first. It's downstairs." Kathleen turned and left.

I looked at Novak, who shrugged, then followed Kathleen down the hall. Downstairs to the dining room, where I stopped dead in my tracks.

All the parts to set up K.I.M. were back, piled on the dining table where they belonged, including the various monitors and our Raspberries—the smartphones connected to her system. I gawked at it, shocked and confused.

"How did you get K.I.M. back?" Novak asked.

Kathleen smiled. "My employer has some pull in a few places. However, this gift is contingent on your acceptance of my offer."

"Which is what?" I asked.

"Come work for us. Help us find Damian again and stop him once and for all."

I met Novak's gaze and saw the same wariness in his eyes that I felt in my bones. Kathleen had betrayed us last week, but she had come through for us this week, and now that I knew she wasn't one of us . . . trusting her again was somehow easier. She'd proved she had resources at her disposal. Resources we'd need if we had any hope of rescuing Jaxon and dismantling everything Damian had built in his efforts to destroy other Paras.

Novak nodded a fraction of a degree.

I faced Kathleen again, hands on my hips, shoulders squared. "Are you asking Chandra, too?"

"Yes, as well as her companion, Hanson," she replied. "His unique abilities may prove useful to us. And on the flight to California, Gideon expressed interest in taking revenge on the man who poisoned him, so he may also be persuaded to join our cause."

"The more the merrier, I guess." Unless he enjoyed his new promotion too much. I turned to where Mom hovered near the window. "Mom? Are you in?"

She blinked at me in surprise. "Me? I'm no secret agent or spy."

"This is your fight too, if you want in. Damian is your father. You don't have to do this, obviously, but you're powerful, and you're sensitive to his magic. You'd be an asset, and we'll do everything we can to protect you."

Mom studied me a beat, before walking over and taking my hand. "I suppose this gives me the best chance to keep an eye on you. That man wanted to enslave my child, so he needs to answer for that."

Excellent.

"Sounds like we're all in, then," I said to Kathleen.

"What about your werewolf friend?" Novak asked. "The guy who brought the witch to California?"

"Will?" As a forced wolf with no Pack, Will didn't seem eager to leave the magical protections of his Colorado ranch, but he had allies and ears on the ground. Irena had connections to a line of very powerful witches. And maybe one or two of his strays would be interested in signing up. "I'll call him."

"Excellent," Kathleen said.

I studied the faces of the people in this room, a new sense of hope for the future stretching out in front of me. I knew who my enemies were now, and I was confident in our collective abilities to fight any battle coming our way. Because mankind had instigated a war against Paras when they began experimenting on them—not only in that clinic, but in what the necromancer had tried to do with Tennyson.

Tennyson. I smiled, hoping he'd agree to join us, as well. He and I made a great team, and I already missed the irritating vampire Master.

"Shiloh?" Mom asked. "You with us?"

"Yup," I replied, grinning with all the newfound confidence bubbling up inside me. A kind of self-confidence I hadn't felt since Julius died and left me in charge of our squad. I could do this. With my friends.

To our newly formed team of private investigators, I said, "Let's get K.I.M. set up and start planning. We've got a warlock to find and a skin-walker to save."

ACKNOWLEDGMENTS

Many thanks to everyone who's made it this far into Shiloh's journey. I hope you've enjoyed the adventure so far; I know I have. Thank you to my wonderful editor, David; the team at Harper Voyager Impulse; and my long-time agent, Jonathan. I couldn't have done this without you.

ABOUT THE AUTHOR

Born and raised in Southern Delaware, **KELLY MEDING** survived five years in the hustle and bustle of Northern Virginia, only to retreat back to the peace and sanity of the Eastern Shore. An avid reader and film buff, she discovered Freddy Krueger at a very young age, and has since had a lifelong obsession with horror, science fiction, and fantasy, on which she blames her interest in vampires, psychic powers, superheroes, and all things paranormal.

Discover great authors, exclusive authors, and more at hc.com.